LETHBRIDGE-STEWART

FEAR FREQUENCY

George Ivanoff

CANDY JAR BOOKS · CARDIFF
2021

The right of George Ivanoff to be identified as the Author of the Work has been asserted by him in accordance with the Copyright, Designs and Patents Act 1988.

Fear Frequency © George Ivanoff 2021

Characters from The Web of Fear
© Hannah Haisman & Henry Lincoln 1968, 2021
Lethbridge-Stewart: The Series
© Andy Frankham-Allen & Shaun Russell 2014, 2021

Doctor Who is © British Broadcasting Corporation, 1963, 2021

Range Editor: Andy Frankham-Allen
Editor: Shaun Russell
Editorial: Keren Williams
Licensed by Hannah Haisman
Cover by Adrian Salmon

ISBN: 978-1-913637-45-3

Printed and bound in the UK by
Severn, Bristol Road, Gloucester, GL2 5EU

Published by
Candy Jar Books
Mackintosh House
136 Newport Road, Cardiff, CF24 1DJ
www.candyjarbooks.co.uk

All rights reserved.
No part of this publication may be reproduced, stored in a retrieval system, or transmitted at any time or by any means, electronic, mechanical, photocopying, recording or otherwise without the prior permission of the copyright holder. This book is sold subject to the condition that it shall not by way of trade or otherwise be circulated without the publisher's prior consent in any form of binding or cover other than that in which it is published.

'For the Doctor Who Club of Victoria and the Doctor Who Club of Australia. These were my gateways into fandom.'

PROLOGUE

THE WAVY lines. The unearthly notes. The way indistinguishable images shot forward at great speed. Everything about it seemed to radiate unease. It made him feel... odd.

Graham pushed away those unmanly feelings and tore his eyes from the television screen, to see his young son clutching a sofa cushion and attempting to hide behind it.

'What are you doing?' asked Graham.

'Hiding,' Tommy replied, his voice a tiny quaver.

'Put the cushion down. Stop being so girly.'

Tommy timidly let go of the cushion.

Satisfied, Graham returned his attention to the screen. It was an old black and white set. Top of the range when he had bought it, but out of date now that the UK was starting to go colour. He'd have to get a new television set soon. The neighbours were already seeing everything in rainbow glory. He didn't want to get left behind. That would be unacceptable.

As the opening titles reached their climax, the music peaked with a long, high, sustained note that seemed to reverberate through Graham's very soul.

CHAPTER ONE
First Night

THE KETTLE shrieked and Bill Bishop jumped, wincing in pain. A constant reminder of the surgeries he'd had to endure two months ago, after... After...

Taking a deep breath, he settled himself and leaned further back into the sofa. And yet, his heart was still racing.

This is ridiculous, he thought. *Unnerved by a silly television show.*

'Tea?' Anne called from the kitchen.

'Um... sure.'

A cup of tea. That would calm him down.

From his position on the sofa, he could see Anne bustling around the kitchen, fetching teapot and cups. She brushed a strand of dark hair from her eyes as she went about preparations. Bishop smiled, watching her. These days he savoured every moment they spent together. Her departure from the Fifth Operational Corps meant that, once he returned to active duty, he wouldn't be spending nearly as much time with her as he used to. That's why evenings like this, even if they were just dinner and watching the telly at her house, were so special. He felt lucky to have her in his life. And, after what had happened to him at the hands of Vaar two months ago, it was like she was looking for any excuse to be by his side. Not that he minded, of course, in fact it was about the only good thing to come out of those traumatic events.

His eyes drifted back to the television. Something was lurking about in a shadowy alleyway making exaggerated grunting sounds as it watched the people walking by out on the main street. As a woman in a very short miniskirt turned the corner and walked in its direction, it slunk back, hiding itself behind some conveniently placed boxes. Then, as the woman passed, it followed, making sure to stay concealed in the shadows.

The creature's grunting became more aggressive and its pace increased. The woman looked over her shoulder and screamed. She attempted to run away, but tripped and fell, her screaming becoming more hysterical. The creature lunged forward out of the darkness.

'Here we are.'

Bishop started.

'Bit jittery this evening,' said Anne, placing the tea tray down on the coffee table. 'You're supposed to be taking it easy. Back to work tomorrow.'

'I'm fine,' Bishop said.

His eyes flicked back to the television set. Anne followed his gaze and burst out laughing. On the screen, the monster had finally been revealed in all its rubbery glory.

'What in the world are you watching?' she asked between giggles.

'It's a new science fiction series. About aliens coming to Earth to... well, I'm not really sure what they want to do yet, apart from savaging pretty young women in dark alleyways. It's been getting quite a lot of promotion, and tonight is the first episode.'

'Really?' Anne sat next to him.

'It's called *Fear Frequency*.'

'That is so obviously a man in a rubber suit,' said Anne. 'It doesn't look anything like an alien. And we should know.'

Bishop smiled. 'Yes, we should.'

'Did you really want to watch it? It's... well... it's preposterous rubbish.'

'No, no,' said Bishop quickly. 'Just curious to see what it was like. And now that I have, I don't really need to see any more.'

'How about we switch over to the BBC for a while?' Anne hopped up from the sofa. 'Food will be ready soon-ish.'

Bishop watched as she changed the channel, still unable to shake his slightly unsettled feeling.

'Yes, I take your point, Madame,' said Gladys, her voice unwaveringly cheery and steadfastly understanding. 'I will make certain to pass your complaint on to the producer. Thank you for your call.'

She quickly disconnected before the old biddy had a chance to say anything more. Gladys huffed as she gazed across the switchboard, alight with incoming calls. Calls that would all undoubtedly be about the same thing.

'Buck up,' she said to herself, her voice tired and strained. 'Only twenty-five minutes until I get to go home. Then Graham can listen to me complaining for a while.'

She connected the next caller and cleared her throat.

'Good evening, London Weekend Television switchboard,' she announced, cheery and welcoming. 'How may I help you?'

'Did you see that new programme that just finished?' demanded the elderly male voice.

'No, sir, I'm afraid I didn't. I've been at the switchboard answering calls. I'm sorry to say they don't allow us to watch television while at work.'

Okay, so that last bit wasn't really something she should have said. The strain was getting to her. But she thought she managed to deliver it without the sarcasm she felt.

'Oh... Well...' The caller was obviously flustered. 'Well, you're lucky then. The opening was completely inappropriate. Much too frightening. It sent chills up my spine, it did.'

'I'm sorry to hear that, sir.'

'And I'm an ex-soldier, I am,' he continued. 'Imagine the affect it may have had on those less hardened.'

'I can imagine,' said Gladys.

It was going to be a very long twenty-five minutes.

Dan Morales hated his job. He hated it with a passion. It wasn't that he was working on a Sunday while most of the UK had their day of rest. It wasn't the fact that he had to cart around heavy boxes. He was young-ish and fit-ish and reasonably capable of physical labour. It wasn't that he was working the late shift, while ordinary people were sitting in front of their television sets having their tea. He was actually a bit of a night owl and rarely went to bed until the wee hours of the morning. And there was never anything good on telly anyway. It wasn't even that he didn't get along with his supervisor. Truth be known, Dan didn't get along with many people. He was not really a people person. He much preferred the company of his guitar. His guitar didn't talk back. His guitar didn't tell him what to do. His guitar let him touch it whenever he wanted, without complaint.

No. The reason he hated his job so much was because working there was a constant reminder of everything he wanted, but had been unable to achieve.

Electric Soundscapes made musical instruments. And those instruments were played by musicians. And those musicians made music. And their music was recorded and played and listened to.

Dan made music too. He played an old six-string acoustic guitar he had inherited after his uncle – a middlingly successful session musician whom he had loathed – had been run over by a bus. He recorded his music using a tape deck inherited after his father – who wasn't a musician, but whom he loathed anyway – had a heart attack. But every time Dan sent a new demo to a record company or radio station or recording studio, they never responded. And anyone of any importance was always busy when he rang. And the useless secretaries were never any help.

So, Dan made unsuccessful music (with artistic integrity) that no one listened to.

And he worked in a warehouse surrounded by electric guitars, electric organs, synthesisers and samplers. That was what Electric Soundscapes made. 'Electric instruments for electrifying musicians,' as their slogan proclaimed.

Dan blew a strand of unruly brown hair out of his eyes. His mother was always telling him to cut it. But stuff that! Musicians, even unsuccessful ones, didn't get haircuts when their mothers told them to. That's why he rarely visited her these days. That and the fact she kept telling him he was too skinny and that he should eat more. She was so annoying! He was thirty-one, for God's sake – too old to have his mother nagging him about his appearance.

A lot of people and things annoyed Dan.

His supervisor, who he didn't get along with, always had the radio blaring pop hits over the speakers in the warehouse. Poorly written songs performed by substandard musicians who made lots of money because the tone-deaf public couldn't get enough of their rubbish. Songs which paled in comparison to what he was writing and playing. At least, that was the way that Dan saw things.

And the song blasting through the speakers at that moment was the worst of the lot.

Listen to me. Listen to me. I'm gonna make you listen to me. Listen to me. Oh, listen to me. I'm gonna make you do what I say. Hey, hey, hey. Do what I say.

Dan Morales stood in a darkened isle of the warehouse holding a box containing a SynthMoods 21-20 synthesiser, while he fumed.

He hated that song more than any other. It was sung by Trev Del. It had been a hit ten years ago. It had made a lot of money for Trev Del, now better known by his real name, Trevor Delacy. And it was Trevor Delacy who owned Electric Soundscapes. So it was, indirectly, Trevor Delacy who was responsible for Dan's misery.

Dan hated Delacy even more than he hated his job. And his malice towards the man was exacerbated by the fact that they were the same age and even shared a birthday. And yet, he was working in a warehouse, while Delacy owned it.

Dan would have liked nothing better than to smash the box he was carrying onto the hard concrete floor. He would have loved the opportunity to punch Delacy in the nose. He would have liked…

'Would you shut up!' said an irritated voice. 'Someone might hear you.'

Dan heard movement in the next isle. He froze and listened.

'It's almost eleven at night in a darkened warehouse,' said a second voice. 'Who's gonna 'ear me?'

'I don't know,' said the first voice. 'There's still a few losers working the late shift. So just shut up and get the bloody synth, would you? Check the serial number. Make sure you get the right one.'

'Yeah, yeah, yeah. Don't get ya knickers in a knot.' There was a grunt as the owner of the voice lifted something. 'Tell ya who I'd like to shut up,' he continued. 'That bloody singer screeching over the speakers.'

'Don't you go talking about the boss like that. If he heard you talking like that he'd—'

Dan heard more sounds as the two men moved off. Unnerved by their odd conversation, Dan shuddered slightly and crept up to the end of the isle to peer around. He saw two large blokes walk to the end of the warehouse and disappear through a door. The door he wasn't allowed to go through. The door that led to the restricted area.

When he had questioned his supervisor about why a musical instrument warehouse had a restricted area with thumbprint keypad access, the terse response had been, 'Prototypes! Obviously! New instruments that could change the face of the music scene. New instruments that our rivals would kill to get a hold of. New instruments that are none of your damn business. So, unless you want me to sack your sorry arse, *keep out!*'

On the spur of the moment, Dan sprinted as the door swung closed, and just about managed to get his fingers in. It was a massive effort not to scream as the door squashed them... but he managed it. Heart thumping away, he wondered what was so special about the synth those two blokes had come to fetch. Was it some sort of special prototype? Or maybe something more sinister. He was burning with curiosity now.

As he pulled the door open, about to enter, a heavy hand came down on his shoulder.

'Didn't I warn you about staying out of there?'

'I better get going,' said Bishop, finishing yet another cup of tea. 'I've got a busy Monday morning ahead of me.'

'Anything exciting?' asked Anne.

Bishop thought she sounded concerned. It was his first day back since he'd been used as an incubator by the Dominator, so it was no surprise that his fiancée was worried. He'd been promised light duties to start with, but they both knew that things didn't always go according to plan at the Fifth.

'No alien threats, rubber or otherwise, if that's what you mean,' Bishop said, smiling at Anne, trying to do his best to reassure her. He rose to his feet. 'Just paperwork and more paperwork. Putting together some files for the Brig to look through.'

Anne stood slowly and gently put a hand on his arm. 'Are you okay?'

'Fine,' he answered a little too quickly, pulling away and heading for the door.

'You've been a bit jumpy this evening,' said Anne, following him. 'Ever since that silly television show.'

'Yes,' said Bishop quietly, stopping at the door, his back to

Anne. 'It was a ridiculous show, wasn't it?' He paused. 'But…'

Anne took hold of him and turned him around. She looked into his eyes.

'But…' she prompted.

'There was something about the opening,' he explained. 'You were in the kitchen. But… Something about it felt… I don't know… Off? It made me feel… uncomfortable… Slightly unnerved. It's hard to explain.'

'And your reaction is what's bothering you?'

Bishop nodded slowly.

Anne was clearly relieved. She reached out and placed a hand to his cheek.

'It's okay,' she said. 'You've been through a lot recently.' She hesitated. Bishop knew she was reluctant to again bring up his experiences with Vaar. 'It's bound to have an affect on how you…'

'Watch television?' Bishop gave her a half-hearted smile. 'You're right. Of course.'

'I usually am.' Anne smiled up at him. She was obviously trying to lighten the mood.

'Yeah.' Bishop gave her a grin.

Anne laughed, and stood on her tiptoes to kiss him.

CHAPTER TWO
Sparking Interest

BISHOP STOPPED in his tracks, files tucked under one arm, to listen to the approaching soldiers. The topic of discussion was a certain TV programme, and its appalling lack of budget. They ceased laughing the moment they saw him looking at them, came to a halt and, hands to their caps, hurriedly saluted.

'Are you two talking about last night's new science fiction programme?' Bishop asked.

'Ah... yes, sir,' Private Goleman said.

'I take it you both watched it?'

'Yes, sir,' they both answered together.

'And... what did you think of it?' Bishop attempted to sound casual, but he recognised the weariness in his tone.

'Well, it was a bit of a laugh, wasn't it?' Private Ashe said.

'All except that creepy bit,' Goleman added.

'What bit?' Bishop asked.

The two soldiers looked at each other uncertainly.

'Those weird images. You know, the opening bit,' Ashe said.

'Yeah,' Goleman agreed. 'I know it sounds daft, Lieutenant, but they were just... Spooky, you know?'

Bishop smiled. 'To tell you the truth, Private, I thought that too. Wouldn't want my little nephew watching it.'

'No, sir.'

'The music, too,' Ashe added.

'The music?' Bishop asked.

'Yeah. It sort of got into your brain, didn't it?'

Maybe that was it, Bishop considered. Only... That was stupid. Music was music. But the opening sequence... He regarded the soldiers thoughtfully, then nodded abruptly. 'Carry on,' he said, dismissing them.

The two soldiers continued on their way silently. Bishop shook his head, watching them.

'A television programme... Silly.'

It was nerves, being back at work for the first time since Vaar. He was understandably out of sorts. That's what it must have been.

Gladys stared at the blinking lights on her switchboard. She could pretty much guess what every call was going to be about. The same topic that had consumed viewers last night.

Imagine, all that fuss over a silly television show, she thought.

She hadn't watched it, of course, but she had already formed a firm opinion that it was utter rubbish. Furthermore, she had decided that anyone who watched it must have very low standards, and that anyone who watched it and then decided that they needed to ring to voice their complaints was a fool.

If people wanted decent entertainment, she decided, they should watch the BBC. If only she worked for them instead of...

She couldn't even bring herself to spell out the initials in her mind.

Gazing at the lights once more, she fixed her smile in place and prepared to deal with the onslaught.

'Here we go again.'

So, apparently Paul McCartney died in 1966 and was replaced by an alien. The other members of The Beatles, fearing for their own lives, could not speak out publicly, but had seeded clues in their songs and album covers. The crossing photo on the cover of Abbey Road, for instance, was actually symbolic of a funeral procession, with the barefooted McCartney as the corpse. Eventually, the McCartney imposter had broken away from the band in order to pursue his plans of world domination. An official announcement of The Beatles breaking up was imminent.

At least, that was what an odd little group of conspiracy theorists had been spreading in their poorly produced, faded purple, mimeographed newsletter pages.

Brigadier Alistair Lethbridge-Stewart stared at the photo. He could not fathom how the whimsical crossing photo could represent a funeral. And McCartney looked very much alive, and not in any way alien. Out of sheer disbelief he flicked through the rest of the newsletter, scanning the headlines.

Turns out Bowie was also an alien... although he had always been one, apparently. And The Rolling Stones were secretly a group of alien-fighters, tracking down and neutralising alien threats in the music industry.

Lethbridge-Stewart almost burst into laughter.

'Poppycock,' he concluded, closing the folder with a definitive slap.

He was seated at his desk with files arranged into three neat stacks. On his left were the ones yet to be perused. On the right were the potential cases to be watched but not yet acted upon. And to their right were the ones that were to be dismissed. It was onto this pile, the largest so far, that he added the alien pop star file.

It was as if everyone was treating the Fifth as a dumping ground for crackpots.

But every file needed to be looked at and assessed. Just in case. Perhaps next time he would get Bishop to vet them, removing the patently more ridiculous ones, rather than just summarising them for him. More light work for the man, which was, quite literally, just what the doctor had ordered. The doctor, in this case, being Captain Lindsay, the Fifth's MO.

Lethbridge-Stewart picked up the next file, Electric Soundscapes, and began to read Bishop's dot-point summary.

A company specialising in electronic musical instruments. About to launch the SynthMoods 21-20, a new synthesiser which they claimed would revolutionise the music industry. Owned by Trevor Delacy, pop singer turned entrepreneur.

Lethbridge-Stewart couldn't seem to get away from pop music today. First it was The Beatles, and now this Delacy chap, whom he had, frankly, never heard of. Still, it wasn't as if he really kept up with pop music. Far too much of it was just noise these days. He preferred something a little more old-fashioned.

Lethbridge-Stewart continued reading, wondering why Bishop would have brought this to his attention, when he came to the final dot-point.

'Ah,' he said. 'Now this makes sense.'

Electric Soundscapes had spent the past three years funding research at several colleges and universities into the use of sound frequencies for 'mood enhancement'.

That was a phrase Lethbridge-Stewart didn't care too much for. It made him think of Moon Blink, of the dream eggs, and, worse, the effect of the Ice Maidens. Messing with such things never boded well, as far as he was concerned. No doubt there were unscrupulous military applications to such a technology… if perfected. But equally there was the detrimental effects…

He flicked through the rest of the file.

There was a short biography of Delacy, promotional material for the new synthesiser, company reports and a thick set of research papers. He couldn't really make heads nor tails of the scientific jargon in the reports, and his mind immediately went to Anne. He would have her explain it to him…

Lethbridge-Stewart let out a grumble. Over two months, and still she was his first port of call. The team she had left behind were all top boffins, no doubt, but none had her tenacity, or her general expertise. Still, they were all Lethbridge-Stewart had now, so he supposed they would have to do.

He returned to the scientific reports, and wasn't surprised to find that each of the conclusions seemed to indicate a lack of successful outcomes to the research.

Lethbridge-Stewart closed the file and put it onto the potential investigations stack.

He picked up the next file. Haltwhistle Aged Care Facility.

It was located on the South Tyne near the town of Haltwhistle, and specialised in the care of patients with senile dementia. The file mentioned eye-witness accounts of miraculously cured patients, but without any notable evidence to back up the claims. There was a report of one patient who was convinced that he'd been abducted by aliens and experimented on. Lethbridge-Stewart rolled his eyes at that, and put the file to one side.

The next one was just as interesting. International Electromatics. The competition for Bryden Industries, and the company who funded a lot of the Fifth's scientific work. Peyton Bryden had insisted he'd heard strange things about IE and, as a result and a favour, General Hamilton had told Lethbridge-Stewart to look into it.

Which he did. In a cursory sort of way.

With that in mind, he opened the file and read.

*

Bishop gulped some tea to wash down the last of his lunch as the BBC announcer continued to relate the details of Janis Joplin's death with detached professionalism. A month had passed already, and still Bishop couldn't quite take it in. He'd always liked her music, but as the voice turned into little more than a droning in the background, Bishop's thoughts moved in different musical direction, and what Goleman and Ashe had said that morning about…

'And it seems there were many unhappy viewers last night after the broadcast of LWT's new science fiction drama serial, *Fear Frequency*.'

Bishop sprung up, suddenly paying attention. His tea forgotten, he moved across the canteen and sidled up to the radio.

'It seems that rubber aliens and science fiction stories may be a little too much for some viewers to bear,' said the announcer, his voice taking on a much lighter tone than before. 'With the recent cancellation of the BBC's own *Doctor Omega*, LWT were banking on their new science fiction programme to get the audience figures the BBC have since lost. However, LWT have been inundated with viewer complaints since the broadcast of the first episode. It appears that the opening titles, in particular, have been denounced as too frightening for teatime viewing.'

Bishop's heart quickened, and in his mind's eye he could see the earie title sequence playing all over again.

'The unusual opening sequence, with a succession of unidentifiable images rushing quickly towards the viewer and wavy, abstract patterns, were accompanied with a distinct theme created on a synthesiser. The synthesiser in question is the SynthMoods 21-20, soon to be released onto the market by Electric Soundscapes, a company owned by former pop singer Trev Del.'

'Electric Soundscapes,' Bishop whispered, the name familiar. Although he couldn't quite remember why.

'In other news today, British Leyland have announced the new Austin Maxi…'

Of course! He'd dropped off a file on Electric Soundscapes that morning to the Brig.

Bishop rushed from the canteen.

*

'Ah, Lieutenant Bishop, perfect timing,' said Lethbridge-Stewart, as soon as Bishop entered the office. 'I've just finished assessing the files.'

Bishop stood to attention before the desk. 'Sir, I've just heard a BBC news report on the radio that pertains to one of the files.'

'Which one?'

'Electric Soundscapes.'

'Take a seat, Lieutenant,' Lethbridge-Stewart said, pulling out the appropriate file and opening it. 'What did the news say?'

Bishop related what he had heard. Then hesitated, again feeling the now-familiar trickle of sweat down his back.

'There's more?' Lethbridge-Stewart asked.

'Yes, sir. I…'

Bishop felt himself squirm under the Brig's inquisitive eyebrow. He felt foolish even thinking about it, but after almost two years of dealing with strange and alien things, Bishop knew to trust his instincts.

'Did you watch *Fear Frequency* last night?'

'No.' One corner of Lethbridge-Stewart's mouth twitched up slightly in amusement. 'Science fiction. Hardly my thing, Lieutenant.'

'Anne and I watched a little.'

Lethbridge-Stewart's mouth tightened. 'And how is Anne? I was only thinking of her today.'

'Yes, sir. Her absence is… noticeable.'

'That it is.'

'But she's doing well, sir. Finding new things to occupy her. Playing nursemaid high among them.'

Lethbridge-Stewart smiled. 'Quite right, too. She's been through a lot this year, wouldn't do to have her lose someone else.'

Bishop looked down briefly. 'No, sir.'

Lethbridge-Stewart waited a moment. 'So, this science fiction nonsense. What of it?'

'There was something… odd. It's hard to explain, sir, but while I was watching it… The opening titles in particular… It made me feel… uneasy. Unsettled.'

'Mood enhancement,' said Lethbridge-Stewart.

'Sir?'

Lethbridge-Stewart pointed to a section of the file, and indicated that Bishop should read it.

'I see,' Bishop said, once done.

'Doesn't necessarily mean anything untoward,' Lethbridge-Stewart said, coaching his words carefully.

'No, sir, just a new part of the viewing experience.'

Bishop waited while Lethbridge-Stewart gave it some thought.

'Very well,' he said. 'Wouldn't be the first time something strange came out of the TV that fell under our remit. Contact the BBC and get a transcript of that news report, as well as any further information they may have.' He passed the file to Bishop. 'Then get this file to…' He stopped to think. The name of Anne's team didn't readily spring to mind. There were a few of them, all with their own different specialities, but he was sure one of them was nominally his new go-to person. But what was the man's name…?

'Jeff Erickson, sir. He helped us out in Keynsham.'

Lethbridge-Stewart nodded. 'Ah yes, that's his name.'

'Adjustment periods are always difficult, sir.'

'That they are, Lieutenant. Very well, pass this on to Erickson. I want his team's assessment before we start making any official enquiries.'

'Yes, sir.' Bishop made to get up out of the chair.

'Just a moment, Lieutenant, there is another matter.'

Bishop settled himself back down.

Lethbridge-Stewart handed Bishop the Haltwhistle old persons' home file.

'I'd like you to pay a visit to this establishment,' he said. He did think about sending Bishop to International Electromatics, be his inside man, but that would have taken a lot more planning and, Lethbridge-Stewart suspected, it could easily become a much longer-term role. On the other hand, the old persons' home was just the walk in the park his adjutant needed. 'Talk to the staff, interview the chap who's claiming alien abduction and check out their records – particularly recent death certificates and any post-mortem reports.'

Bishop flicked through the paperwork. 'You think something's up over there?'

'Possibly. I agree that alien abduction seems unlikely, but

you never know. And I suspect you could do with the fresh air.'

'Yes, sir.' Bishop stood.

Lethbridge-Stewart watched him leave, thoughtfully. The man had been isolated long enough. An old people's home was hardly exciting, but at least it would be a little more interesting than filing.

CHAPTER THREE
Watchdog

HEART POUNDING away like the drum in a top-forty hit, Dan Morales entered the warehouse and scuttled straight to the relative cover of the shelving units. He tried to steady his breathing as he took a moment to lean against a support strut and close his eyes.

So far, so good. He had picked a time he knew his supervisor would not be there. His employment pass hadn't been cancelled yet, so getting through security turned out to be easy. And his key-code for the doors still worked. He hadn't encountered anyone he knew in the corridors. And the only staff in the actual warehouse all appeared to be gathered at one of the open shutters having a smoke.

But, of course, the luck wasn't going to hold out. Life just wasn't like that. He was in the wrong aisle. And, as if taunting him, Trev Del's voice blared over the speakers again.

Listen to me. Oh, listen to me.

He made his way to the end and peered around the corner. He needed to get to the middle aisle. He dashed around and into the next aisle. That was the way to do it, one at a time.

In his mind's eye, he imagined himself playing his guitar, plucking out the first notes of Lalo Schifrin's *Mission: Impossible* theme. He made it to the next aisle. And the next.

Until he finally reached the right one.

Without any mucking about, he went straight to the shelf and grabbed one of the SynthMoods boxes. He patted it like it was a dog or something, a stupid grin on his face.

'Prototype,' he whispered. He was pretty sure that he'd be able to sell it to the competition. That'd teach them for sacking him. For treating him like dirt.

But thoughts of revenge were pushed from his mind at the

sound of approaching footsteps and voices.

Dan frantically looked around for somewhere to hide. There were lots of spaces on the shelves he could squeeze himself in to, but if the approaching people actually came down the aisle, there was still a good chance they would see him. He looked up. There! If he could climb up past eye-level, that would be a better option.

The voices were getting closer and... damnit, he recognised them. In a panic, Dan reached up and gripped the edge of the shelf. He suppressed a shout as a rough bit of metal gouged his left hand. Dripping blood, he hoisted himself up. Wedging himself between boxes labelled 'electric flutes', he wriggled back as far as he could and tried to shift another box in front of himself. Then he pressed his right thumb onto the wound to staunch the bleeding.

The footsteps approached and he held his breath. Damn it, they'd stopped right below him.

'*Get another SynthMoods. Bring it here. Take it there.* I'm not a goddamn delivery boy,' complained the voice.

'Oh, for Christ sake, stop your whinging,' said the other voice. 'We do whatever the boss says.'

Definitely the blokes from last night, thought Dan. There was something about them that sent a shiver up his spine.

'Yeah, yeah, I know. Don't want 'im zapping me with his synth.' He chuckled.

Dan's eyes widened. *Zap?*

'Shhh!' There was a note of panic in the second voice now. 'Bloody hell, you've got to learn to keep your big trap shut. There are workers all over the place.'

'They're all slackin' off and havin' a smoke at the other end.' He chuckled again. 'Maybe the boss should zap *them!*'

'Would you quit it with the zapping. Christ almighty!'

Dan heard the movement of boxes and the footsteps started to move off.

'I wonder who the buyers are?'

'Oh, for God's sake, shut the f—'

And they were out of earshot.

Dan let out a long slow breath and shuddered.

This is something big, he thought. Something that could potentially get Delacy into a lot of trouble.

A smile slowly tugged at the edges of Dan's mouth. He

pulled a used handkerchief from his pocket and bandaged up his hand. He decided that all this undercover stuff might have been a mistake.

Waiting another few minutes, just to make sure the two blokes were gone, he jumped down, his boots slapping onto the concrete. He froze. For once in his life he was actually pleased to have annoying pop music piped in over the speakers.

He dashed to the end of the aisle and peered out. No sign of them. But the other workers looked like their break was ending. He needed to get out of there fast.

He took a deep breath and went back to where the synthesizers were shelved. With shaking hands, he grabbed one of them and took off.

He had to do something. He wasn't quite sure what just yet. But he could work that out later. For now, getting out of there with the evidence was all that mattered.

Dan could hear the other workers moving around, returning to the job. He figured that the best way to handle things from there on was to simply pretend he was meant to be doing what he was doing.

With the box up on his shoulder, he strode out from the aisle, across the warehouse floor and to the exit, whistling in what he decided was an average storeman kind of way. A couple of the workers looked briefly in his direction, one even waved, but most ignored him. He reached the door without incident.

As the yellow and orange Nationwide logo spun out of view, Mike Langley began speaking. His voice, although BBC proper, carried a hint of sensationalism.

'LWT finds itself embroiled in controversy and protest, all thanks to the eerie opening titles sequence featured in its new science fiction drama serial *Fear Frequency*.'

Dressed in a dark three-piece suit, Langley seemed to be relishing the chance to lambast the televisual opposition.

'This is, of course, not the first controversy that LWT has found itself in the middle of; I call to mind all that business last year with *BLIMEY*, Aubrey Mondegreene's last desperate attempt at gaining the spotlight. Spearheading the campaign to have *Fear Frequency* pulled from television schedules, is self-appointed television decency campaigner, Arabella Constance. Miss Constance has been urging viewers who found the first episode to be objectionable, to contact LWT and voice their complaints. Miss Constance now joins us in the studio to tell us a little more of what she is hoping to achieve.'

Langley turned to his right and the screen now revealed Arabella Constance seated next to him. Although only of middle age, Miss Constance had the appearance of someone much older. Her greying hair was pulled up into a severe bun, her eyes were narrow and squinting through her pince-nez glasses, her nose was prominent, and her lips pinched and sour. She wore a mauve jacket with floral embroidery over a cream blouse with frills at the high neck and sleeves. It was an outfit that would have been more suited to an elderly lady.

'I want it removed,' she announced, her voice harsh and bitter. 'Simple as that. It is not fit for public consumption.'

'What is it about this programme that makes it so unfit for public consumption, as you say?'

'Everything!'

Langley waited for her to continue, but when she didn't, he drew in an irritated breath and said, 'Could you be a little more specific, Miss Constance?'

'It is lurid and horrific sensationalism, masquerading as drama,' she said, glaring down the barrel of the camera. 'Completely inappropriate for early evening entertainment, when families, with their impressionable children, might be watching. It will give children nightmares. It gave me nightmares!' She gave a little shiver as if to emphasise the point.

Langley opened his mouth, ready to ask another question, but Miss Constance continued.

'The woman featured as the victim in the first act, was wearing clothing that was inappropriate, and although it was not directly shown, it was implied that the creature removed that clothing when it pulled her into the shadows.'

Langley tried to hide a smirk as he prepared himself to speak. But again, Miss Constance barrelled on.

'Perhaps the most objectionable aspect of the programme was the opening. The combination of images and music was...' She seemed momentarily lost for words. '... objectionable.' It seemed that whenever in doubt, she returned to her favourite word. 'I can only imagine the affect it would have on viewers of delicate sensibilities.'

'Thank you, Miss Constance.' Langley finally interrupted

her, determined to get his next question in. 'Your objections to the programme seem to be based on its unsuitability for younger viewers. Could not the situation be resolved with moving the programme to a later timeslot?'

'That is simply not good enough. Whilst unsuitability for younger viewers is certainly a concern, I fear for the morality of our society in general. By allowing programming such as this to proceed we run the risk of desensitisation to harmful images and potentially the disintegration of the moral fabric of society. It is utterly—'

'Objectionable,' Langley cut her off. 'Yes, I think we get the gist of your argument, Miss Constance.'

Anne switched off the television set and paced the room, her cold cup of tea untouched on the table. She remembered Bill's reaction last night. Perhaps there was more to this than she first thought. Yes, Arabella Constance was obviously unhinged, but there had been much talk about the series and its mysterious title sequence on the radio today. It seemed to have bothered quite a lot of people.

Anne's first instinct was to go and talk to Lethbridge-Stewart about it. Of course, that wasn't really her place to do. She had chosen to walk away from the Fifth. Her choice. Sure, she had things to occupy her the last couple of months – mostly looking after Bill – but she had always had an active imagination, an enquiring mind. She wasn't suited to just sitting back, not anymore – if she ever really was. She couldn't just stop taking an interest in the world around her. Especially when odd things happened.

Anne took a moment to listen to the sound of her breath going in and out. Perhaps she was seeing things that weren't really there. Perhaps she was suffering from too much inactivity. Too much breathing space. She was waiting to hear back from her friend at Cambridge University and the research she had underway. Surely, Anne could just put it to the back of her mind…?

Maybe she could just talk to Bill about it. But should she? He was on light duties, still recovering. She couldn't use her relationship with him to get her foot back in the door – a door she'd firmly closed herself.

Anne picked up her cup of tea, took a sip and grimaced.

Maybe closing that door had been a mistake after all.

'So... you are claiming that Electric Soundscapes is a threat to national security?'

Dan Morales nodded emphatically as he critically studied the young policeman with the podgy face and crisp uniform who had introduced himself as PC Reed.

Young man? Boy, more likely. He looked like he should still have been in school clothes. And just like a schoolboy in class, he seemed thoroughly bored.

'Your connection with them?' Reed didn't look up as he spoke. His head, with its neatly parted dark hair, was down, eyes buried in the notepad on the table.

'I work there...' Dan hesitated. 'Well, I used to work there. In the warehouse.'

Reed finally looked up. 'Used to?'

Dan nodded, avoiding his eyes. He figured that might be a sticking point.

'Why did you leave?'

'I was asked to leave.'

'I see. And when was this?'

'Erm...' Dan looked around. 'Last night.'

'So, you were sacked by them less than a day ago?'

'Well, yes, but only because they knew I was on to them.' Dan immediately realised that he'd responded with a little too much force. Lowering his voice, he continued. 'I'd been snooping around their... They have a secret area. And I found out—'

'We'll get to that in a moment,' said PC Reed, cutting him off unceremoniously. 'First I'd like to address a discrepancy between the personal details form you filled out when you arrived at the station and what you've just told me.' He looked down at the form and poked it with his pencil, pushing down hard, grinding the lead into the paper. 'Right here, under occupation, you have written musician. Yet you have just said that you worked in the Electric Soundscapes warehouse. Until last night, of course.'

'The warehouse job was just a temporary thing,' Dan rushed to explain. 'I needed the money. It was as simple as that. But what I really do... my career...' A distinct element of pride crept into his voice. 'I'm in music. I play guitar. And I sing.

And I write songs.'

'Hmmm.' PC Reed released the form from under his pencil. 'So, you are an unemployed musician.'

'It's a tough industry,' said Dan, defensively. What did this *boy* know of the music industry and the struggles that talent faced? Him with his perfect hair and perfect uniform and job that Daddy probably got for him. 'I get the odd pub gig. But mostly I'm working on getting a demo together.'

The odd pub gig, Dan thought miserably. It had been almost twelve months ago. And it had been an *odd* pub, in that it was mostly empty. The only person listening to him had been the owner. And he hadn't seemed too pleased.

'Right,' Reed said, letting the word stretch out. He pushed the forms to one side. 'Okay, Mr Morales. If you could please tell us about Electric Soundscapes, how they constitute a threat and how we can assist.'

PC Reed leaned back in his chair and folded his arms. The look of utter disinterest on his face made Dan hesitate. He'd obviously been fobbed off onto the junior officer, some kid fresh out of school who didn't know anything and didn't care. He felt cheated. He had important information, damn it! And the kid should be interested… should be grateful that he was reporting what he had found out.

'Well, you see, the SynthMoods 21-20 that Electric Soundscapes is about to launch… well it's… you see, it's a…' Dan faltered. All he had to go on, was the overheard conversation. Which wasn't much, now he came to think of it. Now that the fear and excitement had worn off. In his mind's eye he saw the open box stashed in his bedroom. That was proof, surely. Although it was stolen proof. He pushed away his doubts and pressed on.

'Well, it's not a synthesiser. It's not really a musical instrument. And they're about to sell it off to… someone.'

'So, if it's not an instrument, what is it?' Reed asked.

'Well, it's… I think it might be a weapon.'

'A weapon?' The boy no longer looked disinterested. The expression on his face now clearly said, oh-god-this-guy-is-a-nutter!

'Yes, a weapon. They were talking about zapping people with it.'

'Zapping?' PC Reed stared at him for a few moments, then

sighed – long and loud.

Dan huffed. Maybe going to the police hadn't been such a great idea after all.

'Where?' asked Anne.

'Haltwhistle,' Bill said. 'It's a town about halfway between Edinburgh and Leeds. And I'm off first thing tomorrow morning. Three hours by car to get there, then goodness knows how long to investigate the facility. I'll probably end up staying there at least one night. Possibly more, depending on what I find. Which is why I wanted to borrow your car, since mine is currently at the garage.'

'My *little lady's* car?'

Bill smirked. 'Did I say that? I'm sure it was Samson.'

Anne raised her eyebrows, mockingly. 'Oh, I'm sure it was him.' She rummaged around for the keys.

'I probably won't get the chance to see you now until the weekend,' Bill said.

As Anne searched for the keys, she also searched for something to say. 'Do you think there's an alien presence in an old folks' home in Haltwhistle?'

Bill chuckled. 'No, I don't think so. But after all the things we've seen…Who knows? Besides, there have been some unusual reports and—'

'No, no, no.' Anne cut him off. 'It's okay. You're under no obligation to brief me.' There was, perhaps, a little too much sourness in the way she delivered that. It was her own choice to leave the Fifth. She was happy with her decision to do so. And she really needed to get on with things and not be constantly bothered about what they were doing without her.

'Yes, well… okay, you're probably right. After all, you did leave of your own volition.'

Did Bill seem disappointed? There were a few seconds of awkward silence, as if there was something else he wanted to say. Instead, he went for…

'I'll give you a call when I get back. It's all bound to be nothing anyway.'

'You take care.' Anne handed him the keys. 'Are you sure you don't want to remain here tonight?'

Bill smiled warmly. 'No, I've taken up your bed long enough. You could do with a night away from your sofa.'

Anne reached up and pecked him on the cheek. 'Okay. Can't say I haven't missed my bed.'

She saw him to the front door, where he turned to face her.

'Don't worry, I'll be careful. Anyway, I'm sure it'll be nothing.'

'It better be. You're still not fully healed.'

Bill grinned and kissed her on the forehead. 'What will I do without you?'

Anne didn't answer him, instead she just watched him walk down the pathway from her house and to her car.

Let's not find out, she thought.

It was only after he'd driven away and she had closed the door that she realised she'd forgotten to mention the news reports about *Fear Frequency*. Deciding it could keep, Anne thought of her bed and decided on an early night.

CHAPTER FOUR
Haltwhistle

THE LONG *and Winding Road* started playing.

With a groan, Bishop switched off the radio and Paul McCartney's voice disappeared. He'd already had his fill of winding little roads.

Bishop yawned as he carefully rounded another country corner. He'd had a poor night's sleep, his dreams filled with eerie music, old people turning into aliens, and Anne. He was beginning to worry that her leaving the Fifth would put a strain on their relationship. Things had certainly gone a bit funny last night when he went to borrow the car. It was almost as if she resented him for having an investigation to proceed with, while she didn't.

Of course, last night's conversation had also been difficult as he desperately tried not to mention the fact that the old persons' home specialised in dementia. The last thing Anne needed was to be reminded of her father's final months.

Bishop shifted in the driver's seat and stretched.

Anne's Peugeot 204 Coupe was a nice enough car, he supposed, but it wasn't what he considered to be a proper sports car. It didn't feel powerful enough, it lacked a tachometer, and the transmission was mounted on the column. He smiled, still remembering the great care Samson had taken in helping Anne pick the perfect car. Bishop had driven it before, of course, but the circumstances had been somewhat different and the journey not as long as this one. Now he really appreciated what Samson had meant when he'd said that it was 'designed to be driven by a woman'.

Bishop pulled into a passing area to allow a car from the opposite direction to go by. The roads appeared to be getting narrower... And more winding.

He had already passed through Haltwhistle, a town which claimed to be the exact geographic centre of Britain, and secured himself a room at the local pub. Now he drove towards the South Tyne, and the home itself.

He hoped that this wasn't all going to be a waste of time. He seriously doubted that anyone had been abducted by aliens. And as for mysterious deaths... Well, old people died, didn't they? All the time. It was a part of the whole ageing deal. Still, if the Brig thought it was worth looking into, Bishop wasn't going to argue. Besides, as the Brig had said, the fresh air would be good for him.

Bishop turned onto the road that, according to the map spread out on the passenger seat, would lead to his destination.

And there it was in the distance. It's sprawling grey stonework spread across the greenery like an ugly stain. The road was dead straight, and Bishop could clearly see there were no other vehicles. He put on a final burst of speed.

Bishop parked the coupe under the overhanging branches of a large Mulberry tree, and hopped out. He regarded the building. Prison grey and functional. The sort of building that sapped the joy from the surrounding countryside and, he realised with a thud in his heart, not unlike Sebastian Collins' facility in Southrop. Bishop forced down the nausea, ignoring the pain in his abdomen, and headed through the glass double doors, straight to the reception desk at the end of the foyer. He wondered how long he'd be suffering from his experiences. Oh, sure, physically he'd heal soon enough, but mentally and emotionally...?

The receptionist seemed to be having a panicked conversation with a gruff looking orderly, but as soon as they noticed Bishop, the orderly hurried off and the receptionist was all smiles. She was young and pretty, with a fringe of blonde hair, from under which she gazed up at Bishop with baby-blue eyes.

'May I help you?' she asked sweetly.

'Lieutenant William Bishop.'

The receptionist gasped and her smile disappeared.

'Are you okay?' asked Bishop. He wasn't expecting his presence to elicit such a reaction, especially since his visit had been prearranged.

'Oh... Yes... I'm fine,' she said, recovering herself. 'It's just that your appointment with Dr Quinlan isn't until eleven thirty. And... well... you're not... you know... dressed like a soldier.'

'Ah, the civies.' Bishop chuckled, looking down at his blue blazer and beige slacks. 'This has to be the first time that a lack of uniform has shocked someone. It's usually the other way around.'

'Oh, it's just that I was told to expect an Army officer.' She didn't look at all amused.

'Uniforms tend to draw a lot of attention. And given that I'll be staying in Haltwhistle, I thought it best to keep things casual.'

'I see,' said the receptionist, although her expression indicated otherwise. 'And... you're staying in Haltwhistle?' Now she sounded confused.

'Yes. I wasn't sure how long this would all take. I thought I'd stay at the local pub.' After an awkward moment of silence, Bishop checked his watch and continued. 'I know that my appointment with the director of this home isn't for another—'

'Excuse me, Mr Bishop. This is not a *home*, it is a care *facility*.'

The receptionist looked rather put out by this, so Bishop offered his best smile.

'Sorry, the Aged Care Facility. Anyway, as I am here early, and I need to see the patient who reported aliens, as well as take a look through your records, I thought I could get a start on that before the appointment.'

'I'm terribly sorry,' said the receptionist, 'but you can't see anything or anyone until Dr Quinlan authorises it.'

Bishop hesitated. 'I was under the impression that I already had that authorisation. I do believe that my superior, *Brigadier* Lethbridge-Stewart, spoke to him yesterday.'

'I'm afraid that I've not been informed.' The receptionist's manner was now decidedly cool and definite. 'I'll have to contact Dr Quinlan and check.' She picked up her phone, dialled and waited. After a few moments she hung up. 'I'm sorry to say that he's not responding.'

Bishop thought she didn't look at all sorry.

'If he's not in his office, he must be doing his rounds,' the receptionist explained, getting to her feet. 'I'll just show you to the waiting room before I go and look for him.'

*

Bishop had been waiting almost twenty minutes and was getting rather irritated indeed. The fact that he was sipping on terrible tea and sitting on an uncomfortable sofa did not help his mood. The waiting room looked nice enough, with its floral drapes and window overlooking the garden, but the tea and coffee on the bench beside the kettle were the cheapest one could possibly find. Oh yes, and the biscuits were stale.

Reaching the end of his patience, Bishop put down his unfinished tea and marched back out to reception. There was a buzz of activity, the gruff looking orderly directing several other staff members out through the front doors, and the receptionist talking animatedly on the telephone.

Again, Bishop was uncomfortably reminded of Southrop, and the furtive behaviour on display there following his and Sally's arrival.

He swallowed down a lump. He wasn't too sure who he felt sorrier for. Himself or Sally. She had died there, but he... He wouldn't have admitted it, not even to Anne, but in the past two months there were moments when he wished it was he who'd died instead.

The receptionist saw him approach and, placing a hand over the mouthpiece of the phone, called to him before he had a chance to ask anything.

'I've let Dr Quinlan know you're here. He's just finishing up his rounds and will be with you as soon as he can. In the meantime, there is coffee and tea in the waiting room, as well as a selection of biscuits.'

She resumed her telephone conversation.

Bishop stood where he was for a few seconds. A doctor and nurse hurried along the corridor further up and disappeared through a door. Through the glass in the front doors, he saw the staff fan out into the car park. There was a definite edge of tension in the air.

And he did not like it. Not one bit.

He returned to the waiting area, trying to remind himself that an old persons' home was not the same as Collins' Future Warrior facility. Whatever happened here, it would never be as bad as being held captive by Vaar and experimented upon...

About bloody time, thought Bishop, jumping to his feet. But what he said was, 'Thank you for taking time out of your busy schedule to see me early, Dr Quinlan.' Not that it was that much earlier than the scheduled time. He glanced at his watch. Only about twelve minutes early.

Dr Quinlan, Director of the Haltwhistle Aged Care Facility, stared at him from the doorway, looking not at all pleased to see him. He was tall and slim, with thinning hair, a hawkish nose and suspicious eyes that glared from behind wire-rimmed spectacles. He carried a clipboard and wore a white coat over his nondescript shirt and trousers.

'I'm Lieutenant Bishop.' Bishop stuck out his hand.

'I'm surprised you're not demanding a salute,' said Quinlan, taking his hand and shaking it a little too firmly.

Bishop shrugged the comment off as attempted humour. 'We generally don't require civilians to follow military protocols.'

Quinlan sighed theatrically. 'I still fail to see what business the military have in coming here.' He was making no attempt whatsoever at hiding his displeasure at having to accommodate Bishop.

Which was strangely reassuring. Sebastian Collins at least pretended to be amenable to the inspection.

'Yes, yes, I know,' Quinlan said. 'Grantly is ex-Army. Still seems somewhat tenuous to me.' He sighed again – bigger and more exaggerated. 'So, you want to see our alien abductee?' He actually sneered as he said that, as if mocking his own patient.

'Yes,' answered Bishop, keeping his voice polite, if somewhat cooler. 'I would like to interview Colonel Grantly.'

'He's been suffering from dementia for quite some time and his lucidity varies from day to day, from hour to hour, sometimes even from minute to minute, so interviewing him may prove to be more than you bargained for.' Quinlan paused for a moment. 'There was also some mention of records. As I explained to your brigadier on the phone, financial records cannot be made available without the consent of the Board of Directors and—'

'I'm more interested in death records, post-mortem reports and medical histories.'

'Day-to-day medical records and medical histories are confidential. Technically, you would need approval from each of the families to view those individual patient records.'

'I see,' said Bishop, making a mental note to find out if there was any way around that technicality. 'In that case, I will need to interview some of your staff, particularly nurses and doctors who have dealt directly with Colonel Grantly.'

'Please yourself.' Quinlan glared at Bishop. 'Now, if there is nothing more you need from me, there are other matters that require my attention.'

'Yes, there does seem to be something going on,' said Bishop, deciding to test the waters.

'I beg your pardon?' Quinlan's tone quickly became hostile. 'What exactly do you mean by that?'

'Just that there seemed to be some excitement earlier on. Urgent conversations, orderlies wandering around out in the car park.'

'There is nothing going on that is out of the ordinary. Orderlies check the grounds regularly to ensure our patients are safe.' And with that, Quinlan turned on his heel and stormed out.

'There was music!'

'I beg your pardon?'

Colonel Grantly stared at Bishop as if he were a simpleton. 'There was music. When I was abducted.'

The old colonel was seated in an armchair by the window in his room. His face was gaunt, his cheeks hollow, his eyes sunken. He looked like he hadn't slept in weeks. He squirmed in the chair as if unable to get comfortable, and his fingers constantly fidgeted. He shifted his haunted gaze away from Bishop and out the window.

'They strapped me to a table and played music at me.'

'The aliens...?'

'Mmm.' Grantly nodded his head vaguely.

'And they played music for you?'

'Not *for* us. They played it *at* us. Made us listen to it.'

'Why?'

'Because it changes us. Makes us... different.'

'In what way?'

'I don't know.' Grantly's voice rose in frustration. He raised a trembling hand to his face. 'Just different. It's... it's so hard to remember.'

Okay, it was going to be harder than Bishop had expected.

Asking about the music was agitating Grantly, so Bishop decided to try something else.

'What did the aliens look like?'

Grantly's eyes widened and his hand dropped back into his lap. 'They were in disguise.'

'What were they disguised as?'

'People of course,' growled Grantly. 'What else would they be disguised as? They're disguised as people so that they can move among us.' He lowered his voice to a whisper. 'Some of them are here. They take us away, so that they can experiment on us. And play us their music. And then they bring us back.'

'If they're in disguise, how do you know they're aliens?'

'Well, what else would they be, young man?' Grantly glared at Bishop as if he were an idiot, before turning back to the window.

Bishop didn't know how to respond to that, so he tried to steer the conversation in another direction, again.

'Where did they take you?'

'To the music place.'

'And where, exactly, is that?'

'Away from here.'

Bishop wasn't getting anywhere. He tried yet another change of direction.

'You said *us* before. They take other people from here?'

'Yes. They took Bradley and Simons. And now they've taken Miss Talley.' Grantly turned away to look out of the window again. 'Poor Miss Talley.'

'Who? Who's Miss Talley?'

'Hmmm?' Grantly slowly turned to face Bishop, his eyes glassy and squinty. 'Who?'

'There is no one by the name of Bradley or Simons currently at this institution,' said Nurse Hadley.

Bishop gazed around the common room. A brightly lit area with an old television set at one end, windows looking out over a garden at the other end, and copious shelves along the remaining walls, loaded with books. Most of the patients sat in armchairs, sofas or wheelchairs gazing blankly at nothing, although two of the ladies sat playing cards around a foldout table. There was another nurse, much younger, trying to interest one of the other ladies in a book. Mint-green vinyl dominated the decor.

'What about someone called Miss Talley?' he asked, bringing his attention back to the head nurse.

Hadley suddenly looked less sure of herself. 'I'm... I'm afraid that I do not have the time to be answering your questions at the moment,' she said, eyes darting around at the patients in the common room. 'You're free to talk to any of the patients in here. But there's no Miss Talley among them. If you have any more questions, I would suggest that you direct them to Dr Quinlan.'

Leaving Bishop open-mouthed in the centre of the common room, Nurse Hadley stalked away.

First the receptionist, then the director and now the head nurse. They definitely had something to hide.

All Bishop had to do was work out exactly what it was.

He looked around the common room. It was so normal.

He seriously doubted that aliens were behind anything, music-playing ones or otherwise.

So, what was being concealed...?

CHAPTER FIVE
Miss Talley

BISHOP PICKED up a footstool and took it over to the old lady who had given in and was finally reading, and plonked himself down next to her armchair.

'Hello. My name's Bill.'

The woman slowly looked up from her book and squinted through her thick glasses. 'Eh?'

'Bill! My name is Bill. I've been visiting with Colonel Grantly. Do you know him.'

'Eh?'

'Colonel Grantly!' Bishop repeated, louder this time. 'Do you know him?'

The old woman shook her head and glared at Bishop. 'Who are you?'

'Bill.' He felt very much like he was on a merry-go-round.

'Bill?' The woman looked confused. 'I don't think I know anyone named Bill.' She looked down at her book, bringing the conversation, if you could call it that, to an end.

'The ladies playing cards are chattier than Greta here.'

Bishop looked up to see a young nurse. She looked nervous, he thought, the way her eyes kept darting towards the door where the head nurse had exited.

'They know all the other residents.' She hesitated. 'And... um... People who have died... well... they aren't currently here, are they. At this institution.'

'Sorry?'

'Please, excuse me,' she said moving off. 'I've got work to do.' And she was gone.

'People who have died?' Bishop whispered to himself, curiously. Then it hit him.

Bradley and Simons weren't currently residents at

Haltwhistle. But they may have been in the past. That nurse was obviously hinting at what Nurse Hadley was concealing from him.

Bishop got to his feet and went to the fold out card table.

'Good afternoon, ladies. May I join you?'

'And who are you, young man?' asked the plump lady with the blue-rinsed hair and a distinctly mischievous sparkle in her eyes, which were behind large tortoiseshell glasses.

'Lieutenant William Bishop, at your service.' Bishop saluted. 'But most people, these days, just call me Bill.'

'Well, Bill, my name is Hyacinth and my friend here is Jasmine. And now that we have been properly introduced, we would be delighted if you would join us.'

'Thank you, kindly.' Bishop pulled up the spare seat. 'Such pretty names. Both flowers.'

Jasmine, who was thin, grey-haired and looked considerably frailer than her friend, giggled like a schoolgirl.

'Well, aren't you the flatterer,' said Hyacinth. 'I've often said that Jas and I have managed to be friends for as long as we have because of our mutually floral given names. That, and the fact that, even though we are not related, we share a most common and boring surname in Smith. Although my late husband always pronounced it *Smythe*.' She smiled lovingly at the memory. 'He was such a pretentious prat.'

Jasmine giggled again before saying, 'We may have pretty names, but you do so have a pretty face.'

'Ah.' Bishop blushed, momentarily lost for words.

'So, my dear, what can we do for you?' asked Hyacinth. 'You look like a gentleman with something on his mind.'

'I came here to have a chat with Colonel Grantly. But that didn't go so well.'

'I'm not surprised.'

'Yes, indeed,' chimed in Jasmine, spinning a finger in circles at her temple.

'Jas is right,' continued Hyacinth. 'The poor man has lost his marbles. Mind you, he was already rather vague when he arrived here last year. But he's been getting worse of late. Keeps blathering on about aliens, you know.'

'Yes, I know,' said Bishop. 'But he also mentioned Bradley and Simons and—'

'Oh!' gasped Jasmine, cutting him off.

'Paul Bradley and Mike Simons,' said Hyacinth with a nod. 'They died recently. It rather upset the poor Colonel. They were friends, you see.'

Died recently? Surely, the head nurse should have remembered their names then.

'What about someone called Miss Talley?'

'Ooooh,' squealed Jasmine, practically bouncing up and down in her seat. 'She's escaped!'

'Settle, petal.' Hyacinth patted her friend's hand before turning to Bishop. 'But Jas is quite correct. Miss Talley did a runner this morning. She's one of our younger residents, only in her sixties, so she's still got some vim, verve and vigour. There's been a good deal of excitement, as they've been unable to find her. I mean, residents do wander off every now and then, but they're usually found fairly promptly. You know, meandering around the grounds or ambling off up the road in a bit of a daze. But there's been no sign of Miss Talley.'

Cardiac arrest. Both of them. Within hours of each other. Last week. No autopsies. Both bodies discovered in their rooms by Head Nurse Hadley.

Bishop put down the file. Well, that settled it. Something was definitely going on. Given that Hadley had found both the bodies, on the same day, there was no way she wouldn't have known the names. She was deliberately being obstructive.

Yawning, Bishop flicked through the small stack of files that Quinlan had grudgingly given him access to. There were staff files, procedural files and some resident files. The medical files were not there, as they were confidential, so the resident files mostly contained information such as names, background, date of admission, whether they had signed themselves in or been placed there by a family member. And, in some cases, death certificates.

The first file was on Greta, the lady he had tried to speak with in the common room. He browsed it and moved on to the next. And the next. As he flicked through the rest of the files, something very odd and disturbing stuck out.

There had been a spike in the number of deaths over the last month. The cause for each and every one of them was cardiac arrest. And each one of the bodies had been discovered by Hadley.

Bishop went to the staff files.

Head Nurse Leone Hadley. Forty-three years of age. Unmarried. Began work at the home two months ago. A list of past places of employment. Qualifications and training. Blah, blah, blah.

Closing the file, Bishop ran a hand over his tired eyes, then checked the time. Sixteen-hundred. He decided to call it a day, intending to drive back to Haltwhistle and report to the Brig from there.

'See you tomorrow,' he said as he passed by the receptionist. She nodded curtly in response.

On the spur of the moment, Bishop stopped and turned back. 'So, have you found Eva Talley yet?'

The receptionist's eyes looked as if they would pop from her head. 'What? Um... Oh... well...'

'I'll take that as a no.' And with a pleasant smile, Bishop turned and left.

'It's about time you got here!'

Bishop narrowly missed smashing his head into the sun visor as he jumped in surprise. He twisted around in the car seat, hand going for the pistol that wasn't where it would have been were he in uniform, searching for the owner of the voice. A pair of bright, aged eyes stared back at him from the floor behind the passenger seat, surrounding wrinkles accentuated by the broad grin on the owner's face.

'Miss Talley, I presume?'

'Indeed. And you would be Lieutenant Bishop.' She grunted as she shifted position. 'Is there anyone around out there? My back and knees are killing me. I really need to get off the floor and into the seat.'

Bishop took a quick look around. The car park was deserted. 'All clear.'

'Hallelujah!' Miss Talley groaned again as she pulled herself up out of the ridiculously small space. 'That's better,' she said, and leaned back in the seat and smoothed down her tartan dress.

Miss Talley was incredibly short. Tiny, in fact, which explained how she was able to fit in her hiding spot. Seated in the back, her head barely came up to the window. No wonder she'd been able to evade the orderlies.

'How do you know who I am?' Bishop asked. 'Why are you

in my car? And how, for that matter, did you get into the car? I'm sure I locked it.'

'I know who you are because your name was in Dr Quinlan's diary,' Miss Talley said, eyes twinkling mischievously. 'I found it whilst snooping in his office. I've been doing a lot of that. Snooping. Not just the director's office. All over the place, in fact. Trying to find out what the hell is going on in this poor excuse for an over-the-hill *facility*.' Her mouth was running at a hundred miles an hour. 'Seeing as you're Scots Guards, I thought you'd be a good person to talk to about my suspicions. Not just because you're military, but because I've got Scottish ancestry, on my mother's side, and any branch of the military with Scots in their title is bound to be trustworthy. As for your car... well...' She pointed to the floor where a wire coat hanger lay bent and discarded.

Bishop tried to assimilate all this information. 'How come you know how to break into a car?'

'Misspent youth, I'm afraid,' she said, lowering her eyes deliberately. It was as if she was trying to appear guilty and repentant, when in fact, she just looked thoroughly pleased with herself. 'My first sweetheart was a hooligan with a liking for fast cars. Of course, fast cars back then weren't all that fast compared to what you get today. I dare say, this little beauty would really go!' She giggled. 'Of course, the courting didn't last, but I certainly learned a thing or two. And I've maintained an interest in cars.'

It seemed like nothing today was going quite how Bishop expected.

'Right,' he said, looking Miss Talley right in the eyes. 'I don't suppose your suspicions involve alien abductions, music and mysterious deaths?'

'You must have been talking to Colonel Grantly,' she said. 'No. Maybe. Yes!'

'Sorry?'

'Do try to keep up. You're Scots Guards, so it's the least I expect. But I'll spell it out. No, for aliens. I have no idea where he got that idea from. Yes, for the mysterious deaths. Maybe, for the music, because there is music for those of us who attend the regular recitals, and that includes Grantly; but I don't necessarily think it's got anything to do with the mysterious deaths.'

'So, these mysterious deaths,' asked Bishop, 'do they include Bradley and Simons?'

'They most certainly do.' Miss Talley nodded emphatically. 'And there were several more before them.'

'And what makes their deaths mysterious?'

Miss Talley's brow furrowed as if deep in thought and her eyes clouded over. 'Um...' But then her eyes brightened again. 'Well, for starters, they lie about them. I've heard the nurses telling their families that they died in their rooms when no one was around. But they didn't, you see. They died somewhere else. I've seen their bodies being brought back by Nurse Hadley and that Neanderthal orderly of hers.'

'But their death certificates list this institution as place of death.'

'Lies!' Miss Talley took a deep breath and held it. She suddenly looked quite strained and tired.

'Are you okay?' asked Bishop.

'Not really.'

'What's the matter?'

'I have dementia. Alzheimer's they call it. Not a very helpful name, is it? Doesn't tell you anything about the problem. Doubt it'll catch on.'

Miss Talley may well have been right. Bishop certainly wasn't familiar with the term. He looked at her in confusion. She did not strike him as someone whose mental faculties were deteriorating. Certainly, she appeared lucid and in command of her memory.

'This facility specialises in this Alzheimer's, which is why I am here,' she explained. 'But recently, the effects have... faded. My condition went into remission to the point of being non-existent. My memory returned and my ability to think things through and focus, all improved. Now, this has happened to other people as well, including Bradley and Simons. And Grantly.'

'But Grantly...'

'Yes, I know,' Miss Talley said, cutting him off. 'Grantly has regressed. As did Bradley and Simons, just before they died. And, I fear that I am headed in the same direction. I'm beginning to have moments of memory loss and difficulty in concentrating. I can feel my grip on my mind beginning to loosen again. And... and...' Her eyes were haunted now, her hands shaking. 'I am so very scared.'

'You're worried that you'll become one of the mysterious deaths?'

'No. At my age death no longer holds the fear it used to. I'm scared of losing my mind. This condition is... It's so insidious. Because you know it's happening. Oh, you try to deny it, but... but you can feel it chipping away at your mind. And there's not a damned, bloody thing you can do about it.' She took a deep rattling breath and leaned forward. 'I should be getting back.'

'Wait,' said Bishop. 'You don't have to go back.'

'No. But I want to. Whatever happened to me and Grantly and the others has something to do with this place. I want to... No, I need to stay here. I need to find out what's happened to me. With each subsequent person who has gone into remission, that remission has lasted longer and been more definite. I am hopeful I might not regress completely, if I stay here.'

Bishop got out of the car, bringing the front seat forward so that Miss Talley could climb out.

'Are you sure?' he asked, wanting to give her one last chance to change her mind.

Miss Talley nodded and smiled warmly at him before shuffling off back to the home.

Bishop repositioned the seat and sat behind the wheel. Through the windscreen, he watched her slowly crossing the car park, his mind a whirl of new information. As she neared the door an orderly came running out. He took hold of her arm and began leading her inside. As they went through the door, the orderly looked back over his shoulder.

Right at Bishop.

Bishop took a deep draught of his pint and put the glass down on the counter as the publican pushed the telephone and a moneybox towards him. Bishop nodded his thanks, and the publican moved off to pull more beers.

Seated at the end of the bar, up against the wood-panelled wall in the shadow of several beer barrels mounted in a display above him, he readied himself to make his report.

What he really wanted to do was call Anne, speak to his fiancée. But first he had to make his report. He was, after all, still on the clock. No doubt, despite saying that they wouldn't speak for a few days, Anne would be waiting on his call.

Bishop smiled at the thought of her voice.

He popped a coin into the money box and nodded again to the barman, who was still eyeing him suspiciously. With a hmm, the barman disappeared into the back of the pub.

'Lethbridge-Stewart,' said the clipped voice at the other end, within moments of Bishop dialling the Brig's direct line.

'Bishop here.' He deliberately avoided using his rank or addressing the Brig by his rank. That would attract almost as much attention as a uniform.

'Ah, Lieutenant Bishop. Good. What's the progress?'

Bishop turned to the wall and kept his voice down.

'There's definitely something going on.'

'Speak up a bit, man.'

'Sorry, sir. There's no phone in my room, so I'm down in the pub. Trying to keep a low profile.'

'Understood. Carry on.'

'As suspected, there's nothing in the abduction claims. But there is something odd going on with remission and subsequent regression of Alzheimer's in patients.'

'Of what?'

'It's a specific form of dementia, sir. I was going to find out what exactly it is from Anne.'

'No, let's not bother her. I'm sure it's still a sore subject. I'll make some enquiries.'

'Yes, sir. Ideally, we also need to get access to the patient's medical records.'

'I'm sure we can get that organised. Anything else?'

'There's definitely a cover-up with recent deaths as well. Death certificates appear to have been falsified in terms of location and possibly with cause of death. I'd like to organise the exhumation of the most recent body and have a post-mortem carried out.'

'Tricky.' There was a pause before Lethbridge-Stewart spoke again. 'Perhaps it might be a good idea for you to brief Captain Lindsay tomorrow morning. Give him more details on what you've discovered. Is there a less public telephone you could use?'

'I'll see what I can do.'

'Very good. Now, get on to Anne, and then have a well-earned bit of rest. And that's an order, Lieutenant. Don't overdo it.'

'No, sir.' Bishop disconnected the call, but kept the receiver to his ear. He closed his eyes a moment, then dialled Anne's number.

CHAPTER SIX
Reports and Interviews

FIRST THING the next day, Lethbridge-Stewart leafed through Erickson's notes on the Electric Soundscapes file, as he spoke on the phone to Lindsay, who had yet to leave his own home, about the situation at Haltwhistle.

'Lieutenant Bishop reported in yesterday and seems to think we need to go through their patient medical files, as well as conduct an exhumation and post-mortem. Take a look at the file and get the ball rolling on that, Captain.'

'Yes, sir. I'll make sure it's the first thing I do when I report in.'

'Yes, sorry about disturbing you and your lady wife,' Lethbridge-Stewart said, 'but I want us to get the jump on this.'

'Of course, sir. I do have a long list of things that require my attention, but I can see how this should take priority. If I may ask, sir, how is my patient?'

'As far as I can ascertain, he's doing well. No action, just sitting down talking to old people and reading files. Now then, Bishop will contact you today to give you a more detailed briefing on what he's discovered.'

'Yes, sir.' There was a momentary pause on the other end of the line. 'I'll be leaving in about ten minutes. Just need to drop the misses off, and I'll head directly to the Madhouse.'

'Thank you, Captain. Oh, just one last thing. Have you heard of Alzheimer's?'

'Of course, sir. Named after the German psychiatrist Alois Alzheimer who first identified it sixty years ago, or thereabouts. It's not a commonly used term, really, most people just use dementia as a catch-all, but it's not quite as straight forward as all that. Can I ask why you want to know, sir?'

'I'm sure it'll make perfect sense when Lieutenant Bishop

rings you later.'

'Very good, sir. I shall wait on Mr Bishop's call then.'

No sooner had Lethbridge-Stewart hung up the phone, ready to go through Erickson's notes, when a quiet rap on his door announced the arrival of Colonel Walter Douglas. He poked his head in.

'Got a moment, sir?'

'Yes, yes. Come in, Dougie. What is it?'

As one of his oldest friends, Lethbridge-Stewart had no trouble reading Douglas' expression. He had quite a story to tell. Lethbridge-Stewart pointed to the chair before his desk, and Douglas sat.

'I've just had a very interesting chat with a police officer about a report they took the other day.'

Lethbridge-Stewart raised an eyebrow. 'And since when have civilian police been in the habit of briefing the Fifth Operational Corps on reports made to them?'

'Ah, well...' Douglas chuckled nervously. 'It's not really official. Just a contact of mine in Scotland Yard I've known for a few years. Always seemed prudent to have a man on the inside, as it were. It's not like we haven't needed to call on civilian police before.'

'Can't argue with that. Go on.'

'He mentioned in passing that they'd had a report made by some nutter, his word, not mine, who'd just walked in off the street. Completely out there accusations.'

Lethbridge-Stewart wasn't sure he wanted to hear this. Was the Fifth going to become the dumping ground for all insane reports? Still, Douglas wouldn't have brought this to him, unless he thought there was something to it.

'We would've just had a laugh about it and I wouldn't have paid it no mind normally,' Douglas went on, 'except that he mentioned Electric Soundscapes.'

Lethbridge-Stewart's eyebrow immediately shot up, and his eyes landed on the notes before him. 'Did he now?'

'This fellow, a musician or something, used to work for them. And now he's claiming that they're making musical instruments that are actually weapons.' Douglas hesitated a moment. 'Now I know it all sounds a bit daft, but given the file we've got on Electric Soundscapes...'

'You thought right,' said Lethbridge-Stewart. 'I hesitate to tread on the Met's toes, but… See if you can get this contact of yours to send us a copy of that report.'

Douglas smiled. 'Already on its way.'

'I'll need to set up an office,' said Bishop, smiling pleasantly and putting as much sweetness into his voice as he could manage. 'With a telephone.'

The receptionist stared up at him, aghast. 'Why?'

'I need to be able to receive phone calls,' he said. 'I need somewhere to continue my investigation of the records. And a space in which to interview staff… Privately.'

'I'll need to check with Dr Quinlan.'

'You do that,' said Bishop. 'Please let him know that Brigadier Lethbridge-Stewart is available to discuss the matter, should he have any concerns about my needs.' He clapped his hands together and rubbed them eagerly. 'Now, I don't suppose there's a staff area I can make myself a decent cup of tea in?'

Having read the notes Erickson had assembled from his team of experts, which included copious amounts of scientific jargon on the theoretical possibilities and probabilities of sound being used to affect the way people thought, felt and behaved, Lethbridge-Stewart was now reading the statement made to the police by Dan Morales.

By the time Lethbridge-Stewart finished, there was no longer any doubt in his mind that something was going on. He didn't have enough yet to warrant a full-on investigation, but his gut told him he had to do something.

He snatched up the phone. 'Get me Colonel Douglas.' He waited a moment until he was connected. 'Dougie, I want to bring this Morales chap in for an interview.'

Bishop made himself another tea and returned to his *office*. He shared the windowless room with some old filing cabinets and cardboard boxes stacked along the walls. A small table and chair had been squeezed in there for him, with a stool positioned in front of the table for interviews. A telephone had been grudgingly provided, its cord running under the door and down the corridor to a connection point in a real office.

Negotiating his way past the boxes, he circled around the table and looked down at the chair. What was this obsession with uncomfortable, mint-green vinyl? He settled himself into it anyway, took a sip of tea (which was decidedly better from the staff kitchenette than the visitor waiting room), and placed the mug down on the table next to a pile of staff files. He glanced at his watch. Sixteen-twenty-three-hours. He yawned and stretched.

It had been a long day. He had spent an hour or so on the phone with Lindsay, filling him in and getting an overview of what he should be looking for in medical files, which according to the MO he would soon have access to. Bishop had spoken to several more of the residents with varying degrees of lucidity, but there had been little joy there. Greta had been more friendly and chatty this time, but even with a greater clarity of mind, she didn't really know anything of value. He had searched out Miss Talley, who had not been in any of the common areas, and eventually found her sitting alone in her room. But she displayed none of the mental acuity she had the day before. In fact, she had barely even recognised him. He had noticed three discarded paper medicine cups in her otherwise empty wastebasket. He had attempted to interview some of the staff, but they had been mostly reticent and obstructive. Even Nurse Greyson, the helpful young nurse from yesterday, was unhelpful today, nervously fidgeting the entire time and timidly shrugging in answer to most of his questions.

It was all very frustrating.

He was considering packing it in for the day, when his door burst open and Dr Quinlan stalked in. If looks could kill, Bishop would have been dead on the spot. The director's right hand was clenched into a fist, the knuckles white.

'You appear to have some very influential superiors.' His voice was cold and controlled. He glared at Bishop, obviously not wanting to continue. After a moment's silence, he thrust his fist forward and opened his hand. A key hit the table, skittered across the surface and over the edge onto the floor. 'The medical files are in the next room.' Turning on his heel, he stalked out, not bothering to close the door.

Bishop watched him stride out of view. A moment later, a door slammed loudly. Picking up the key, Bishop smiled.

Things were looking up.

His hair was blond, long and tied back with a black ribbon. His eyes were a twinkling blue with a jovial intensity, made more startling by his eyebrows and lashes which were so blond as to almost disappear. Although thirty-one years of age, his skin was flawless, with a youthful glow. And as he smiled, straight, very un-British white teeth sparkled in pearlescent glory. He was dressed in a tailored suit. Blue to match his eyes.

'Former-pop idol, transitioned to successful entrepreneur. Head of Electric Soundscapes. Mr Trevor Delacy.' The announcer paused. 'And now he finds himself embroiled in controversy over the theme tune to a new television series. Over to you, Mr Delacy.'

Delacy smiled his dazzling smile, before launching into his speech. 'I think that *controversy* is a bit of an overstatement. My company has created a new musical instrument, a revolutionary new synthesiser, which has been used to perform the theme music for *Fear Frequency*. The series tells a scary science fiction story about invading aliens, and the brief was to create a piece of music that reflected the emotional state of that series. And that brief has been met with startling accuracy. People have been unnerved by it. People have been scared by it. And I say: Terrific! It demonstrates the power and influence of music. It demonstrates the power and influence of the musical instrument. It demonstrates the power and influence of the SynthMoods 21-20. Providing twenty-first century sounds for twentieth century music! However...'

He paused, gazing intently into the camera.

'There has been some concern. Yes. In deference to their advertisers, who want to sell their products to the viewers rather than frighten them off, LWT has asked me about the possibility of modifying the music. I see this as an opportunity. An opportunity to demonstrate the versatility of the SynthMoods 21-20. Yes, it can produce music to scare you with. But it can also soothe and calm viewers, placing them in the right frame of mind to be advertised at.' His smile made a comeback. 'So, it is with great pleasure that I can announce that LWT has been able to secure permission to rescreen the first episode of *Fear Frequency* tonight. Along with a brand-new theme to accompany a new opening sequence, which, I should add, caused much more of a stir. And the music will, again, be created on the versatile SynthMoods 21-20.' His smile widened, becoming even more dazzling. 'I hope you will all be watching.

I know I will be!'

'And... cut!' the production assistant called after receiving the instruction over his headphones from the director in the booth.

Delacy's smile switched off and the twinkle was gone from his eyes, his ponytail swishing from side to side as he weaved his way across the studio floor, dodging cameras, cables and people. He had almost made it to the exit when Merv Chatley, *Fear Frequency's* producer, cut him off.

'Nice speech, Trev. Nice speech,' said Merv, trying to put an arm around Delacy's shoulders. A task made difficult by the fact Delacy was a good head taller than him. He quickly gave up. 'A little heavy on the *demonstrates this* and *demonstrates that*, but on the whole, nice speech.'

Delacy gave him a curt nod of acknowledgment and tried to head around him. But Chatley moved to block.

'I just wanted to check about the new piece of music. It *is* ready to go, isn't it?'

'Yes, of course.'

'Excellent, because you know, changing the title sequence at such short notice wasn't easy. And let's not forget the difficulty we had in getting a repeat screening of the episode not even a week later. Thames does not repeat LWT's output. Do you know how rare this is? That they agreed to do so? Especially for science fiction. The last time I can recall such a thing was seven years ago, and *that* was the BBC!' Merv scratched nervously at his prematurely greying beard. 'Any chance of a listen?'

'No.' Delacy's tone was about as matter-of-fact as you could get. 'You know the score. Pun intended. You get the music in time for the broadcast. No one hears it prior to the broadcast. That was the arrangement.'

'Yes...' Merv continued scratching. 'But we have to make sure it fits in with the new title sequence, and given what happened last time—'

'And what did happen last time?' Delacy looked down on Chatley. 'You had the music right on time. For free. Remember? You didn't have to pay for it, which, given your shoe-string production budget, must be a considerable boon. And, if I may say so, it fit the title sequence perfectly. Perfectly! The music was broadcast. It got a reaction. A reaction that has brought your little serial a great deal more attention than it actually deserves.'

'Well, that's a little...'

'It's quite simple,' concluded Delacy. 'Do you want the music or not?'

Merv nodded, almost desperately.

'Well then. Get out of my way.'

Delacy pushed past Chatley, who now stood with his mouth agape, obviously unused to people speaking to him like that, and strode out of the studio.

Bishop opened Miss Talley's medical file. Scanning through, he stopped at medications. Aside from heart tablets, there was nothing else listed.

He had a hunch that someone was meddling. Drugging her. Possibly to stop her from giving him any more information than she already had.

He noted that her daily dose was delivered at 9:30am each day, and made up his mind to stop in and visit her again tomorrow.

'Just on the table there.'

Douglas watched as Private Ashe manhandled the television onto the table that had been set up in the corner of the office.

'Will that be all, sir?'

'Yes, dismissed.'

The private saluted and headed off.

Douglas checked his watch. Not long to go. He went over to the set, plugged it in and switched it on, to be greeted by the hiss of static. He pulled up the rabbit ear aerials from the back and manoeuvred them until he got a fuzzy picture. It was just a portable black and white set, but it would do. Having read the Electric Soundscapes file, he thought it best to actually watch the show for himself. And since he was working late, a television in his office was the way to go.

He checked his watch again. Just enough time to nip out and make himself a cuppa.

Dan Morales dumped his bags onto the floor, plonked himself onto the bed and gazed about. The compartment was small, but not as cramped as he had expected. In fact, it had a distinct touch of luxury about it, as far as he was concerned. There was a rich, blue, patterned carpet on the floor, with a paler blue on the wall above the bed. The other walls were an off-white. He'd never experienced anything quite like this. It was out of his price-range. Not that he'd ever needed to travel to Edinburgh before. He still found it all quite unexpected.

He'd received a phone call earlier that day from a Colonel Douglas, telling him that some military chap, quite high up with a fancy title – Brig-a-something-or-other – wanted to chat to him about the report he'd made to the police. And then the next thing he knew, he was booked onto the Caledonian Sleeper that very night.

Dan was quite excited about finally being taken seriously. And not a little too pleased with himself for having scored an all-expenses-paid jaunt to Edinburgh. He had plans to make use of his time there to try and peddle his demo tapes. He wondered briefly if a military endorsement would help.

Still... getting someone to look into Electric Soundscapes was the important thing. Wasn't it? He needed to focus on that.

His eyes, after doing the rounds of the compartment, came to rest on his second suitcase. Yes, that's what he needed to focus on.

He leaned back and sprawled himself out on the bed, visions of soldiers raiding the warehouse dancing through his mind. He imagined his supervisor being carted off in handcuffs along with Trevor Delacy, as that blasted song blared out through all the speakers.

The thought of Delacy's music empire crumbling down around him, gave Dan an undeniable thrill.

Graham was prepared this time. He had lectured his son about how men were not supposed to have their fears on display, that they had to control and overcome them, and that if he ever wanted to grow up to be a real man, as opposed to some nancy boy, he needed to start now. And he had steeled himself as well. Yes, he was prepared for the repeat broadcast of *Fear Frequency*.

He tensed as the strange imagery of the opening titles began. They were different, he noticed, not quite as spooky and weird, but still very unusual. And the music was different this time, too. Although still a dark and ominous collection of wavering notes that reverberated through his core, the music did not make him feel in any way uneasy or fearful. Pleased with what he presumed to be his own resolve, Graham glanced over at Tommy, to see the boy gazing eagerly at the screen. That talk he had with his son had obviously been just what the boy needed. Congratulating himself on his parenting techniques, he returned his attention to the television set.

As the images and music reached their climax, Graham felt something. A want. No, a need. A burning desire, in fact. For… he couldn't put a word to it. But there was certainly an emptiness within him – a gaping void in need of filling. It puzzled him and it frustrated him. So much so, that he found his attention wavering as he watched the show.

He tried the push the gnawing want from his mind and focus on the story unfolding in front of his eyes. But even though he had seen the original broadcast of this episode, he found that he just couldn't follow it.

It was with some relief that he greeted the advert break, and nice calming images of boats on crystal-clear waters, of happy people smiling and laughing on the decks… and then a cigarette being lit in slow motion. Of those happy people enjoying the flavour and social experience of their Morleys King Size Filter, puffing away, breathing in the sweet aroma and exhaling joyous little clouds.

Graham began to salivate.

He hadn't smoked a cigarette since he was at school, even though all his friends and workmates did, hanging out by the back fence with his mates. It seemed a lifetime ago to Graham now, and in all those years, he'd never craved one. But now… right now… he could suddenly taste them. And damn it. He wanted one.

The advert ended, but Graham was left with the craving.

'Daddy,' said Tommy. 'I wonder what a cigarette tastes like.'

CHAPTER SEVEN
Craving

GRAHAM STOPPED by the corner shop on his walk into the office.

'I'll have a pack of Morleys King Size Filter, thanks Jim.'

Jimmy Maggs stared at Graham, a regular customer for years, with a curious look. 'Didn't realise you smoked, Gray.'

'Oh well... Used to when I was a kid.' Graham was a little flustered. 'Stopped pretty much after school. But I dunno... Just suddenly got a craving for them.'

'Yeah?' Jimmy looked at him intently. 'You an' everyone else, by the looks of it.'

'Sorry?'

'I'm out,' explained Jimmy. 'Every last pack. There's been a run on 'em this morning.'

'Oh!'

'Get you somethin' else?'

'Um...' Graham surveyed the shelf of cigarettes. 'I don't know. Give me the closest thing you got.'

Jimmy reached up for a packet of Embassy Filters.

'It was bad enough the first time,' complained Arabella Constance. 'But repeating that first episode was just rubbing salt into an open wound. A wound that was still festering, I might add.'

'I find your imagery more horrifying than the actual television show,' joked Freddy J, the radio announcer.

'You may find humour in all this, but I do not. It is a serious matter.'

'Well, at least they changed the opening sequence and theme music. Surely that must count for something?'

'A token effort. And while they replaced one objectionable

piece of music with another objectionable piece of music, they also added in cigarette advertising.'

'And just what is your problem with that?' asked Freddy. 'There's a lot of cigarette advertising on television.'

'It's a filthy habit,' ranted Miss Constance. 'And besides, advertising shouldn't be allowed on television anyway. And—'

'I can't help but wonder,' interrupted Freddy, 'given how objectionable you seem to find almost everything on television, why you even bother to watch it.'

'What...? Well... I...'

As Miss Constance was lost for words, Freddy took his opportunity.

'Well, thank you so much, Miss Constance, for ringing in this morning, as you have done on so many other occasions, and giving us all your opinion. Now, on to today's weather...'

Anne sat in Ruth McGrath's living room enjoying a nice cup of tea. Up until now it had just been small talk, while Ruth's husband, Richard, got the twins ready to take a walk to the local supermarket. Now they were gone, Ruth returned to the living room.

'So, how are you and Bill? Set a date yet?'

Anne smiled. 'We're great, and no we haven't. No rush.'

Ruth sat in the armchair and picked her own cup off the tea-table. 'And he's healing well?'

Anne hadn't told Ruth the full circumstances behind Bill's injuries, but she knew the basics.

'He'll be fine. Taking it easy, in so much as his work will allow. He's on assignment right now. Talking to people, no action.'

'That's good.' Ruth was quiet a moment, watching Anne.

Normally Anne would be annoyed that Ruth was casting her professional eye over her, but in truth Anne knew that was why she came to see Ruth. To get some things off her chest.

'Civilian life not working out for you?' Ruth asked. 'You seem at odds with yourself, and the only reason I can think of for that is that you regret stepping down from your position.'

'Yes. I thought it would be easy to find another post. But so little compares, and then, of course, there was Bill. I couldn't just leave him after what happened.'

'Anne, I doubt Bill would have begrudged you looking to

advance your career. No more than you begrudge him returning to work.'

Anne let out a breath. 'That's the thing,' she said. 'I think I do. A little. It's silly, I know, but he's back in the thick of it, and me... I'm thinking of returning to Cambridge.'

'Ah. I see the problem. Bill won't be able to go with you, will he?'

'No. Well, I suppose he could ask to be reassigned, and for me I suspect he would. But... I couldn't do that to him. Take him away from his current posting. The work he does. It's important.'

Ruth leaned forward. 'And so is yours.' She chuckled slightly. 'It always was, no matter where in the world you went.'

Anne slumped back into the sofa. 'Long distance. You hear so many stories of how it kills relationships...'

'It can,' Ruth said slowly. 'But not always. Depends on the people involved, on their dynamic, the strength of their bond. Do you not trust yours and Bill's is strong enough?'

Anne considered all they'd been through. Things that most people couldn't even imagine, and all it had done is serve to bring them closer. They'd both face certain death – together and apart.

'I think I miss it,' she said. 'The risk involved in my previous post. The work I was doing. Ruth, I wish I could tell you, but it was important. More important than I can explain.'

Ruth was silent a moment. 'Anne, dear, you have some tough choices to make. Things to weigh up. I can't make the decisions for you. I can only listen, offer some advice perhaps.'

'I know.' Anne sipped her tea. 'I can't just walk backwards, though. Nobody gets anywhere like that.'

'True. But sometimes it takes strength to admit a mistake, and to fix it. And that could well mean taking a step backwards, so that you're truly happy again.'

Anne nodded. So much to think about.

Dan Morales was met at the train station by a coloured soldier, a sergeant major no less. It surprised him somewhat.

'Oh. You... You're...'

'Yes? Go on, son, I'm what?' The soldier glared at him, as if daring him to make an issue of it.

It wasn't like it bothered him or anything. Dan was in the

music scene, so he was used to seeing all types of people. It was just that, well, he'd never met a coloured soldier before. And it took him by surprise. That's all. Nothing more to it.

'I'm taking you straight to see the brigadier,' the soldier announced, leading Dan to the Army Land Rover parked outside the train station.

An awkward drive ensued and, after a few minutes silence, the fellow switched on the radio. Some nutty woman was carrying on about the dangers of television and smoking. Dan didn't really pay attention, instead he gazed out at the sights of Edinburgh city.

They drove through the streets until they pulled up outside a small, but expensive looking, hotel. Dan recognised the name as the hotel he was staying at – all bills paid by the Scots Guards. Confused, Dan climbed out of the Land Rover and grabbed his bag and suitcase. The coloured sergeant major led the way through the hotel, past the reception desk, and into the dining room.

It was empty but for one man sitting at a table at the far end. The soldier stopped, and waved Dan on.

'You can leave your things here,' the sergeant major said. 'One of the lads will take them to your room and bring your key to you.'

'Erm...' Dan looked down at the suitcase. He really didn't want to let it out of his sight, but he supposed the military could be trusted. After all, they wouldn't have forked out for his travel and accommodation if they didn't need him, right?

'Thanks,' he said, and crossed the dining room to the man at the table.

The man looked up and scrutinised Dan. He was in a soldier's uniform, of course, but with shiny gold things on the epaulettes. He had a no-nonsense face, although it wasn't harsh. And he had a moustache. Dan wondered if it was real.

'Take a seat, please, Mr Morales. I'm Brigadier Alistair Lethbridge-Stewart.'

'Ah, thanks.' Dan shuffled forward and plonked himself into one of the wooden chairs.

'Mr Morales,' said Lethbridge-Stewart, looking down at the papers spread out on the table in front of him and shuffling through them. 'I have here a copy of your statement from the Met.' He looked up. 'I was wondering if you'd mind telling me exactly what it is you are accusing Electric Soundscapes of?'

'But you just said you've got my statement.'

'Indeed.' Lethbridge-Stewart gave him a curt smile. 'But I would like to hear it from you personally. Here. Now. If you don't mind?'

'Um. Sure.' Dan suddenly felt rather nervous, like a schoolboy being interrogated by his headmaster. He nodded, swallowed hard and launched into his story.

Lethbridge-Stewart made notes as he spoke, asking the odd question for clarification, and occasionally running a thoughtful hand over his moustache.

'That's quite a story,' he said, when Dan had finished. 'But unfortunately, you don't appear to have any evidence.'

'Well… Actually I have!'

'Really?' Lethbridge-Stewart raised an eyebrow. 'Go on.'

'Ah… I sort of got the impression the police didn't really believe me when I told them. I knew I needed some proof, but wasn't sure if I should bring it to them, since I kind of pinched it. You see, my security pass still worked, so I went in and took one of the SynthMoods.'

Lethbridge-Stewart leaned forward onto the table. For the entire interview, up to this point, his expression and demeanour had been fairly neutral –*a military tactic, no doubt*, thought Dan – but now there was definitely interest in his eyes.

'You stole property from a private company?'

Dan wasn't sure if the officer's expression was one of a man impressed, or if he was simply bemused that someone like Dan could do such a thing.

'Well. Yes.'

'And where exactly is the sample you procured?'

'It's in my suitcase,' said Dan. He looked over at the doorway, where his bag and suitcase no longer sat. 'Which has already been taken to my room.'

Lethbridge-Stewart immediately stood up. 'Samson!'

The coloured soldier appeared a second later. 'Sir?'

Lethbridge-Stewart almost smiled. 'If you could go and grab Mr Morales suitcase and bring it to me?'

'Yes, sir.' Samson disappeared as quickly as he appeared.

Lethbridge-Stewart sat again, looked at Dan, and raised an eyebrow.

*

Bishop strode down the corridor in the residents' wing. The alarm in his room hadn't gone off and he'd arrived at the home later than he would have liked. It was just after oh-nine-thirty. He stopped outside Miss Talley's room as he heard voices. The door was ajar.

'Now be a good girl and take your meds,' said an impatient male voice.

'I really don't like these new tablets,' said Miss Talley. 'I don't like the way they make me feel.'

'And I don't care whether you like them or not.' The unfamiliar voice was getting harsher. 'You need to take them. So, take them.'

'If you don't mind, I'll wait and speak to the doctor first. He never mentioned a change of medicine to me.'

'As if you can remember anything.' The voice was mocking now. 'Just shut up and take them. Or do I have to make you?'

That's it, thought Bishop, as he pushed the door open.

'I really don't think you should be making anyone take anything they don't want,' he said, stepping into the room.

The large orderly turned to face him. He looked momentarily guilty, as if he'd been caught out doing something he shouldn't. But that was quickly covered with a scowl. Bishop noted that it was the same young orderly who had taken Miss Talley back into the facility after their meeting in the car.

'Back off,' he demanded. 'This isn't any of your business.'

'Actually, since I am investigating this facility, you're damned right it's my business. Besides, Miss Talley is a friend of mine.' Bishop looked around the orderly and gave the elderly little lady a wave. 'Aren't you, Miss Talley?'

'Oh, yes indeed,' she piped up. 'Lovely to see you again, Bill.'

'And I don't care who you are,' persisted the orderly, taking a step towards Bishop. 'She needs to take her meds and that's that.'

Bishop remembered Miss Talley's comment about Nurse Hadley's 'Neanderthal orderly' and assumed that was the man before him. He was certainly larger than Bishop. But if push came to shove, Bishop was pretty sure the man wouldn't be a problem for him, no matter how big he was. Bishop had been trained to handle bigger men than him.

Bishop held up the file that he had under his arm.

'Well, if this is the medication that she is supposed to be taking, then you won't mind if we first check it against the medical records. Which I just happen to have right here with me.'

'Here.' Miss Talley passed the medicine cup over to Bishop.

He looked down at it. 'There are four tablets in here. But according to the records, she is only supposed to get two.'

The orderly's face fell. 'Well... I don't know about the records. I just give out what I'm told to give out.'

'And who told you to give these tablets to Miss Talley?'

'That would be me,' said Nurse Hadley from the doorway. 'The extra tablets are a sedative and a calmative. She's been rather unsettled lately.'

'I'm feeling just fine,' said Miss Talley with determination. 'And I don't want those.'

'The patient is under no compulsion to take the extra medication,' said Nurse Hadley, her face unreadable.

'Excellent,' said Bishop. 'But you might want to make sure your orderly is aware of that.'

Nurse Hadley glared at the orderly, who shrivelled under her gaze.

'I'm sorry, Nurse,' he said, his voice low and submissive. 'I thought she had to take them.'

'An honest mistake. Continue with your rounds.'

'Yes, Nurse.' The orderly made a hasty exit. Bishop marvelled at how this bulky young man now looked small and cowered.

Nurse Hadley went to follow him out.

'Oh, and Nurse,' said Bishop. 'I'll need to talk to you later today, if you'd wouldn't mind dropping by my office.'

'Very well,' she said without turning around.

After she'd gone, Bishop handed the medicine cup back to Miss Talley.

'Thank you,' she said, fishing the two heart tablets out and popping them into her mouth, tossing the other two into the bin.

'My pleasure. I came to see you yesterday and you just didn't seem yourself.'

'I can't really remember anything from yesterday.' Miss Talley sat in her armchair. 'And while I know I'm regressing, yesterday was... different.'

'Yes. At a guess, I'd say they don't want you talking to me anymore.' Bishop paused and smiled. 'So. How about a little chat?'

'I would be delighted. What shall we chat about?'

'Music,' said Bishop. 'I was hoping you could tell me a bit more about the music therapy.'

'I'm afraid there's not a lot I can tell you.' Miss Talley frowned thoughtfully. 'We get taken to the conservatorium in the van that horrid orderly drives. Nurse Hadley always comes with us. They always take us in wheelchairs, even if we don't normally use them. I mean, look at me. I'm still quite capable of walking. Quite briskly in fact. And when we get there, we listen to music.' Her frown deepened. 'And then we come back.'

'Can you remember any details?'

'The conservatorium is in a lovely old house that's been repurposed. Well, more like a mansion really. Quite beautiful. Reminds me of the family home belonging to one of my suitors. He was a Lord, you know. I could have become accustomed to living in that place. But alas, he was so damn boring. But I'm getting side-tracked. Back to the music. Ah... I don't actually remember the music. Other than it being rather pleasant. Calming.'

'Is it live or recorded?'

'Oh, now that's a good question, isn't it? And I should know, shouldn't I? But...' She shrugged. 'But I don't. Sorry.'

'Anything else you can remember?'

'Well...' Miss Talley paused. 'Bright lights. I remember lights.'

'Thank you, Miss Talley. You have been very helpful.'

'Oh, really?' She looked surprised. 'How nice. But I didn't actually tell you all that much.'

'I think the fact that you can't remember, is the significant thing.'

Jeff Erickson stifled a yawn as he entered the briefing room. Lethbridge-Stewart watched him take a seat.

'Didn't sleep well?'

'No,' Erickson replied. 'I couldn't stop thinking about cigarettes.'

'And let me guess. Morleys King Size Filter.'

'Yes, but how did you—?'

'Colonel Douglas came to see me this morning with a similar story.' Lethbridge-Stewart cleared his throat. 'And… I also experienced it. You watched that damned show last night, didn't you?'

As Erickson nodded, Douglas walked in. 'My ears are burning.'

'Perfect timing, Dougie. Take a seat,' Lethbridge-Stewart said. 'Professor Erickson here seems to have had a similar experience to you and I.'

Erickson smiled slightly. 'Hardly much of a professor these days. Haven't taught anybody in what seems like an age.'

'Something tells me that will change now,' Douglas said. 'Science isn't really my thing at all.'

Erickson nodded. 'I appreciate the thought, Colonel, but I'd rather be referred to as *doctor*, as I do have a PhD in geomorphology. Seems more apt while I work at the Madhouse.'

'Very well, Doctor,' Lethbridge-Stewart said.

Dr Erickson smiled. 'As to my experiences since last night. Cigarettes are rather bad for your lungs. I've been trying to give up. And I was doing just fine until last night. So, to find myself desperately wanting one, was rather disconcerting. In fact, the desire is still lingering. Do you smoke?' he asked, suddenly looking up at Lethbridge-Stewart.

The question caught him a little off guard. And what's worse, is that he felt slightly guilty as he answered. 'Not cigarettes. Although I do enjoy the occasional cigar.'

'Well, they're just as bad for you, you know.'

Scientific chaps did have a way of taking the joy out of life sometimes. 'I trust we're not about to get a lecture on the evils of smoking.'

'What?' Erickson asked, clearly surprised. 'Oh no. It's just…' He stopped a minute, and opened his own file. 'I've been doing some reading, trying to make sense of what we know about Electric Soundscapes, and this strange effect that has been reported by several people after *both* transmissions of *Fear Frequency*.' He looked at Lethbridge-Stewart and Douglas, making sure he had their attention. 'Now, I do dabble in physics, which is probably why Dr Travers suggested I be the leader, as it were, of our little scientific cabal here at Dolerite, but my speciality is geomorphology. In so many ways I'm way out of my depth here.'

'I'm sure your candour does you proud, Dr Erickson, but I can't say I'm feeling particularly reassured,' Lethbridge-Stewart pointed out.

'Sorry. I just want you to understand why I needed to reach out, talk to people not directly connected to HAVOC.'

'HAVOC?' Douglas asked.

Erickson blushed. 'Sorry, isn't that what we call the Fifth Operational Corps?'

'It most certainly is not,' Lethbridge-Stewart said forcefully.

'Oh.' Erickson pointed at the regiment patch on Douglas' sleeve. 'But that does say HAVOC?'

Lethbridge-Stewart regarded it. He supposed the Roman numeral for five did look rather like a V between the HA and OC. He hadn't really noticed before. He let out a hmm, and turned back to Dr Erickson with a slightly quirked eyebrow.

'I think the Fifth sounds fine.'

'Okay.' Erickson nodded, glanced down at his open file and cleared his throat. 'Very well. I had to speak to people outside the Fifth, get their opinions. Obviously I was careful to not mention the work I was doing.'

'Obviously,' Lethbridge-Stewart agreed.

'Yes. Um. So, I read a few files relating to events from before I was, ah, drafted to the Fifth and coupled with the input from outside, I've come to the conclusion that what's happened is a direct result of the transmission of *Fear Frequency*.'

Douglas leaned forward. 'In what way? I mean, I get how advertising works, and an advert for cigarettes may make smokers want more. I've been on the phone this morning making enquiries, after I kept hearing people talking about smoking – people whom I know to not be smokers – and it seems that there's been a high demand for Morleys King Size Filter cigarettes.'

'Yes, the advertised brand. Don't you think that's weird?' Erickson asked.

'Clearly, Doctor,' Lethbridge-Stewart said, 'as that's why we're here.'

Erickson looked down at his files again. Lethbridge-Stewart wasn't impressed. Was Dr Erickson really the best choice to head the Fifth's scientists. Oh, he wished Anne were there.

'I don't suppose either of you have read Norma Vine's paper

on quantum harmonics?' Erickson asked, and the blank looks from both Douglas and Lethbridge-Stewart was enough of an answer. 'No, I don't suppose you would have. Anyway, I'm getting ahead of myself.' He took a breath, and started again. 'I was thinking about a term I'd read in the Electric Soundscapes file: *mood enhancement.*'

'Yes,' Lethbridge-Stewart said, 'I had a similar thought, and was reminded of the Moon Blink from last year.'

Dr Erickson suddenly looked excited. 'Precisely. Of course, there's nothing to suggest drugs are being used now, and seeing how many people have reacted to the transmission of *Fear Frequency*, I think we can rule that out. However, I thought about what else tends to affect moods so easily, and music was an obvious choice. Which reminded me about Vine's paper which Dr Travers showed me late last year. About the vibrational frequencies of the universe. What if, that could somehow be used against people?'

'And you think that's what we're dealing with?' Douglas asked.

'No, not quite. But maybe something similar. You both remember the effect the Keynsham Triangle had on people, and that was down to vibrational frequencies. What if, somehow, the music produced by Electric Soundscape's new synthesiser can, quite literally, influence how people feel? Not only influence, but *make* them feel things.'

'Is that possible?' Lethbridge-Stewart asked.

'Why not? We've all experienced the consequences of long-term exposure to infrasound.'

Lethbridge-Stewart remembered that clear enough. At the beginning of the year when Sunyata, an alien entity that usually manifested as the Great Intelligence, attempted to break through from another dimension. As it broke through it used infrasound, a low frequency sound wave that people couldn't actually hear, but could *feel.*

'You think this is deliberate?' he asked Erickson.

'I can't see how it could be anything else. Both times *Fear Frequency* was transmitted people responded differently.'

'Quite. The first time the music made people scared. This time people were influenced to buy cigarettes. And not just smokers, but, it seems, anybody who watched the programme.' Lethbridge-Stewart paused, and considered. 'What will it be next time?'

All three were quiet a moment, and then Douglas said what they were probably all thinking. 'It's like they're testing it.'

'Yes, but that doesn't feel right to me.' Lethbridge-Stewart was beginning to form a different idea, and he didn't like it one bit. 'No, not testing it. They could do that with small groups of people in more discrete ways. Using a national broadcast like this brings attention to what they're doing. This isn't a test. It's a demonstration.'

'Why would they do that and risk exposure?' asked Dr Erickson.

'Perhaps they have buyers lined up?' Douglas suggested. 'Buyers who require to see practical applications in effect.'

'Of course, that fits with what I learned this morning.' Lethbridge-Stewart frowned.

'Which was…?' Erickson prompted.

'I had a meeting with a chap called Dan Morales. He used to work in the Electric Soundscapes warehouse, and believes that they are making sound weapons and disguising them as synthesisers.'

'Weapons…' Erickson was silent a moment, and Lethbridge-Stewart and Douglas waited for him. 'Yes, that makes sense. It certainly fits with my hypothesis that the music produced by the synthesiser was being used on people.'

'Yes,' Lethbridge-Stewart said. 'And as Douglas suggested, Morales believes they are preparing to sell them. And, as I have since discovered, he's not wrong. They're due to be released onto the market in two weeks' time.' Lethbridge-Stewart lifted a suitcase off the floor and carefully placed it on the desk. He opened it and let them see the *instrument* within. 'The SynthMoods 21-20, the company's new synthesiser. Doctor, I want you and your team to examine it. Find out how it works.'

Erickson joyfully reached for the suitcase. Lethbridge-Stewart placed a warning hand on it.

'Remember, it's potentially a dangerous weapon.'

'Of course. We'll take every precaution.'

'Are we thinking,' Douglas asked, 'that this is alien?'

Lethbridge-Stewart nodded. 'I think that's very probable.'

'If you don't mind,' Erickson said, 'I'd like to call in a colleague, if I may. He's far more versed in the area of experimental sound uses than any of my team.'

'Very well.' Lethbridge-Stewart proceeded to detail the course of their investigation, assigning each of them a different task. When he finished, he added, 'Oh, and Dougie, make sure the doctor's colleague gets the required clearances.'

Douglas nodded, and Lethbridge-Stewart stood.

'Right. It seems we all have much work ahead of us.'

CHAPTER EIGHT
Transcripts

'TELL ME about this music therapy.'

'I don't really know anything about it.' Nurse Hadley stared coolly at Bishop, not a hint of cooperation on her face.

Bishop tapped the medical records on the table before him. 'Well, according to these, you're the one who initiated the programme. And Miss Talley tells me that you always accompany the patients.'

Hadley pursed her lips, but didn't reply.

Right then, thought Bishop, *time to bring out the big guns.*

'I've had a background check done on you. It's interesting, don't you think, that your employment file from this facility doesn't mention why you left Bainbridge Hospital?' He smiled sweetly at her, as she glared daggers at him. 'I believe you were caught stealing drugs from the hospital supplies in order to sell them on the black market.'

'I was not convicted,' snapped Hadley. 'I wasn't even prosecuted.'

'No. But you were dismissed. I wonder if I should request an inventory of supplies for this facility?'

'Please yourself.'

'Look, Nurse Hadley,' said Bishop, folding his arms. 'Either you tell me what I need to know about this music therapy, or I talk to Dr Quinlan about it. I will be sure to let him know how uncooperative you have been, and about your past.'

'I do not know anything about the music therapy. I merely arrange the patients' transport to and from the conservatorium. Yes, I go with them, but I wait in the foyer. They have a nice selection of the latest magazines.'

'But it says here...' Bishop pointed to a document. '...that you initiated the programme.'

'That doesn't mean I know anything about it. The director of the conservatorium contacted us and offered a free music therapy programme for some of our residents. He is of the belief that there is therapeutic value in music. Hence the term "music therapy". Beyond that, I know nothing.'

'Not all residents attend these music sessions, do they?'

'No.'

'From what I can gather by reading through the medical records, it's only those with advanced Alzheimer's.'

'If you had already gathered that, then why ask me?'

'Well, I was hoping that you might be able to elaborate on things.'

Hadley continued to stare at him.

'But, seeing as you don't seem able to tell me anything else, you're free to go.'

Hadley stood and headed out.

'But, Nurse,' said Bishop, making her stop at the door. 'I may need to speak to you again.'

She left without any further acknowledgment.

Bishop shook his head slowly. The music therapy was the only link he could find between the patients who had experienced improvement in their symptoms. Each of the patients had shown improvement not long after beginning. But then each patient had declined again, although at varying rates. And several of them had died. There had to be a connection.

The thought of OAPs being abused by those into whom they'd placed their trust... No, not just abused, but probably being experimented upon...

Bishop's head went light and he staggered forward, reaching out for the table for support. In his mind he saw Dr Rowland Chivers attempting to save his life, stitching him up... Of course, it was an imagined scene. Bishop had barely been conscious when the dying Chivers performed the life-saving operation. His hand reached under his shirt, felt the jagged scar that was still healing.

Experimented upon. The thought of others undergoing anything even slightly similar to what Vaar and Sebastian Collins had put him through made Bishop's blood boil.

He would find out what was going on, and put a stop to it.

Head now clearing, Bishop straightened his shirt and made a decision. It was time for him to arrange a visit to the conservatorium.

'To be perfectly honest,' Professor Marshal said, 'I'm not sure that I'm your man.'

'Oh.' Erickson was completely deflated by those words. But he had to persevere. He needed someone with the right expertise, and unfortunately none of his team (when did he start thinking of them as *his* team?) had it. What he really needed was Anne Travers – but he couldn't contact her. If he did, it'd make him a failure. And he had only recently been authorised to tell his father, Commodore Robert Erickson, of his work at the Fifth, and was overjoyed at the pride on his father's face at the revelation that, at last, his son had finally joined the military – after a fashion. Erickson couldn't let his father down, which meant he couldn't admit defeat and call on Dr Travers.

He tightened his grip on the telephone receiver. 'But I read your paper on ultrasound and infrasound potential,' he said to Marshal. 'And when we met at that conference in Cambridge you were—'

'Yes, that's all very well and good, old chap, but my expertise is in practical applications, mostly medical. From what you've said, you really need someone with a much more… how should I put this…? A much more theoretical approach. Someone like that fellow with the German name. Fry-something-or-other. He delivered a paper at the conference as well. It was all a bit out there, really. At least from what I can remember. Controlling emotions and such stuff. I have a vague recollection that there was some completely untenable medical application. I don't think he got much joy at the conference from the other academics. Not from me, at least. But still, he sounds more like what you're after.'

He's fobbing me off, thought Erickson. Still, maybe the German scientist was worth pursuing.

'Any idea where I might be able to contact him, James?'

'Oh, now, let me think. He was from Glasgow, I believe, *Jeffrey.*'

That was a telling-off. Clearly Erickson had, in his enthusiasm, been a little too informal.

Marshal continued. 'But I've not heard anything from him since that conference. If you check the conference papers, that should set you on the right track. Hmm. Fry... Fry... High. Fry-High. Something like that. Definitely a Kraut.'

Erickson listened for another few minutes as Professor Marshal rambled on about how his own research was far more important than anything this foreign chappie had ever done. When Erickson finally managed to get him off the phone, he was actually quite relieved that Marshal wasn't interested.

After only a few minutes on the phone, Erickson couldn't imagine trying to work with him. It was interesting how different a person could be at an academic conference, when on show, than otherwise.

So, he would have to try and search out the academic with a German name. But first he had other things to get on with. Erickson glanced at his watch. Mr Simons' body would have arrived at Dr Lindsay's lab by now. He should go check on that.

He glanced at the shiny new SynthMoods 21-20, unpacked and sitting on his workbench, ready to be examined. He shook his head in wonderment as he stood. How had Anne Travers managed all of this?

'You mean, there's actually something in it?' Reggie Dwight's voice was incredulous over the phone.

'Yes and no,' said Douglas, keeping his voice level and unconcerned. Much as he hated lying to an old contact, he really wasn't in a position to give away too much. But he also needed Reggie's help. 'I dare say that they're not actually producing musical weaponry. But there is something going on at Electric Soundscapes, but not in the purview of civilian police. Most likely nothing more than a bit of corporate espionage. But we thought we should take a look, so if there's any information you could provide, it would be appreciated.' He paused for a moment. 'But I've actually called about another matter as well. Something on the QT.'

'Oh yes?'

'Yes. Look, I'm sorry but I can't actually tell you what it is we're investigating, but...'

'But... You need some intel?'

'I hate to ask, but yes.'

'What do you need?'

Douglas smiled. This is why he'd kept in contact with Reggie through the years. His willingness to help.

'Has there been any sort of indication that there might be something new on the market. In the underworld? Something that might be of interest to criminals, or even terrorists.'

'Not really my area. But I can ask around for you.'

'That would be very much appreciated.'

'There is one condition though.'

'Yes?' Douglas was worried about what that might be.

'Next time we get together, the Guinness is on you.'

'Nothing?'

'Nothing out of the ordinary at all,' insisted Lindsay. 'The man died as a result of a cardiac arrest just as the death certificate says.'

'Are you sure?'

'Quite sure, Jeff. I'm not a simple Army medic, you know.'

Erickson raised his hands in mock surrender. 'No, sorry, of course not. I didn't mean it to sound like that, Doctor. It's just that I'm surprised.'

'Captain.'

'What?'

Lindsay smiled. 'How long you been with the Fifth now?'

Erickson wasn't quite sure what Lindsay was getting at. 'About fifteen months, I suppose. Why?'

'And you've still not worked out the difference between ranks and titles?'

'Ah.' Erickson smiled. 'It's funny you should say that.'

'I am the medical officer here, but my rank is still captain. Not doctor.'

Erickson let out a sigh and sat on a nearby stool. 'I'm sorry. Pressures of the new position getting to me.'

'Well, you are looking rather tired.'

'Tell me about it.' Erickson shook his head. 'Between all the extra work, the lack of sleep and trying to give up smoking... It's all catching up to me, I'm afraid.'

'Sounds like you need to go back to smoking,' Lindsay said. 'It'll calm your nerves and probably help you sleep. God knows, it helps me at home.'

'Trouble and strife?'

'Isn't it always?'

Erickson shook his head and laughed. He looked at the clock on the wall. 'Blimey. Where does the time go?'

Lindsay smiled at him, and patted his knee. 'A loaded question in the Madhouse.'

Trev Del: I want to make people feel with my music. Get it?

Interviewer: Isn't that the object of all music?

Trev Del: [laughter] Yeah, I guess. Most music is about reminding people of the feelings they already have. Love. Loss. Grief. Whatever. I want more than that. I want my music to influence people. To introduce new feelings. Thoughts, even. There's so much power in music. I find it exciting! Exhilarating!

Interviewer: Ah. [pause] Interesting. And how do you propose to achieve this influence?

Trev Del: Well, it's trial and error, really. [laughter] But I believe that if you can combine the right lyrics, the right verbal suggestions, with the right notes... Well, it could be the start. And from there, who knows what the future might hold.

Interviewer: Well, you certainly are enthusiastic and passionate about your music. But we seem to have come to the end of our time. Trev Del, thank you for your time today, and best of luck with the new single.

-- END TRANSCRIPT --

Interesting, thought Douglas as he finished reading the first of the transcribed interviews he had obtained from the BBC.

On his request, they had provided all the interviews they had conducted with Delacy over the years, from the release of his first, moderately successful single in 1957 at the age of eighteen, to his big hit in 1959, to his transition from pop star Trev Del to entrepreneur Trevor Delacy.

He moved on to the next transcript.

BBC Television Interview with Trev Del
13 November 1959

Interviewer: Thank you for joining us today, Trev Del. First of all, congratulations on your new single, *Listen to Me*, making it into the Top 10. How does it feel?

Trev Del: It feels rather marvellous, really. Very exciting! After having a few songs make it into the Top 40, it's great to finally get to the Top 10.

Interviewer: This one's a little different for you, isn't it?

Trev Del: Well, yes, I suppose it is. I think it's the first song to really represent me as an artist.

Interviewer: Ah well, I was actually thinking in terms of subject. Your previous songs have all been about falling in love and finding that special someone. *You and Me, and Me and You* and *Say You Love Me Always* and so on.

Trev Del: Yes. [laughter] They were rather frivolous really. This one goes a bit deeper. Has more meaning.

Interviewer: And how would you sum up the meaning?

Trev Del: It's about the power of music. Something I feel really passionate about.

Interviewer: The power of music. Yes indeed. Well, his song has certainly shown its power, rocketing to number 6. Let's take a listen to it now.

[*Listen to Me* plays]

— END TRANSCRIPT —

Douglas skimmed through the next batch, which were all pretty similar and superficial, until he came to an interview from the following year, which took a more in-depth approach.

BBC Home Service Interview with Trev Del
Interviewer: Michael Grimes
1 October 1960

Interviewer: After a string of minor hits in 1958, Trev Del went on to hit the big-time last year with *Listen to Me*, which not only made it to Number 1 here in the UK, but also sold millions of records in America and Europe. And he joins us here today. Welcome, Trev.

Trev Del: Thanks.

Interviewer: What's the difference between this song, which has been such a worldwide hit, and the previous ones, which didn't quite hit the mark?

Trev Del: Control. I had had very little influence with those earlier songs. I was under contract to a label, and it was the producer who made all the decisions. He chose the song, the musicians, the background singers, everything. It felt like I was little more than an afterthought. But with *Listen to Me*,

I had complete control. I wrote the song, both lyrics and music. I play all the instruments on the track, which are then mixed together.

Interviewer: And that was quite a risky move wasn't it?

Trev Del: Well, yes, I suppose it was. When my contract came up, the label I was with wanted to renew it with the same restrictions. And I thought, no way! I didn't want to go through all that again. So, I went out on my own. My parents had recently passed away and had left me their house. So, I re-mortgaged it in order to pay for the recording, production, release and promotion.

Interviewer: And that certainly paid off.

Trev Del: Yes. Yes it did. Because there were no other parties involved, I got to keep all the profits. Which was quite a change. A pretty good change. With the earlier songs, I only got a small percentage as the singer, while the record company made most of the money. But this time it's all mine. And given that it's been a global hit, that's a fair bit of money. Which is really rather nice!

Interviewer: It's been almost a year since the hit single, but there's been no follow-up. So, what does the future hold for Trev Del?

Trev Del: Well, things have been pretty busy, promoting the single overseas. Doing appearances and interviews and stuff. So, I've not really had the chance to do much else. But I have been thinking a lot. Giving lots of consideration to the future. And I think I'm going to invest the money in the music industry. In the future. I'm really pleased that my music has been able to influence people, but I'd like to have a greater impact.

Interviewer: But what about the music? Will there be another record? An album perhaps?

Trev Del: You know what…? No! I don't think so. [pause] I think there may be other ways for me to tap into the power of music.

Interviewer: [hesitant] Oh, well then, good luck with whatever it is that the future holds for you.

-- END TRANSCRIPT --

And that appeared to be his last interview for quite some

time. The next one was from 1965.

BBC Third Programme Interview with Trevor Delacy
Interviewer: James Ricks
4 June 1965

Interviewer: Pop star turned entrepreneur, Trevor Delacy has just launched a new business venture, Electric Soundscapes. And he's here now to discuss that with us. Thank you for joining us, Mr Delacy.

Trevor Delacy: My pleasure.

Interviewer: It was not all that many years ago that your voice was gracing our airwaves with songs such as *Say You Love Me Always*, *Be True to My Heart* and, of course, your number 1 hit, *Listen to Me*. Back then you were known as Trev Del.

Trevor Delacy: That was the record label's idea, to shorten my name like that. They thought it sounded more appealing. And I ended up keeping it for my independent single release.

Interviewer: Now you're back on the music scene, but in a very different way. Manufacturing and making musical instruments.

Trevor Delacy: Electric instruments, specifically. Electric guitars, electric violins, etc, as well as theremins, synthesisers and sequencers. I feel that this is the way of the future, which is why the company slogan is: Providing 21st century sounds for 20th century music.

Interviewer: So why this change in focus from performing to creating instruments?

Trevor Delacy: It's a matter of control and influence. In my early career as a musician I had little of either, as it was the record label that held all the cards. Producing music independently gave me greater control and influence. This is the next logical step. In making the instruments and developing new ones, my level of control and influence increases. In terms of the music industry, musicians and listeners.

Interviewer: That's... That's quite the ambitious approach.

Trevor Delacy: I suppose it is.

Interviewer: So, what's next then? Is there another level of control and influence that you aspire to?

Trevor Delacy: Oh yes. There is always a new level to

aspire to. But that's not something I would be wanting to talk about just yet. No sense in letting the cat out of the bag too soon.

Interviewer: Very well. So... ah... Why don't we now have a listen to a recent product of Trevor Delacy's control and influence. This piece of music is a reinterpretation of the Third Movement from Tchaikovsky's Symphony No. 6, played entirely with the first range of instruments created by Electric Soundscapes.

[music plays]

Well, that's a bit ominous, thought Douglas as he finished reading the transcript.

The interviews certainly indicated a little bit of an obsession on Delacy's part. They also showed quite a change in him personally over the years. Gone was the enthusiastic, music-loving young man of the earlier interviews. Replaced by a far more serious and sinister individual.

An individual who now, it seemed, had the ability to manipulate peoples' feelings in a very real and, quite possibly, dangerous way.

Douglas continued to dig into Delacy's past.

CHAPTER NINE
Discoveries

'**WE'VE HAD** some progress with both the Electric Soundscapes and the Haltwhistle cases,' Lethbridge-Stewart announced once he took his place at the briefing room table. 'Let's begin with the latter. Lieutenant Bishop reports that he believes there is indeed some sort of cover-up underway at the home. He's had the chance to go through medical records, and it seems there's some truth to the stories of miracle recoveries, although always with a subsequent relapse. He strongly suspects that this is linked to the sudden deaths of several patients and to the falsifying of their death certificates. However...' He stopped and looked to Dr Erickson.

'Well...' The scientist took a moment to get his thoughts in order, then looked from Lethbridge-Stewart to Douglas. 'You both have copies of Captain Lindsay's post-mortem report. The cause of death is exactly as recorded on the death certificate. Cardiac arrest.'

'Bishop, however, insists that at least the place of death has been falsified,' said Lethbridge-Stewart. 'The certificates list the old persons' home, but he has a witness that says otherwise.'

'Neither Lindsay nor I think it would be a good idea to exhume any more bodies,' said Erickson. 'That sort of thing can be rather traumatic for the family of the deceased. So, unless there is any evidence to suggest the other bodies are any different, best to let them lie, so to speak.'

Lethbridge-Stewart agreed. 'I'll let Bishop know. Right then, on to Electric Soundscapes. What have you found out, Colonel?'

'My contact at CID says that there is something going on in the underworld. A general buzz, is what he called it. But he can't say what. A number of organisations that they're watching have representatives conglomerating in London at the moment. But they don't know why. That's all he could give me.'

Lethbridge-Stewart grunted.

'There is a similar buzz in the advertising world,' continued Douglas. 'Morleys International have been approached by Electric Soundscapes with an offer to take over music direction for their television and radio advertising, at a fee of about five times the going rate. They are currently wrangling over exclusivity clauses in the contract. Delacy is offering a tobacco industry exclusive, while Morleys are arguing, given the asking price, for an across-the-board exclusive. Apparently other advertisers are set to meet at Electric Soundscapes later today. Oh, and Morleys claim that their advertisement was booked months in advance, long before the announcement that Electric Soundscapes would be providing the theme music for *Fear Frequency*.'

'Besides,' Erickson added, 'that repeat showing was a last-minute decision, so the odds of Morleys being able to secure such a spot...'

Lethbridge-Stewart hadn't considered that. So many things to juggle in the air. 'Therefore, Wednesday night's broadcast *was* a demonstration,' he said. 'And if it was designed to bring in advertising contracts, then what does that mean for the original broadcast on Sunday?'

'Well, it did stoke up feelings of fear,' Erickson said, 'capitalising on the title of the programme. But it must be more than that.'

'I think you're right, Jeff,' Douglas said. 'And it would explain the general buzz in the underworld. Think about it. We've seen enough reports of what it did to the general populace who watched the programme, but what if, as Morales said, it's turned into a weapon. A sound weapon that could instil fear in opponents? Now that would be something which would have a considerable market in the UK's murky underworld.'

'Except that there is no weapon,' Erickson said. Lethbridge-Stewart and Douglas both turned to look at him. 'My team and I have gone over the SynthMoods device multiple times, and it is an ordinary musical instrument. There is nothing extraordinary about it whatsoever. In fact, it's not even a cutting-edge synthesiser. There are other brands that exceed its specs.'

'Are you sure?' asked Douglas.

'One hundred percent. We examined every inch of that machine. Compared it with several other models and brands. Took it apart and put it back together. And then finally, out of a loss to do anything else, we tested its complete range of sounds on me. I did not feel frightened. I did not feel the need to rush out and buy cigarettes. I did not feel anything out of the ordinary. Except maybe frustration at not being able to find anything.'

'Damn!' Lethbridge-Stewart clenched his fists. 'I was relying on that blasted machine to give me a reason to raid their warehouse.' He wondered if Erickson could possibly have missed something. But didn't want to actually voice that concern; the man was clearly still nervous about trying to fill Anne's shoes. 'What about your sound expert? Have you had a chance to get him to look at that instrument?'

Dr Erickson winced, no doubt feeling his judgement being questioned. 'That didn't quite work out. Professor Marshal wasn't available and, although he did point me towards someone more qualified, I haven't been able to locate them.'

'I'm sure you're quite capable of handling this on your own,' Lethbridge-Stewart said, trying to reassure the man. He mentally berated himself for having brought up the expert.

'What do we do with Morales?' Douglas asked.

'I think he's told us all he can. And given that the synthesiser he procured turned out to be useless, we might as well let him go home.'

Douglas nodded, making a mental note to follow that up. 'One last thing,' he said. 'I did a bit of digging into Trevor Delacy, and I can say for certain that he is one very strange man. Seems quite obsessed with control and, as he himself puts it in numerous interviews, influence. He's obviously intent on making an impact. As you know from the original file, Electric Soundscapes has investments in a number of research ventures, but in looking into Delacy's background, it seems that he has also financed projects through other dummy companies.' Douglas took out a sheet of paper from the folder in front of him and handed it to Lethbridge-Stewart. 'This is a list of the university and independent research programmes that he's put money into and the names of the companies he used. There is quite a variety. He seems to have had a proverbial finger in every pie.'

Lethbridge-Stewart glanced over the list and handed it on to Erickson. 'Look in to these.' Then he turned back to Douglas, thoughtful. 'Dougie, we need to know more about the meeting between Delacy and the advertisers.'

'Agreed. What we could do with is an inside man.'

'Any ideas?' Lethbridge-Stewart asked.

Bishop drove through the expansive but overgrown grounds of the Haltwhistle Music Conservatorium. They obviously didn't spend any money on gardening. Perhaps if they charged for their music therapy, they'd have the funds to keep the grounds in better condition.

There was no visitor car park as such, just an area of gravel in front of a grand old building that had obviously seen better days. There were no other cars.

Bishop hopped out of the Peugeot and strode up the stone steps leading to the enormous front door. The green paint was peeling from the wood and the bell-pull was quite rusty.

This does not look like an operating conservatorium, thought Bishop, as he yanked on the bell-pull. He couldn't hear anything, but gave it a minute before deciding that it must be broken. He tried the door, and it gave way with a creak.

The interior was in better condition. Standing in the large foyer, a grand staircase spiralled up before him, a chandelier dangling from the ceiling. The lights were off. To the left was a desk with a phone, both covered in dust. If that was reception, then no one had manned it for quite some time.

'Hello!' called Bishop, deciding on a direct approach.

There was no response.

The door behind the desk led to some offices, all empty, all dark with blinds drawn. The door on the right of the foyer led to a small auditorium, fold-up chairs packed away and leaning against the walls, the stage scattered with a few music stands but otherwise empty. Bishop tried the stairs next. The second and third floors were a maze of rehearsal rooms of various sizes, some with instruments, some empty. The place was definitely not in use.

Heading back down, Bishop noticed a set of double doors under the stairs on his way out. He tried them, but they were locked. He considered shouldering them open, but thought better of it. What was the point? There weren't any music therapy session being held here. So where in the world were the residents being taken?

It was time to talk to Nurse Hadley again. And he intended to get answers.

But as he headed for the exit, Bishop thought he heard music. He stopped and stood very still, listening. Yes, there was definitely music. Muffled. Indistinct. Faint. But somewhere in the building.

He walked back slowly, trying to determine the origin. It was coming from under the stairs. He made his way to the doors and pressed his ear to them.

The music grew clearer.

This is different, Erickson thought. Since being drafted by Dr Travers, he'd done all sorts for the Fifth, and it always involved science. Not phone calls and faxes. He didn't mind. A change was as good as a rest, and all that.

He was busy trying to track down information on each of the research programmes that Delacy had financed, and was now reading information from Glasgow's University of Strathclyde as it slowly printed out on the fax machine.

'Good lord,' Erickson said, as the name Professor Waldo Freiheit appeared. 'He was in charge of the programme.'

Erickson took hold of the paper, continuing to read, impatient to yank it from the machine.

The programme was quite wide-ranging, looking at a number of hitherto unexplored applications for high and low frequency soundwaves and the possibility of focusing them through crystals. Although Freiheit's special interest was medical applications, the programme was also researching mood enhancement and mind control.

Erickson's previous attempts to track down Professor Marshal's *kraut* had ended at the university, his last place of employment, but he hadn't made the connection when he'd first read Douglas' list. But it made sense that Freiheit would be working on this research programme.

The programme had failed to deliver any workable results and the university had shut it down at around the time that Freiheit had left.

As soon as he'd finished reading, Erickson was on the phone again. After going through the switchboard, secretary and research assistant, he finally got through to Professor Madson in the Audiology Department. He had worked under Freiheit for the duration of the project.

'I was wondering if you could tell me where I might find Professor Freiheit?' Erickson asked.

'No idea, I'm afraid. He wasn't dismissed. He didn't resign as such, either. One day, he just never showed up. And no one heard from him again. We assumed it was because his pet programme had been defunded. Then again, it might have been more personal reasons. I believe he had an ill parent. Mother, I think. Every time her condition worsened, he'd get more difficult to work with.'

'And why did the university stop funding the programme?'

'Well, it's not as if the university ever wanted it in the first place. The Chancellor regarded the science behind it as somewhat suspect and not really in line with the university's reputation for scientific excellence. The only reason it was up and running in the first place was because it received some external funding from a private company.'

Erickson looked at Douglas' list. 'That would have been a company called Future Investments?'

'That's right,' said Madson. 'There was a clash over the direction some of the research should take and when Freiheit refused to budge, the company pulled funds. And the rest, as they say, is history.'

'What was the clash, if I might ask?'

'Freiheit wanted to concentrate on sound as a treatment for mental illness, inducing a calmative state, enhancing and repairing memory, stabilising erratic behaviours, that sort of thing. While Future Investments wanted to focus on influencing behaviours in a more direct way. Instilling desires, fears and other emotional states. I think they had military application in mind.'

'Thank you, Professor, you have been a great help.'

As he hung up the phone, Erickson allowed himself a moment of excitement, clapping his hands and rubbing together as he grinned. He was finally getting somewhere.

Future Investments was, unsurprisingly, one of Electric Soundscapes' shill companies.

*

Lethbridge-Stewart regarded the man before him, their soon-to-be inside man. 'I trust Dougie has brought you up to speed with the Electric Soundscapes investigation?'

'He has,' Samson said.

'Good. How would you feel about a spot of undercover work?'

Samson grinned. 'It would give me a chance to put my acting skills to the test.'

'And your music skills.'

'I'm not sure that I have any of those.'

'Oh, come now, Samson.' It was funny how easily they slipped into their friendship-mode as soon as the office door closed. Ranks instantly dismissed. Lethbridge-Stewart could only think of one other that happened with. 'I seem to remember you telling me your grandmother forced you into music lessons as boy. Saxophone, if I remember rightly?'

Samson winced. 'Trust you to remember that, Al. Didn't last, though, boxing was much more my thing.'

Lethbridge-Stewart smiled. 'I remember. Well, you won't actually have to play. You just need some background knowledge in order to play the part of a musician turned entrepreneur. We thought that by mirroring Delacy's situation, it might help get his attention. And Dougie has managed to get you a meeting with him.'

'And how did he manage that?'

'Posing as your personal assistant.'

'I have a personal assistant now?' Samson laughed. Dougie must have loved that. They'd only known each other since Lethbridge-Stewart had brought Samson into the Fifth, and they'd built a healthy amount of respect for each other. Being long-term friends with Lethbridge-Stewart was what initially bonded them together. 'I'm liking this mission more and more.'

'*Posing* as your personal assistant, he rang the Electric Soundscapes head office. He wasn't able to talk to Delacy himself, but he left a message with enough key triggers to make sure that a return call with an invitation for a meeting was forthcoming. Delacy has swallowed the bait rather keenly, as he's set the meeting for tomorrow.'

'On a Saturday?'

'Well, from what we can deduce, Delacy is somewhat of a

workaholic.' Lethbridge-Stewart nudged a folder across his desk. 'Your cover story's in here. You can learn it on the way to London. I have transport standing by, so get your things together straight away. You'll get in rather late, but that can't be helped, as the meeting is set for 10am tomorrow. The file also contains everything we have on the layout of Electric Soundscapes. Which isn't much, really.'

Samson picked up the file and flicked through it. 'Sounds fun.'

'Yes. In the meantime, I'll be heading down to the Loony Bin first thing tomorrow.'

'Right-oh,' said Samson, getting ready to stand.

'Sam.' Lethbridge-Stewart leaned forward. 'I need some indication about what he is selling. *Whatever* it is that he's selling. And where he's keeping it. Push him if you have to.'

Samson grinned. 'Hey, have I ever let you down, Al?'

Lethbridge-Stewart smiled in return. 'No. No, you haven't.'

'And I won't this time. In fact,' Samson added, 'I'm looking forward to it. Nice change from drilling the troops at Stirling.'

CHAPTER TEN
The Angel of Death

'NURSE HADLEY tells me you're leaving.'

Bishop started, looking up from the files he'd been packing into a box, to see Dr Quinlan leaning in the doorway.

'That's right.'

'So, your investigation is finished.' Quinlan was looking quite smug. 'I assume you've found nothing out of the ordinary.'

'Nothing out of the ordinary?' Bishop rubbed at his tired eyes as he tried to put his thoughts in order. 'Generally speaking, yes. Although there may be some follow-up.' He paused, trying to remember what it was that still needed following up. 'With regards… to… medical records.'

'I see.' The smug expression quickly disappeared from Quinlan's face. 'Well. You know the way out.' He turned and left.

Bishop sat down in the chair, put his elbows on the table and rested his head in his hands. He was so tired and fuzzy-headed, he was having trouble thinking straight.

He'd need to make sure he got a good night's sleep before his drive back to Edinburgh.

The cabin looked exactly the same. He knew it wasn't, because it had a different number, but it looked the same. Dan Morales spread out on the bunk, the movement of the Caledonian Sleeper churning up his thoughts.

Everything had suddenly changed from 'you can stay in Edinburgh until we need to speak to you again' to 'you're going back to London tonight'. The only thing they wanted him to do before he left, was sketch the layout of the Electric Soundscapes warehouse and accompanying offices. He knew little of the office building layout, other than the fact that

Delacy's office was on the third floor. (Of course he had to be on the top floor, looking down on everyone.) But Dan gave them a reasonable idea of the warehouse building, all except for what was beyond the restricted door. As soon as he had done the drawing, they had packed him off to the station.

When he'd questioned the soldier – a different one this time, not coloured; a colonel, he thought – he was told that there was nothing special about the SynthMoods 21-20 he'd given them. That it was just an ordinary synthesiser. There was something funny in the bloke's voice when he'd said that – it was accusatory. As if it was Dan's fault that the instrument was just an instrument and not a weapon.

All Dan's fantasies of his supervisor and Delacy being arrested had been cut down, like a pub band suddenly having their amps go dead.

It was not fair. How dare he be treated like this. He had to do something about it. He *needed* to do something. But what?

As he closed his eyes and drifted into sleep, he imagined how he might be able to turn things around when he got back home.

The Angel of Death and her minions swept through the chill, drizzle-soaked streets of the Harringay Warehouse District of North London in an armour-plated black van. She was, of course, driving. As she always did when on a mission. She was, after all, a control freak. This was her operation, and her men were here only as backup (in case things didn't go to plan) and muscle (if things did go to plan). Things always went to plan. That's why people relied on her to supply what they wanted.

She drove the van up to the Happy Pets supply depot, where a lone security guard opened the gates to let the van in. It had all been prearranged. He had been bribed to keep the German Shepherds locked up and to let the van in, no questions asked. She would, of course, dispose of him on the way back. It was her policy to leave no loose ends.

The men in the back of the van would be similarly dealt with once it was all over. It was not surprising how she had acquired her nickname.

Her real name, although there were none left alive who knew it, was Angela van Loon. Although a South African of Dutch extraction, she had left many years ago, and now considered herself a citizen of the world. She kept apartments in many cities, and safe houses in many more. None of her clients knew what she looked like. They didn't even know she was a woman. Arms dealing was, after all, a man's game. And she loved the fact that she played it better than any man she had ever met (or killed).

At the back of the depot was an old warehouse (little more than a glorified tin shed, really) that backed on to the electrified wire fence that was the border between that property and the one owned by Electric Soundscapes.

Once inside, her men cut an opening into the back wall and she got to work circumventing the electricity in the fence and the security surveillance devices beyond it. Then it was a short dash across a concreted area to a side door of their target warehouse.

She led the way, ready to eliminate any unexpected guards, her six men following behind, each of them carrying a portable, reinforced trolley. The security system on the door was bypassed in a matter of seconds and then they were inside. She had memorised the layout of the building, so knew exactly where to go – along several corridors, through the main warehouse (empty in the small hours of Saturday morning), and to the door, which would lead to the secondary storage area where all the special merchandise was kept.

The fingerprint scanner on the door took a little longer than the keypad on the outside door – four point five seconds longer. And they were through, down a dim corridor to yet another door, which was heavy, like a vault. It made sense, she thought, given what she expected to be stored here.

The air within smelled funny, like antiseptic, but with the underlying odour of discharged electricity. She didn't switch on her torch just yet. She knew the number of steps she needed to take. But six steps into the required twenty-three, there was a loud clattering behind her.

She whirled around. Her men.

The wan light from the corridor was enough for her to see that they were all on the floor. They had collapsed simultaneously. How could that be?

The door closed, taking away the light.

The Angel of Death tensed, drawing her pistol and her knife. Her heart rate increased. Not by much, as she had trained herself to remain calm under any circumstance, but enough to give her that extra little kick. Her senses were fine-tuned and alert. There was someone in here with her. She could feel it. She readied herself for a confrontation.

The lights snapped on to reveal a grizzly sight. Her men were all quite still, blood pooling around each of their heads as it dripped from ears and noses.

She whirled around again. There was a man, hands behind his back, standing calmly at the end of the empty room. Empty? She gaped. This was meant to be a storage facility. Her heart rate increased that little bit more. She was not used to being wrong.

'No, this is not actually where I store the weapons,' said the man. 'That's just what I tell people. They're actually out there in the main warehouse, in instrument boxes, identified by special serial numbers. You would have passed right by them.' There was a hint of amusement in his voice that vanished with his next words. 'This is the testing area.'

The man was dressed in white, almost blending in with his surroundings. It was Delacy. She recognised him from the dossier she had put together. He appeared to be unarmed. He was dead already, she told herself. She would make him pay for the fact that things had not gone to plan.

She gasped. She couldn't move. She couldn't fire her gun or throw her knife. She couldn't run or turn. She couldn't blink. She was even finding it hard to breathe.

What was going on? Why was this happening? How could control have slipped away from her?

Her heart was now racing, even though it felt like it was being squeezed.

'Don't fight it,' Delacy said. 'And take short, shallow breaths. I think I have the setting right so that you can still breathe. Just.' He smirked.

There was such arrogance in him, she thought. Even more than in her. Perhaps she could play on that? Turn it to her advantage? If only she could make her mouth work, her lips move.

'I knew that putting these weapons on the black market for criminals and terrorists to bid on would come with dangers. With the risk of something like this. But I also knew that I could turn it into an opportunity to up my prices. Imagine my delight when I found out that the Angel of Death was in town. Although, I must admit, you're not quite what I expected.'

Delacy's eyes wandered up and down her sleek, black-clad form. She would have ripped them out if she could move.

'But think how much more I'll be able to charge, when my potential clients see how my weapons and I dealt with the Angel of Death.'

He smiled. Damn him. He smiled.

'Thank you so much for being part of my little demonstration. This is being transmitted, by the way. Live.'

Delacy chuckled as he brought his hands out from behind his back. He was holding something. Some sort of device. She couldn't tell what it was. She was so unused to being at this much of a disadvantage that she didn't know how to cope with it. Her mind kept trying to find a way of turning things around. But there was no way.

'You can do almost anything with sound, you know. Move things. Destroy things. Reshape things. Influence and control things. And people, of course. You can direct it. Sweep wide, as with your late friends behind you, or focus in narrowly on your target, as I'm doing now with you. So, let's begin.'

Delacy adjusted a setting on the device.

Angela could feel a tremor pass through her body. She barely had time to finally acknowledge the fact that she had fatally underestimated an opponent. And then all her muscles went limp. Her bowel and bladder voided instantly, and she collapsed. Her diaphragm relaxed and all the air left her lungs. And her cardiac muscle stopped.

A man sat in a room, the orange embers of a cigarette creating a glowing point of light in the darkness. He had just switched off the monitor on which he had watched the special live transmission. The Angel of Death was no more.

Less competition, he mused.

That Delacy fellow was certainly resourceful and shrewd. But also reckless. There were not many men who would be willing to risk the ire of his profession, but Delacy seemed blissfully unaware of the hornet's nest he had potentially poked a stick into.

The Angel of Death had been careless. She had obviously started to believe in her own reputation a little too much. She

had underestimated Delacy.
He would not make the same mistake.

CHAPTER ELEVEN
Going In

OH-SIX-HUNDRED HOURS. Breath steaming in the chilly air, Douglas was outside the New Barracks ready to see off Lethbridge-Stewart.

'Bright and early start, Alistair.'

'Want to make sure I'm at Imber in plenty of time,' Lethbridge-Stewart said, loading his bag into the back of the Land Rover. 'We need to be ready to act, depending on what Samson finds.'

'There's a thermos of strong coffee waiting in the vehicle. Should help with the journey.'

'Penny has you well-trained.'

Douglas smiled. 'Wives have a tendency to do that. I'm sure Fiona will do the same with you.'

Lethbridge-Stewart looked around, just to make sure nobody was within earshot. Still, he lowered his voice just in case. 'Early days yet, Dougie. Barely two months really. That said,' he added with a grin of his own, 'I am hopeful.'

Just then Lethbridge-Stewart's driver emerged from the barracks' building, saluted the officers and headed straight for the Land Rover.

'Right then,' Lethbridge-Stewart said, swinging the passenger door open. 'All set to go. Bishop and Erickson will keep you updated, Colonel.'

'Sir. And if anything changes, I'll be in touch.'

Lethbridge-Stewart nodded and climbed into the vehicle.

Samson tugged at his suit. It felt wrong going out on a mission in civvies.

He flashed his ID as he strolled up to the front door from the car park. 'Francis Logan. I have an appointment with Mr

Delacy.'

The guard mumbled into his walkie-talkie, waited for an answer, then pointed him to reception.

'I am terribly sorry, Mr Logan,' said the receptionist. 'But I'm afraid that Mr Delacy is not here at the moment. He was called away to do a television interview. It will be at least an hour before he returns. He sends his apologies and trusts that you will be able to wait until he returns.'

'Sure,' said Samson, then mentally flinched. He was supposed to be playing the part of an important, ruthless businessman. He tried to cover it up. 'I'm not used to being kept waiting, but for Mr Delacy I'll make an exception.'

The receptionist smiled understandingly and took him to a waiting room.

'There's a television, if you'd like to watch the interview. Tea and coffee facilities, and a lovely selection of biscuits. Today's papers and a range of magazines. Toilet is through the door at the end. You should have everything you need, right here. But if there's anything else you want, simply dial oh on the phone and you'll get straight through to me.' The receptionist paused before leaving. 'It would be appreciated if you could stay here. Mr Delacy would prefer not to have unaccompanied visitors wandering around the premises.'

Samson looked around. It certainly was a snazzy set-up – comfy looking sofa, window looking out onto an enclosed courtyard full of greenery. He switched the television on, without sound, then perused the biscuits. There really was a 'lovely selection', as the receptionist had indicated. He chose an Abbey Crunch. He liked the golden syrup flavour. He noticed a little bar fridge, like you get in hotel rooms, under the counter. Beer and wine, as well as milk. A little too early for booze, he decided. He wandered over to the door as he munched on the biscuit.

Locked.

They really didn't want people snooping about.

Samson was about to have a go at tackling the lock, when he noticed Delacy's face on the television. He went to turn the sound up.

'And so, in order to further demonstrate the power of music, tomorrow night's episode of *Fear Frequency* will have yet another new theme tune. But more than that…' Trevor Delacy smiled down the barrel of the camera. 'I have made the decision, in order to showcase the versatility of the SynthMoods 21-20, to provide a unique piece of music to accompany each new episode of the series.'

Delacy glanced to the side of the camera to see Merv's eyes widening, the Morleys Filter cigarette almost falling from his lips. There would be no avoiding *Fear Frequency's* producer after this broadcast.

'As with the previous pieces, they will be composed and performed by Yours Truly. Consider it a gift to loyal viewers.' Delacy smiled again.

'And… cut!'

His smile vanished. And Merv stalked forward.

Delacy held up a hand before Merv could open his mouth. 'It will keep viewers interested. It will create publicity. It will get you new viewers. And, it is still at no cost to you.'

Merv stood there, mouth agape like a goldfish. But before Delacy could leave, he found his voice. 'Wait! I appreciate the fact that this is not costing me. But, seriously, a new theme tune for every episode.'

'Every episode? I'm sorry. I meant every screening. The weekly repeats will each have a new piece as well.'

'*Weekly* repeats?'

'Well, of course. ITV had some of its best mid-week figures last week, they want to continue that, so LWT has agreed.'

'Why…? Why wasn't I informed?'

Delacy shrugged. 'Why not just be glad, Merv. More figures, more longevity for your little show.'

'But…' Merv shook his head. 'Fine. Fine. But still… new music each time? It's ridiculous. There will be no recognition. Viewers need an identifiable theme. Something that will immediately signal the start of their favourite programme. Something to—'

As Merv spoke, Delacy slipped his hand into the pocket of his blazer, his finger finding the coin-like device, tapping the raised corner.

'Aagh!' Merv was cut off mid-sentence as he clutched his head and closed his eyes, his cigarette dropping to the studio floor. 'Sorry,' he said, eyes still closed. 'Sudden migraine.'

'Perhaps you should go lie down,' suggested Delacy.

He walked off without waiting for the producer to reopen his eyes.

'More demonstrations,' whispered Samson, as he switched off the television.

It had only been about ten minutes since he'd been shown to the waiting room. So, at least another fifty minutes until Delacy was due back. He'd make sure he returned to the waiting room with time to spare.

He examined the door. Thankfully, it was just an ordinary lock.

The corridor outside was empty, and so he slipped out. He quickly scanned the ceiling and walls for cameras, but all he could see were smoke detectors and fire sprinklers. It seemed like it would be safe enough to explore a little.

Hearing voices from up ahead, he adopted a confident manner and a purposeful stride. In his experience, people rarely questioned a man who acted as if he belonged exactly where he was and knew where he was going.

Along the way, when there was no one around, he tried random doors. Most were locked. Although he had skeleton keys, he didn't want to take the time unlocking all the doors, which were likely to be ordinary offices. The first unlocked door he came across was a stationary supply room. The next was a kitchenette. And the third was an occupied office.

'Sorry, wrong room,' he said, while bidding a hasty retreat.

Finally, he managed to find a room full of filing cabinets. Deciding to take a quick look, he slipped inside. But the files were just records of sales, so he continued on.

Passing a lift, with a number of men in suits waiting for its doors to open, he carried on, thinking the warehouse was probably a better bet. But when he came to the end of the corridor, he was greeted with a locked door. This time there was a numeric keypad.

Given how far he'd come, he assumed it must lead out to the warehouse, but there was no way for him to bypass that lock.

He backtracked to the lift, deciding to see what was upstairs. As he entered and examined the controls, he realised that he'd need a pass card to use it. He was about to head out again when another man entered. He appeared to be in quite a hurry and, not paying any attention to Samson, he swiped his card and pressed level two. Samson quickly pressed three.

After the other passenger alighted on level two, Sampson continued up. The *ding* that announced the lift's arrival on the third floor seemed very loud. Samson felt strangely jittery as he got off and looked around the large, spacious area — a bit like a cross between a foyer and a lounge. There were wingback armchairs along the walls, each with speakers set into their wings, and doors between them.

He walked to the nearest door, his heart fluttery and a headache beginning to take hold behind his eyes. There was a keypad on the door. In fact, there were keypads on all the doors. He tried one. Locked, of course. As he went to the next, his headache worsened. He grabbed the edge of a chair as a wave of dizziness assaulted him.

Taking a deep breath, he moved on, only to find himself stumbling, his legs jittering beneath him. He slumped into one of the armchairs. There was soft music playing through its speakers, barely audible. It was undeniably soothing, and he felt his headache receding. It was a comfortable chair, and he felt quite relaxed. His eyes grew heavy. His mind wandered.

What was he doing here?

Oh yes, the mission. A recce round the offices. But he was so tired. He tried to fight it, but the lethargy dragged his eyelids down.

Perhaps he could rest for just a moment.

But, as his eyes closed, he lost consciousness.

This time I will do it, Dan told himself. This time he would get proof. This time, he'd get into the restricted section of the warehouse.

He walked up to the side of the gatehouse and flashed his old ID, half expecting to be turned away. The guard held up a hand as he spoke into his walkie-talkie, paused, then waved him through.

Heart thumping, breath coming faster than normal, Dan went through the gate and around the side of the main building, towards the warehouse at the back. He tried to saunter nonchalantly, but it more than likely came across as a nervous stumbling sort of walk. The moment he was out of sight of the gatehouse, he quickened his pace.

He keyed his code into the panel by the side entrance, hurried down the corridor and into the warehouse. Being a Saturday morning, stock was being prepped for shipping out, so that it would arrive at retail stores on Monday morning. The staff were very much focused on that, and no one paid him any attention as he strode towards the door that led to the restricted area.

Just stay cool, he told himself. Look confident. Look like you belong. It worked last time.

But when he arrived at the door, he realised that he was sweating and trembling. He had no real plan. He didn't know what was beyond the door or if he would be able to find a weaponised instrument. He didn't even know if he'd be able to get in, as the keypad wasn't numeric – it required a thumbprint.

Dan came to an abrupt halt at the door, staring at the thumbprint-pad, sweating even more, wondering what he should do. Run away? Try his thumbprint? Knock? Glancing over his shoulder, he noticed a couple of the blokes looking his way. Whatever he did, he had to do it right away.

What the heck? He had nothing to lose. He pressed his thumb onto the pad and held his breath.

Click!

Hardly believing it was possible, he tried the door.

It opened for him.

Dan took another glance over his shoulder. Those two blokes were still watching him. He took a deep breath and stepped into the corridor beyond. The door swung shut behind him.

Click!

He whirled around and tried the door. It had locked. He stabbed his thumb at the pad. This time, nothing happened. Damn. What had he got himself into?

Turning slowly, he shuffled warily along the corridor towards the door that stood open at the end. He entered a large white space that smelled a bit like a hospital, but also like something else. Like the concreted area behind his block of council flats just as a thunderstorm was about to start. There was a wingback armchair in the centre of the room.

The door behind him clanged shut.

'The prodigal employee returns,' said a voice from unseen speakers. 'Please have a seat, Mr Morales.'

He'd been caught. He knew it and he suddenly felt incredibly daft for having returned. Why, why, why had he come back? Stupid, stupid, stupid!

'Sit!' the voice commanded, less friendly this time, making Dan jump.

Fear compelled him to rush for the chair and throw himself into it.

The voice sounded so familiar. The lyrics of *Listen to Me* sprung up in his mind. Trev Del. Trevor Delacy. It was his voice.

Dan thought he heard music. But it was so soft, he wasn't sure. He concentrated, trying to work out if it was his imagination or if the chair was serenading him.

'Now, Mr Morales. Why have you come back?'

'To steal one of your synths,' Dan answered without really thinking. 'One of the ones that's really a weapon and not a musical instrument.' He inhaled sharply.

'This isn't the first time you've stolen from us, is it, Mr Morales?'

'No! Yes!' Dan blurted out. 'I mean, no it's not the first time and yes I stole a SynthMoods 21-20 a few days ago. And stationery before that. Since starting work here, I've taken three packets of pencils, a retractable measuring tape and a stapler.' He was babbling now. He couldn't stop himself. He wanted to confess. 'I've also taken food from the staff refrigerator. Although technically that's not stealing from Electric Soundscapes 'cause the food belonged to other workers. And then there was—'

'Enough!' Delacy's voice commanded. 'Mr Morales, please tell me everything you think you know about Electric Soundscapes and who you have shared your suspicions with.'

Dan couldn't hold back. He didn't want to hold back. He had a deep desire to tell the disembodied voice of his employer anything and everything that it wanted to know. And he did. He told it of the overheard conversations, of his report to the police, of his return to steal a SynthMoods 21-20, of his visit to the Scots Guards Special Support Group, and of his return to Electric Soundscapes.

'Thank you, Mr Morales. That will be all.'

That will be all? Relief washed over Dan. That will be all. Was he about to get released? Since he had been so cooperative, was Mr Delacy going to let him go?

Dan made a move to get up out of the armchair, but found that he couldn't. Something was keeping him there. He fought against it.

'Oh. Did you think I was going to let you go? No. I can't do that.' Delacy's voice was mocking.

The tone reminded Dan just how much he despised the man. He had the sudden urge to confess again.

An odd feeling washed over Dan. Like a deep vibration in his skull.

'*I hate your song!*' he yelled.

Then his eyeballs popped, and his brain began to boil in its own cerebral fluid.

Hey, hey, hey, sung Delacy's voice.

CHAPTER TWELVE
Red Handed

SAMSON YAWNED and stretched, his eyes still closed. That nap was just what he'd needed. He felt refreshed and ready to proceed with the mission.

Mission?

His eyes snapped open.

Trevor Delacy regarded him from the other side of a large wooden desk, its surface reflecting the light from above. Samson could smell the wood polish. There was a complex set of controls taking up more than half the surface of the desk. Was he in a recording studio?

'What happened?' he demanded, jumping to his feet.

'You appear to have dozed off, Mr Logan.'

'What? How?'

Delacy smiled. 'You sat down in one of our relaxation chairs. They play smoothing music, designed to calm the mind and encourage it to rest.'

'Oh.' Samson tried to regain his composure.

'Mind you,' said Delacy, his smile switching off, 'you were not authorised to go wandering around the building.'

'My apologies,' said Samson, slipping into the character of Francis Logan and sitting back down. 'But I got impatient. I'm not used to being kept waiting. And I figured a little look around might give me an advantage.'

'Really?'

'I like to know as much as I can about prospective business partners.'

'Business partners? Interesting. Well then, Mr Logan—'

'You can call me Frank.'

'Okay... Frank.' There was a hint of amusement in Delacy's eyes as he studied Samson. It made him feel decidedly uncomfortable. 'Firstly, let me apologise for keeping you waiting so long. The interview was a last minute thing and rather important. And then I had to deal with another wandering visitor.'

Samson did not like the way he said 'deal with'. It was most certainly a threat. He mentally berated himself for having been caught. He felt a flush rise at his collar as he imagined telling the Brig that he'd fallen asleep on the job.

'Anyway,' Delacy continued. 'I am rather curious about your interest. Your PA told my PA that you were aware of yesterday's advertising meeting and that you wanted a meeting of your own. I wonder who blabbed about the advertising get-together? Morleys, perhaps? I might have to raise their price. There was also an indication that you were aware of other even more confidential meetings regarding other products that you might be interested in. So then, tell me, Frank, what exactly is it that you want?'

Delacy knew. Or at least suspected. But until he said something directly, Samson had to continue with his cover.

'You may or may not have heard of me, Mr Delacy, but I am a musician-turned-producer. I've always believed in the power of music.' He tried to slip in the key words he knew would get a reaction. 'The power to influence. And that is something that I am seeking to exploit. Your little demonstration with the *Fear Frequency* theme was quite… dramatic. It got my attention. And it got me thinking. So, I made a few enquiries, found out all I could about you and your operation. My initial thought was that your unique synthesiser could be used on singles that I produce in order to make them irresistible. Imagine a pop song that, when heard on the radio, made everyone who listened to it *want* to buy it. I'd use session musicians of course, so that we'd keep all the profits.'

Delacy steepled his fingers and leaned back in his chair, but didn't say anything.

'But then I found out that you had other products on the market,' continued Samson. 'Products that could potentially be used against the competition.'

'Corporate espionage? Interesting angle. I was wondering how you were going to manoeuvre this beyond the mind control.'

'I beg your pardon?' said Samson.

'Oh come on, *Frank*, give me some credit. I know that you're not a musician or a producer. And I doubt that you actually know the extent of my operations. Amusing as this little game has been, I think it's gone on long enough. Time for you to drop the pretence and give the real story. I strongly suspect that you're from that Scots Guards Special Support Group that Dan Morales visited the other day. Am I right?'

Stay calm, Samson told himself. He kept his face neutral. 'I have no idea what you mean.'

Delacy reached out to the controls on his desk and Samson suddenly felt a pressure descend on him. It wasn't painful, but he found that he couldn't move. Faint music began to play through the speakers in the chair wings. It was calming. His heart rate slowed. He felt relaxed. All his worries, all his cares, were melting away. He looked across the desk at Delacy and realised that he could trust this man. He could trust him completely.

'Now, Frank, tell me everything.'

A mass of electronic equipment was spread out on the bench in front of Erickson. To the left was a pile of research papers with his notes in the margins and page corners bent over to mark relevant sections. To the right was an ashtray. He stubbed out a cigarette. He was disappointed with himself for having given in, but Lindsay was right. Now was not a good time to be giving up. He needed to stay calm and focused, to get the job done, and if a few cigarettes were what it would take, then so be it.

He picked up a soldering iron and began attaching wires to a small metal casing. If what he had gleaned from Freiheit's research was correct, he should be able to rig up a device that would offer some protection from the influence of the *Fear Frequency* music and anything of a similar nature.

He glanced at his watch. He needed to hurry if he was going to be ready in time to test it.

'Welcome back, Lieutenant.'

'Sir.' Bishop climbed out of the Peugeot and stood to attention. 'Good to be home.'

'What's the situation at Haltwhistle? Did you get anywhere with Nurse Hadley?'

'Nurse Hadley?'

Bishop had woken refreshed that morning, feeling better than he had in ages. He had enjoyed the drive back to Edinburgh, singing along with the radio, feeling quite carefree. But as he tried to think of what he'd been investigating at Haltwhistle, he felt weary again – as if all those thoughts were weighing him down. He struggled through the lethargy.

'Oh yes. Turned out to be a dead end. She's not exactly a wonderful human being, but she wasn't doing anything wrong.' He thought for a moment. 'As for the patients, they were receiving a new therapy, which seemed at first to be helping with their dementia but, in the end, it was temporary. So, not exactly a miracle cure. I think there may have been some exaggeration there.'

'What about the deaths?'

'The deaths?' Bishop was confused.

'The deaths,' repeated Douglas. 'There was a discrepancy over the time and place of death with several of the patients. We had one of the bodies exhumed.'

'Yes, that's right. Turned out to be a storm in a teacup. The witness who disputed the time and place of death... Well, she's quite elderly and has Alzheimer's. Not really reliable.'

'So, we can wrap this up and close the case?'

'Yes. I think so.'

'Good. Things have become rather busy with the Electric Soundscapes investigation.'

'And what's happened with that?' asked Bishop, his tiredness ebbing.

'Quite a lot actually. Go and get back into uniform and I will brief you over a nice strong cup of coffee.'

'Yes, sir.' Bishop turned to Anne's car to collect his things, then rushed into the New Barracks.

Samson woke with a start. Falling asleep on the job was becoming a thing; lucky he wasn't a commissioned officer. He thought a moment, trying to remember what had happened... He'd been telling Delacy about... Oh no, he'd been telling Delacy about everything.

Samson looked around. He was in a different room. In a different chair. The room was white and spacious with an odd smell. The chair was more like a dentist's chair than the comfortable armchair he had been in before. Speakers were pressed up against his ears. He couldn't hear anything through them, but he could feel the rhythmic vibrations. Again, he couldn't move.

'Now then, Sergeant Major Samson Ware, try to relax. This will only hurt if you attempt to resist.' Delacy's voice was mellow and soothing. 'Of course, I know you will. But that's fine. I do rather enjoy the process.' He chuckled. 'So... I have a little job for you, Sergeant Major. I need you to deal with a problem for me. A problem that needs to be removed. Disposed of. Would you do that for me?'

Part of Samson still wanted to trust Delacy, to do what he asked. But he also knew that he was being influenced by the sound, just like Erickson's report had said. And he'd be damned if he gave in without a fight.

As he thought those thoughts, the pain began.

Erickson attached the reel of magnetic tape and fed it through the recording heads, wound it a little way on to the empty spool, then flicked a few switches. Standing back, he admired the set up. Everything was ready to record this afternoon's broadcast of a *Fear Frequency* promo. More than that, he was all set to examine the music in great detail. He had put together this special equipment, including a state-of-the-art sound frequency analyser. Now all he had to do was wait for the broadcast. He switched on the television and checked his watch. Twelve minutes to go.

It would have been simpler if he'd been able to get a recording from LWT, but they were unable to provide one with the music. Apparently, the music arrived by special courier, just before the broadcast, on a self-erasing tape that could only be played the once. So, he needed to make his own recording. They had, at least, been able to provide the exact time of the scheduled promo spot.

Erickson was also planning on testing another piece of equipment. He went to his workbench and picked up a set of headphones. He examined the connections from which wires snaked out to a small metal box with a switch. Satisfied, he placed the headphones over his ears. The sound of the television was still quite clear. He then flicked the switch on the box.

He smiled a satisfied smile, thinking that Dr Travers

herself would be proud of this little set-up, and clipped the box to his belt. He returned to his equipment to await the arrival of the other participants in his little experiment.

Merv Chatley's eyes kept nervously flicking to the wall clock. Seven minutes until the scheduled broadcast and still no music. He wouldn't normally be at the studio just for a promo spot, but the whole situation was just so damned odd. He felt the need to micro-manage every aspect that he actually had some control over. And that included the broadcast of a promo.

He lit up another Morleys.

An alternative piece of music was all cued up on standby. Not as atmospheric or effective as what Delacy had been providing him with, but adequate enough. If the courier didn't show, they would just go with that. Part of him would actually be happy if that happened. He could stop dealing with Delacy. And he wouldn't have to listen to creepy music that made him feel so damned uncomfortable. He could return to a more normal approach.

But he couldn't deny that the SynthMoods music delivered bucket loads of attention. Controversy, he acknowledged, was fuel for the television industry. And, damn it, if someone was willing to hand him the fuel, he'd throw it on the fire.

With five and a half minutes to spare, the tape arrived. Merv was certain that Delacy had done this deliberately. He was flaunting his power. God, how he hated that man.

'It's very exciting,' said Liz's voice over the phone.

'It sounds it,' Anne agreed. 'And I am very tempted.'

'Only tempted…?' Liz laughed. 'Come on, Anne, you didn't get in touch just because you were tempted. Cambridge needs you. I need you.'

Anne laughed good naturedly at her old friend's claim. 'Cambridge is lucky to have you running research programmes there,' she told her. 'What is it Professor Jensen said to us?'

Now it was Liz's turn to laugh. 'One day you'll run the scientific community,' she said, doing a very good impression of Professor Rachel Jensen's precise tones. 'Which only proves why you need to join me. We shouldn't be competitors, we should be allies.'

'I assure you, Elizabeth, the work I do does not compete

with yours.'

'The work you used to do.'

Silence, and Anne felt the pit threatening to swallow her.

'Sorry,' said Liz. 'That was mean of me. But it's your own fault for not telling me what it was.'

'Top secret. I told you that.'

'Producing invisible ink, were you?'

Anne didn't want to tell Liz that invisible ink had been developed a couple of years ago. Just one of the things Anne had discovered while working for the Fifth.

Oh, who was she kidding? She had already made her decision. She wasn't quite sure how she would approach Lethbridge-Stewart about it, but she wanted back in.

'Liz. We must arrange a tea date soon.'

'Well,' Liz said, resigned now, 'that way you'll at least visit me in Cambridge, and I can show you what I'm doing.'

'Yes, you certainly can.'

'Good. One day, Annie, you will tell me what you're doing.'

'One day,' Anne said, with a smile, 'perhaps you'll find out first-hand.'

Tommy was out in the back yard kicking the ball around. A good manly thing for his son to be doing on a Saturday afternoon, Graham decided. His wife, Gladys, was in the kitchen rustling up some lunch. And Graham was taking a moment to catch the football preview on *Grandstand*. As commentator Sam Leitch finished his summary and Fight of the Week began with highlights of the 10-rounds at Shoreditch Town Hall, Graham got up to turn off the telly. But on the spur of the moment, he switched it to LWT instead.

The Morleys advertisement assaulted him. As he watched it, Graham felt angry. Furious with himself for giving in to his sudden craving the other day. He made a vow to never, *never* give in to his weaknesses again. It lessened him as a man and was a poor example to his son. But before he could switch off, the advertisement transitioned into a promo for *Fear Frequency*. It was an odd cross-fade, with the music beginning before the cigarette imagery had faded.

Graham froze, his fingers on the knob. He wanted to switch it off, kill the music. But he couldn't. The music held him, penetrated him, violated him. Made him watch. He felt the terror building. Something terrible, unimaginably horrible would happen if he didn't act.

And within seconds he knew that he would watch the advertised episode tomorrow night and he knew, with absolute certainty, that the moment the music finished, he'd be out the door and down the street to get a packet of Morleys King Size Filter.

CHAPTER THIRTEEN
Debriefing

ERICKSON REMOVED the headphones. They had worked perfectly. He'd been able to hear the music, and felt no ill effects. So, it was possible to circumvent the influence of the insidious sounds.

He turned to face the other two.

Sergeant Jean Maddox, who was usually in charge of the girls who manned the phones and radios, was taking off a large pair of industrial, noise-cancelling headphones.

'Didn't hear a thing,' she said.

'Any strange feelings or cravings? Heightened emotional state?'

She shook her head.

Bruce Baxendale was another matter. One of the younger scientists on Erickson's team, the grizzled-looking man with his shoulder length fair hair had volunteered to watch and listen without any protection. His face was haunted – pale and sweaty with wild eyes.

'Well?' Erickson asked.

'Fear,' Baxendale said. His face relaxed as he looked at Erickson, and a barely contained excitement began to build. 'But more than that. There was a… a desire to smoke cigarettes. Specifically, Morley's King Size Filter. The two things were mingled… *Are* still mingled. It's like…' Erickson watched him pause, wringing his hands, as if trying to get his thoughts in order. 'I'm scared that something bad will happen if I don't get those cigarettes. It's fascinating.' Baxendale took a deep breath. 'I know what's going on, and yet I'm finding it hard to fight these feelings.' He turned to Jean. 'Can you imagine what it's like on unsuspecting members of the public?'

'Terrifying, in a word,' she said.

'Yes,' agreed Erickson. 'Which makes it all the more important to analyse the sounds in the music and try to isolate the frequency or frequencies that are causing this.' He tapped the headphones he was still wearing. 'These are very general, covering a range of frequencies. But like a broad spectrum antibiotic, they won't work as well as something more targeted.'

'Are you okay?' Jean asked, putting a gentle hand on Baxendale's shoulder.

He gave her a weak smile.

Erickson turned his back on them and gave his attention to his equipment. He wound the tape back, adjusted some settings, and switched the television over to input. He took off his headphones and handed them to Baxendale.

'I need to hear this for myself,' Erickson said. 'But there's no sense you being exposed a second time.' He looked at Jean. 'You should either put yours back on or leave.'

She held up her hands. 'Oh, I think I've had enough of this for one day. I'll leave you two gentlemen to your music.'

'Thanks,' Erickson called after her as she left.

He hit the playback. But the screen showed nothing but distorted static.

'What?'

He checked the readings on the instruments.

'I don't believe it. The tape is blank.'

'How is that possible?' asked Baxendale.

'I don't...' Erickson ran a frustrated hand through his hair, and thought a moment.

'Did the music...?' Baxendale shrugged. 'I know it sounds mad, but could the music somehow have *wiped* the magnetic tapes while it was playing?'

Erickson balked at the idea. 'I don't see how. But...' He indicated the TV. 'If it does, then we cannot record the music. Which means...'

'We're stumped.'

Erickson sat down, dejected and annoyed. 'Yes. Up the proverbial creek.'

Samson rubbed at his eyes as he drove. It had been a long and fruitless day.

His wander around the Electric Soundscapes offices had revealed nothing out of the ordinary. And his meeting with

Trevor Delacy, who had been charming and effusive, had resulted in very little.

Delacy was offering nothing more than a contract to custom develop music that reflected the feel that advertisers wanted to create for their products. Pricey, yes – but the pieces of music promised to be unique. No matter how hard Samson had pushed, there was not a hint of anything untoward. Certainly, nothing along the lines of mind control or, heaven forbid, weaponry. In retrospect it seemed like a ridiculous notion.

Samson couldn't understand why the Brig had sent him on this undercover mission. With the benefit of hindsight, it seemed like a complete waste of time and resources. Not to mention, an insult to Trevor Delacy. The man didn't deserve this kind of suspicion. He was a hard-working businessman, that's all. He wasn't any kind of threat. And besides, he seemed like a nice bloke.

The sun began to set, as Samson approached Imber Base. He decided that he would have to set the Brig straight on the matter of Trevor Delacy and Electric Soundscapes.

Delacy sat in his office. Things were coming to a head. Advertising contracts were almost at the point of a signature. The other arrangements – there were no written contracts with these sorts of deals – were also on the verge of agreement. He would need more weapons, of course. But he would bring pressure to bear to ensure that happened.

The only other thing requiring his attention, assuming of course that Samson Ware accomplished his mission, was *Fear Frequency*. He still needed to send the music for tomorrow's episode. He picked up the phone to arrange the courier. He would send it early, he decided, if for no other reason than to mess with Merv Chatley. The last time, he had instructed the courier to wait outside the studio until seven minutes to the scheduled broadcast. He chuckled. Yes, he'd get it delivered earlier this time, to Chatley's private residence.

'Nothing?' Lethbridge-Stewart was more than surprised. He couldn't believe it.

'There is no evidence to suggest that there is anything untoward happening at Electric Soundscapes,' Samson said.

'Then how the blazes do you explain the effects of that music on people throughout Great Britain?'

'Excessive imagination.'

Lethbridge-Stewart regarded Samson with disbelief, momentarily lost for words. 'This will make it difficult to justify a raid on their warehouse.'

'I don't see any need to go ahead with the raid. Not now that we know everything there is above board.'

'Is that so, Samson?' Lethbridge-Stewart shook his head, and looked around Major Leopold's office. Unbelievable. 'Well, thank you for your considered opinion on the matter. As it is, the decision is not yours to make.'

The muscles in Samson's neck tightened, his jaw clenched and Lethbridge-Stewart noticed the right side of his face twitch oddly.

'Are you quite all right?'

'So you plan on conducting the raid anyway?'

Lethbridge-Stewart harrumphed loudly as he strode around the desk and sat in the chair. 'Not without clearance from higher up, damn it.'

He wasn't sure if he was imagining it, but it seemed as if Samson relaxed at Lethbridge-Stewart's words, and his hand fell back down by his side. As if he'd been reaching under his blazer.

'Are you sure you're okay, Samson? You don't seem yourself.'

'Fine, thank you.' Samson's smile was not very convincing.

Lethbridge-Stewart studied him a moment longer before saying, 'Very well, then. Dismissed.'

Something was definitely wrong. Lethbridge-Stewart had seen too much to so easily believe Samson.

Lethbridge-Stewart reached for the phone, just as Samson opened the office door.

'Get me General Hamilton.'

What followed was so quick, Lethbridge-Stewart hardly wanted to believe it. But his training kicked in and he responded in an instant.

Samson's hand went for his pocket and he whirled around, pulling out an odd-looking gun. Lethbridge-Stewart was already on the move. He quickly pulled out his service revolver and ducked down behind the desk.

An odd thrumming sound reverberated through the room. The glass in the picture frames above the desk shattered, raining shards onto Lethbridge-Stewart.

'I can't let you raid the warehouse,' said Samson.

Lethbridge-Stewart could hear Samson's shoes on the floor. If he timed it well… Lethbridge-Stewart shoved the desk forward, slamming it into Samson's midriff. The lamp came crashing down and the drawers sprung free, scattering paperwork, pens, pencils, an enormous amount of paperclips, and a bottle of ten-year-old Glenfiddich. Samson doubled over, his torso landing on the top of the desk. Lethbridge-Stewart was up in seconds, knocking the strange gun from Samson's hand and pointing his revolver.

'I think you've got some explaining to do, Sergeant Major.'

Samson groaned, slowly rising up, and launched himself over the desk. He grabbed Lethbridge-Stewart's wrist with one hand so that the revolver pointed off to the side, and went for his throat with the other. They stumbled back hard into the wall. Glassless frames fell to join the shattered shards on the floor.

With his free hand, Lethbridge-Stewart clawed at the fingers on his throat, but Samson's grip tightened. Lethbridge-Stewart's vision swam and he struggled for breath. Samson smashed Lethbridge-Stewart's hand against the wall repeatedly, until he was forced to let go of the revolver.

In response, he kneed Samson in the groin. His grip loosened and Lethbridge-Stewart twisted free, shoving his attacker to one side. Samson landed on the floor and immediately scrambled for the strange weapon he'd dropped.

Lethbridge-Stewart jumped over him, landing on his hand just as his fingers reached it. There was a sickening snap, and Samson screamed as he pulled his hand back.

Lethbridge-Stewart scooped up the strange gun and levelled it at his friend.

'I realise you've been brainwashed,' he said, between breaths, grim determination on his face. 'But I will shoot you if I have to.'

Samson looked up and nodded. Cradling his left hand, he managed to get to his knees. But rather than continuing to his feet, he rolled forward, knocking Lethbridge-Stewart's feet from beneath him. Again, the gun clattered across the floor, as

Lethbridge-Stewart landed on top of Samson.

The two men continued to struggle, slamming into walls, knocking into the desk and chairs, and crunching over the glass shards and splintered wood from the picture frames.

Samson managed to pull free and lunged for his weapon. Revolver out of reach, Lethbridge-Stewart grabbed the closest thing he could, the smashed desk lamp. He brought it down heavily onto the back of Samson's head.

Finally, he slumped to the floor, unconscious.

The door flung open and Captain Younghusband and a corporal ran into the room. They both stopped at the sight before them.

'Well, you took your sweet time, Captain,' Lethbridge-Stewart said, staggering to his feet.

'A disagreement, sir?' Younghusband asked.

'If only,' Lethbridge-Stewart said, with a grim smile. 'Well don't just stand there, Corporal. Take Sergeant Major Ware to the sickbay.'

'You heard,' Younghusband said, already moving towards Samson, 'give me a hand, Seager.'

'Sir.'

'Be careful, I think I broke his hand,' Lethbridge-Stewart said. 'Captain, make sure a guard is on him at all times, until we find out what happened to him.'

'Yes, sir.'

Samson groaned, semi-conscious as Younghusband and Seager picked him up by the armpits and dragged him off.

Lethbridge-Stewart rubbed at his bruised throat and surveyed the damage. He was pleased to see that the bottle of Glenfiddich lay safely in the corner of the room.

'Thank goodness for small mercies.'

He picked up the bottle and took a swig. The familiar burn of the liquid down his throat paled in comparison to the burn of his anger.

He wondered what exactly had happened at Electric Soundscapes. Evidently their music could do more than just alter peoples' mood.

'That,' he said to the empty office, 'is all the justification I need.'

'He tried to kill you?' Nick Ellery was aghast.

'His mind has been tampered with,' Lethbridge-Stewart explained.

'Ah, the sound waves. Jeff filled us all in. I should be up in Scotland, myself,' Ellery said, 'only it's my niece's birthday.'

'Lucky for me, since I need someone with some expertise. Samson's in the sickbay under guard and Corporal Fenn is tending to him. But Fenn's just a field medic. I don't suppose there's anything you could do to help?'

'I'm a seismologist, Brigadier, not a physician. I've got a pretty general science background, but nothing that could possibly help in this case.'

'It was worth asking.' Lethbridge-Stewart turned to the desk and retrieved the strange gun. He handed it to Ellery. 'See what you can make of this weapon.'

Ellery tentatively took it.

'I'll see what I can do. But, like I said, this is well out of my expertise.'

'Maybe so, but you're all we have down here at the Loony Bin right now.'

Ellery gave a smile with little mirth. 'Thanks.'

The scientist had barely been gone a minute before there was a knock on the door.

'Come in,' Lethbridge-Stewart called.

Bishop marched in with a box under one arm and saluted. He looked around at the mess. 'What happened here, sir?'

Lethbridge-Stewart looked up from the papers he was shuffling through on the desk. The lamp was back in place and, remarkably, with a new globe was still operational. But the office did look rather worse for wear. The shattered glass had been swept up into a corner and the broken frames and drawers stacked up against a wall. Despite a cursory clean up, the place still bore the marks of the recent encounter.

'I was attacked by Sergeant Major Ware.'

'Samson?'

'Yes, Lieutenant. They got to him. Did something to his mind.'

Lethbridge-Stewart indicated that Bishop should place the box on the desk. It was a delivery from Erickson.

Bishop took a seat while Lethbridge-Stewart explained about Samson's new change of mind.

'I assume the raid is going ahead, sir,' said Bishop, when he had finished.

'Indeed. I'd like to have you with me, but first I want to know if you feel up to it. Investigating an old persons' home is a far cry from a raid.'

'Potential risk and danger.' Bishop smiled. 'With all due respect, sir. When do we head out?'

Lethbridge-Stewart nodded. He still wasn't sure about taking Bishop, but he needed his best people on the raid. And Bishop was one of them.

'I want to be at Electric Soundscapes by oh-one-hundred. The last warehouse shift finishes at twenty-three-hundred, but I want to make sure there's no one there other than the security guards.'

Bishop nodded. 'I think I'll be okay to handle a few security guards.'

'Let's hope that's all the resistance we do receive, Mr Bishop. Captain Younghusband is getting the men ready now.'

'Would you like me to attend his briefing, sir?'

'Shortly. First,' Lethbridge-Stewart said, sitting himself down and reaching for the box on his desk, 'let's see what Dr Erickson has come up with.'

Having tested it on the firing range, Ellery deduced that the gun shot short bursts of intense sound waves. It was a compact, close combat weapon, it's effectiveness drastically declining after a few metres. But close up, it could shatter glass, splinter wood and even put a dent in the softer metals.

There were no seams, no screws, no nothing. How in the world was he going to figure out how it worked, if he couldn't get inside it? He drummed his fingers on the workbench as he thought.

Making a decision, he dug through the supplies and came back with a vice and a hand drill. He clamped the weapon to the side of the workbench and then, choosing a narrow bit, started to drill into the casing. *Like a skewer through butter*, he thought. Next step would be to insert a tiny surgical camera and take a look at the innards.

But he never got to that stage.

Accompanied by a high-pitched whining that hurt his ears, the weapon dissolved into a puddle of goo.

'Oh dear,' whispered Ellery. 'The brigadier is not going to be pleased.'

CHAPTER FOURTEEN
The Raid

'**No. No!** *No!*'

The RSM's shouts brought Corporal Seager running. He'd been sitting just inside the sickbay on an uncomfortable wooden chair, leaning up against the wall.

He looked down at Ware, strapped onto the bed with restraints, his left hand bandaged, two of the fingers in splints. Seager was worried about his old training RSM. They had bonded over a few pints at *The Bell Inn* on several occasions. There was a sheen of sweat across Ware's brow and an expression of agonised concentration on his face. His eyes were screwed up tight as he thrashed his head from side to side.

'I. Will. Not!' he growled through gritted teeth.

Apart from Seager and RSM Ware, the sickbay was empty. Seager looked across to the phone attached to the far wall. He should probably call Fenn.

Lethbridge-Stewart sat in the passenger seat of the lead Bedford. On the benches in the tarp covered rear were a squad of men. He peered out through the windscreen at the darkened Harringay Warehouse District side street, searching for movement. The raid was only minutes away and he felt the adrenaline begin to make its way through his system. This was more like it. Better than being couped up in an office reading files, making calls and holding meetings. Mind you, his office meeting with Samson had been a little more energetic than he had bargained for.

Lethbridge-Stewart spotted movement up ahead, and then the figure of Bishop appeared through the gloom, approaching the vehicle at a jog. He did his best to hide the pain on his face, but Lethbridge-Stewart recognised it. He trusted Bishop would know when he'd pushed himself too far.

He climbed into the driver's seat and passed the night vision binoculars to Lethbridge-Stewart. 'Looks like our intel was spot on. One security guard in the gatehouse. Reading a newspaper, but it looks like he's close to dozing off. And there appears to be another patrolling the grounds on foot with a dog. A German Shepherd, I think. He's passed the office building and is now going round back towards the warehouse.'

Lethbridge-Stewart spoke into his walkie-talkie. 'This is Mayhem One to Mayhem Two and Mayhem Four. Mission is a go-er. Mayhem Four, Babysitter is in the Nursery. Mayhem Two, second Babysitter is walking the dog along your intended route.'

Bishop started the engine.

'Maintain radio silence until target is secure. Follow our lead. Mayhem One, out.'

Lethbridge-Stewart put down the walkie-talkie and snatched up a pair of headphones from the dashboard. He placed them over his head and positioned the padded circles over his ears. Taking the lead running from them, he plugged it into a small unit attached to his belt and switched it on. Bishop did the same. They glanced at each other, and Lethbridge-Stewart saw his own 'let's hope these actually work' expression mirrored on Bishop's face.

Erickson had sent the headphones over with Bishop. They allowed ordinary sound to reach the ears, but the signal from the belt units supposedly blocked a broad range of ultrasounds and infrasound. They were prototypes that the scientist had cobbled together in a hurry. And there were only four pairs. Captain Younghusband and Lieutenant Dashner had the others.

'Right,' said Lethbridge-Stewart. 'Let's go.'

Bishop pulled the truck out from the curb and proceeded down the street at a slow pace. Behind him, another Bedford and a Land Rover followed. Reaching the end, he turned the vehicle onto the larger road and planted his foot on the accelerator.

Up ahead, Lethbridge-Stewart could see the closed chain link gates and lowered boom rapidly getting nearer. He braced himself for the impact.

Samson's eyes opened wide as he yelled another, 'No!'

A soldier came running into view. Samson recognised him from training sessions at Imber, but it took him a second to remember the name.

Seager. That's right. Corporal Samuel Seager. Sam. Of course Samson knew the man; they always joked about sharing the same name. More or less.

'Sir? Samson? Are you okay?'

'Sam. What's going on?' Samson asked, struggling against his restraints. 'Why am I strapped down?'

'Try to relax. You're in the sickbay. I've just called Fenn. He should be here any moment.'

'What? Why?'

The look on Seager's face said it all. Whatever Samson had done, it was bad. So bad, that Seager wasn't sure whether to look worried or angry.

'You assaulted the Brig.'

Samson felt a weight drop on him. 'I did what?' And then the memories flooded back. He almost screamed again when he remembered the pain of the sound. That sound that invaded his mind and made him think things he didn't want to think. Feel things he didn't want to feel. Do things he didn't want to do. He closed his eyes again and groaned. He couldn't stop the jumble of memories assaulting him.

He heard Delacy's voice in his head. 'You must stop Brigadier Lethbridge-Stewart from launching the raid. Talk him out of it if you can. Kill him if you can't.'

Samson's eyes snapped open. 'Alistair!' he barked urgently. 'I must talk to the Brig right away.'

'I'm sorry, Samson, you can't,' Seager said. 'He's not here.'

'Well where is he, man?'

'He's leading the raiding party.'

'But he can't,' Samson shouted in desperation. 'I was supposed to telephone Delacy once I was certain the raid wasn't going ahead.'

Seager stared at him blankly.

'For God's sake, Sam, listen to me,' Samson said. 'I didn't call. Delacy knows the raid is coming.' He struggled against the restraints. 'The Brig is walking into a trap.'

Sergeant Keil Langdon quickly glanced over at Private Finnegan. He was young and naïve, and B Company's latest recruit. Langdon had sort of taken him under his wing when he'd arrived at Imber – not his usual way, of course, as it wasn't proper behaviour for a sergeant, but there was something about Finnegan that made Langdon want to protect him. Not a great position for a private, really, to be so fragile. But now, here he was, on his first mission, looking a great deal more eager than he should.

Didn't the stupid lad realise the danger? Langdon never quite understood why some people, particularly younger people, seemed to equate risk with excitement. He generally preferred safe boredom.

'Get ready,' he said.

Finnegan wound down his window and readied the tranquiliser gun.

Langdon returned his attention to the road ahead. They were following the two Bedfords towards the lowered boom and the closed gates behind it. With an almighty crash, the first truck smashed through. As the gates were thrown wide open, the first Bedford veered left as it headed for the office building entrance. The second was close behind, the rebounding gate hitting its sides as it sped off to the right, following the road around to the warehouse at the back.

The security guard in the gatehouse jumped so high, Langdon was amazed that he didn't hit his head on the ceiling. Then he gaped through the glass as the trucks sped on. He was just stumbling out into the night air as Langdon brought the Land Rover to a screeching halt. Finnegan leaned out of the window and dropped the guard with one well-aimed shot. Langdon had to give Finnegan his due – young and foolish he may have been, but the lad was one hell of a sharpshooter.

Langdon drove onto the property and around to the left to park behind the gatehouse. Jumping out of the vehicle he ran to the open gatehouse door and quickly surveyed the cramped, glass-enclosed area. No siren. No blinking lights on the console. Looks like the guard hadn't set off any alarms. Perfect! They might get away with an easy night.

'Right.'

He turned back to the Land Rover. Finnegan and the three from the back stood at the ready.

'Grimes, Davenport and Frost. Get the remains of the boom cleared away and then close the gates.' It was important to make the property look as normal as possible from the outside. 'Finnegan, in the gatehouse. Let me know if you hear anything on their radio.'

Langdon looked around. The second truck was out of sight. The first was parked right up near the office building doors. He heard the sound of smashing glass as Lethbridge-Stewart and his team entered.

Langdon drew in a lungful of cold night air. Nothing more for him and his team to do until the two main teams had secured their areas. He was just about to congratulate himself on a job well done, when the speakers on the outside of the gatehouse crackled into life. A high-pitched whine filled the air.

Langdon's head felt like it was about to explode.

Thinking fast, he threw himself through the gatehouse door and slammed it shut behind him. Through the soundproof glass he saw the three soldiers collapse to the ground, clutching their heads. He felt a warm trickle at his ear, lifted a hand to dab at it and then examined it. Blood.

He looked into Finnegan's surprised eyes with resignation.

'Well, lad. Here's that excitement you wanted.'

Lethbridge-Stewart marched across the foyer, his boots crunching over the shattered glass. Passing the unattended reception desk, he made his way into the building. Bishop was at his side, six soldiers behind them. Each of the soldiers carried a dart gun with tranquilisers, as well as their standard issue rifles, slung over their shoulders. The early hours of Sunday morning meant that it was unlikely they would encounter ordinary employees, but given that it was a civilian property, Lethbridge-Stewart didn't want to take the chance of bystanders being accidentally shot. He led his men down the corridors until they came to the lifts. He indicated the door marked 'stairs' to the right.

They started up the narrow concrete stairwell, intended mostly as a fire escape. Delacy's office, according to Mr Morales, was on the third floor, which was where they were headed. As they reached the door, Lethbridge-Stewart allowed Bishop to take the lead. Bishop listened at the door and then, taking hold of the handle, nodded at two of the men. As he yanked the door open, they charged in, guns at the ready, and took up positions on either side of the entrance to the floor.

Bishop entered next, followed by Lethbridge-Stewart and the remaining men. The place looked like a lounge area to Lethbridge-Stewart – plush carpet underfoot, wingback armchairs against the walls, a warm, subdued lighting. There were no windows. Just closed doors, presumably leading to offices.

'Check the other doors,' he instructed as he headed for the larger door on the opposite wall.

As the other men fanned out, Bishop stayed with him. Of course, the door was locked. He was about to kick it in, when a high-pitched whine filled the air. The six soldiers immediately fell to the floor clutching their heads in agony.

Only Lethbridge-Stewart and Bishop, with their headphones, were immune.

Bishop ran to the closest man, who was now lying still, and checked him.

'Unconscious,' he reported.

'Blast!' Lethbridge-Stewart drew his pistol and shot out the lock.

Of course it wasn't going to be anywhere near as simple as he'd first hoped. Bishop was back at his side, pistol drawn as well.

Lethbridge-Stewart kicked open the door, and the two of them stepped forward, weapons out in front. They were greeted by an empty, darkened corridor.

No, not empty. There was something at the far end. In the gloom, it looked like a camera set up on a tripod.

Lethbridge-Stewart felt a vibration in the air. 'What the blazes?'

Before he even thought of moving again, Lethbridge-Stewart and Bishop were knocked back off their feet, the sonic blast hitting them head on.

Two shots and the security guard and his dog were down.

Dashner pulled the dart gun back in through the window.

'That chap was talking into his radio when we got him,' Younghusband called to his men in the back of the truck. 'Chances are that he's alerted his colleagues. We don't know how many of them are here. So be ready!'

He sped up, heading for the warehouse. Bringing the vehicle to a screeching halt by the semi-trailer-sized roller door. He was out of the truck before his men. The door beside the roller door looked pretty solid, and was locked with a numeric keypad.

'Blow the door,' he commanded, as his men came up behind him.

Lance Corporal Woolverton ran up with the plastic explosives, moulding a square of it around the keypad and lumps at the hinges. He then attached the wires and strung them out to the truck, where he connected them to the small plunger. Once all the men were sheltered behind the truck, he lifted the plunger handle.

'Clear!'

He brought the handle down, and the explosion blasted the keypad out.

'Get that roller up,' Younghusband ordered.

As Dashner and two of the men headed in, he climbed back into the truck. Once the roller raised, he drove the truck in.

'Right,' he said, once they were all assembled in the warehouse by the Bedford. 'Fan out and search the shelving. Anything that looks suspicious or even remotely like it might be a weapon, load it onto the truck.'

As the men dispersed, Younghusband and Dashner headed for the door at the far end. The door that Morales had reported as leading to the restricted area. It had a thumb print lock, but otherwise seemed like an ordinary door. Using his pistol, Younghusband shot out the lock and pushed the door open.

It led to a darkened corridor. There was another door at the far end. The two men made their way to it, and discovered it was ajar.

'It's like the door to a vault,' said Dashner.

'Yes. But at least it's open.'

'Don't you think that's a little strange, sir?'

'Probably, Lieutenant.' Younghusband peered through the gap without touching the door. 'And it's dark in there.' He didn't like this. It felt off. But he was in command, he decided, so he would take the risk. 'Wait here.'

'Sir.'

Younghusband edged the door open, just enough to slip inside, the wedge of light from the corridor showing up a white tiled floor. He took a couple of steps, peering into the gloom. Was that a dentist's chair up ahead?

Clang!

The wedge of light disappeared, plunging him into complete darkness.

Before he knew what was happening, the door slammed shut in front of him. Dashner banged his fists on the metal. 'Captain! Captain, are you okay?' There was no response.

A high-pitched whining sound echoed into the corridor from the main warehouse. Not willing to just abandon Younghusband, Dashner stepped back, aimed his pistol and fired off three shots in quick succession, then ducked down as they ricocheted off the metal.

'Bloody hell!'

Examining the door, he found barely a scratch. He slammed his fist uselessly against the metal once more.

He raced back along the corridor to check on the men. The whining had stopped by the time he got there. Looking out into the open space, he immediately spotted two of them, lying prone on the concrete floor. He sprinted to the first. There was a trickle of blood from each ear. He checked breathing and pulse. Still alive. Well, that was something.

He ran to the second man. Same situation – unconscious with bleeding from the ears. That whining sound. It must have caused this. Dashner lifted a hand to touch his headphones. He hadn't really believed they'd protect him, but now he was very thankful to have been wearing a pair.

He searched the aisles to find the other four men in the same situation as the first two.

Dashner had, at best, field medic training, but he didn't know what to do about the unconscious soldiers. And he couldn't get through that vault-like door to Younghusband.

Knowing he was risking disobeying orders, Dashner had little choice but to race back to the truck and grab the walkie-talkie. Static hissed at him. They were being jammed.

Delacy returned to his office, slightly out of breath. Although there were a couple of security guards on the grounds, he was alone in the office building.

He now settled himself behind his desk, which looked more like the control console in a recording studio — lots of dials and sliding controls, meters and gauges, with a small black and white monitor to the side. He nudged a switch and the screen flickered into life.

There was a man lying crumpled on the floor of a sound booth, where Delacy had unceremoniously dumped him a few minutes earlier. The little room was padded with soundproofing foam. The man was a lieutenant. Delacy adjusted the settings on his controls, then hit the switch for the monitor again. Another identical sound booth. Another unconscious man on the floor. This, he was certain, was Brigadier Lethbridge-Stewart. Again, Delacy adjusted settings on his controls. He flicked the monitor switch. The screen went black.

He adjusted another control and lights came on, the screen now showing a man in military uniform standing in a white room, looking around in confusion. Delacy wasn't sure who this one was. But he didn't care.

'Time for the fun to begin.'

'Thank you so much for volunteering to be part of this experiment.'

Younghusband took up a position by the locked door, weapon drawn, eyes darting from side to side, looking for the source of the voice. It seemed to be coming from everywhere.

'This room is soundproof and escape proof, so you might as well put away the gun.'

Not likely, thought Younghusband, tightening his grip, still searching for something he could fire at.

'Have it your way.'

There was a short sharp thrum, and the pistol was knocked from his hand, sent skittering across the tiles. It felt like someone had slapped him.

There was another sound, warbling up and down in pitch, and the gun melted. Younghusband couldn't hold back a surprised gasp.

'Now then. Let's see what sort of intensity your little toy is able to withstand.'

A high-pitched whine filled the air. Slowly the pitch rose. Younghusband remained pressed up against the door, mind trying desperately to think of a way out. The sound rose to an uncomfortably high level before disappearing. But the discomfort remained. In fact, it intensified. Became painful.

Younghusband winced.

'Ah. We have a reaction. Excellent.'

And then the pain stopped.

'Let's try the opposite direction.'

A low humming filled the room. Younghusband could feel the vibration. It got lower and lower, until the sound itself was no longer distinguishable. The vibrations, however, intensified. His muscles felt like jelly. He stumbled forward a few steps, and vomited.

There was an insistent hum. Electronic. Annoying. All pervading.

Bishop screamed through the darkness, his voice drowning out the electronic hum.

His body resisted. But to no avail.

Flesh was sliced.

Pushed and prodded.

Implanted.

Violated.

Something grew within him. Fear and revulsion consumed him.

But he was helpless. He had no control. He could do nothing.

He was useless. He was more than useless. He had no more purpose in and of himself.

Bishop's eyes snapped open, his voice hoarse, his throat like sandpaper and razor blades. And yet he continued to scream.

The horror of what Vaar had done to him played through his mind. He relived every moment, every second. The pain. The violation. The trauma.

He tried to take a breath, to blot out the memory, but he couldn't. Couldn't shut down the feelings of revulsion, of horror and helplessness.

Deep down, he knew it was all in the past, that he needed to move beyond it... But he couldn't.

He dropped to the floor, and in his mind's eye he saw Vaar looming over him. And it started all over again.

Bishop screamed; the pain very real.

Lethbridge-Stewart floated in darkness as the hum drilled into his brain. A darkness so thick and restrictive and everywhere. He was lonely. So very lonely. He felt as if a piece of him had been taken away. Forcibly removed. Like a bullet to the heart, leaving an empty space in its wake. A wound that could never be entirely healed. And it was his fault.

Lethbridge-Stewart swam in darkness, trying to get away from the feelings. Feelings he had tried to suppress. But no amount of burying himself in work could really remove them. They were there with him, under the surface. Even as a new relationship formed.

Lethbridge-Stewart sank through darkness. A new feeling surfaced. It gnawed at him. Snapped at him. Tried to devour him. Pulled him down. Down. Down. Into despair.

He forced himself to open his eyes.

He was in a room. But his location didn't matter. What mattered were the feelings that battered over him like a tsunami. Violent. Devastating. All-consuming.

Loss.

Guilt.

Despair.

He knew he had to fight them. Knew that they were being imposed on him. Knew he had dealt with them already. Dealt with them and come to terms with them. Knew he had to move on.

And yet he couldn't.

She was gone. Taken out of his life. Taken out of the world. Taken out of existence. Dead.

Sally was dead. And it was his fault.

He shouldn't have allowed her to go on that mission with Bishop. She had wanted to prove herself, to be her own person. And he had let her. His guilt over the way their engagement had ended overriding his common sense judgement.

Another wave of guilt crashed into him.

Fiona Campbell.

How could he betray Sally's memory? How could he move on? What right did he have to happiness, when she was gone?

The despair washed over him. Why was he even trying to fight it? It made no sense.

It would be easier to just give in, let the guilt consume him. And so, he did.

CHAPTER FIFTEEN
Retaliation

PRIVATE DERMOT Finnegan watched in astonishment as Langdon ransacked the gatehouse. He emptied the draws from the tiny desk, checked the cupboard under the console and upturned the cardboard box in the corner.

'Bugger!' grumbled Langdon, as he surveyed the mess. 'Was hoping to find a pair of earplugs or something.'

Finnegan, meanwhile, had pressed his ear to the door. Of course, he couldn't hear anything, the gatehouse was soundproof. He grasped the handle and opened it just a little, ready to slam it shut again if necessary.

'That sound has stopped.'

'Right,' said Langdon. 'Stay in here, while I check the gatehouse guard. If they've got a security system which blares out sound like that, he's got to have something for protection.' He paused at the door. 'Close it the moment I'm out. Just in case.'

As Langdon dashed out of the gatehouse, Finnegan closed the door. He watched as Langdon went over to the prone body and rifled through his pockets. He looked back at Finnegan and gave him the thumbs up signal and a big smile, before stuffing something into his ears. He then ran to check on their fellow soldiers before coming back to the gatehouse.

'They're alive but they're unconscious,' he shouted.

'You don't have to yell.'

Langdon looked like he was about to say something, then paused and pulled the rubber plugs from his ears.

'There's nothing we can do for the men at the moment. We should regroup with either Captain Younghusband or Brigadier Lethbridge-Stewart. Let them know what happened.'

'What if the sound comes back?'

'Take these.' Langdon held out the plugs. 'In the briefing we were told there were likely to be guards patrolling the grounds, but unlikely to be any inside the office building. With any luck Younghusband will have taken them out before the sound hit. So, we might be able to score another pair of these.'

Langdon headed out.

Finnegan wiped the wax off the plugs before inserting them in his ears, then followed.

They headed around the side of the office building and towards the back of the property. Sure enough, it wasn't long before they came across the unconscious forms of the guard and his dog lying in the dark grounds. Langdon pulled the plugs from the man's ears.

'Right,' he said, straightening up. 'Let's get to Captain Younghusband.'

Dashner moulded the last of the plastic explosive around the door seam, where the hinges should have been. He saw no point in targeting the thumb print pad as it was on the wall beside the door. It was bound to have its own security, and unlikely to lead to the door unlocking if it was damaged. He just hoped there was enough explosive to deal with the vault-like door.

He attached the wire, led it back along the corridor and out into the warehouse. Attaching it to the plunger, he partly closed the door and set himself up against the wall beside it. He pulled up the handle and was about to press down, when he heard running footsteps. He turned to see a large bearded man about the size of a gorilla running towards him.

'One of 'em ain't down,' yelled the gorilla as he took a swing.

Dashner dropped the plunger, avoided the fist and rammed his elbow into the gorilla's gut. As the first bloke doubled over, Dashner saw another come running out from behind the truck. This one pointed a weird looking gun. There was a loud thrum and the door to the corridor splintered.

Dashner return fire with his pistol. As the man ducked back behind the truck, the gorilla began to recover, so Dashner brought the butt of his weapon down onto the man's head.

The gorilla collapsed onto the plunger.

The handle went down.

The explosion slammed the remains of the splintered door into Dashner's face. He collapsed onto the concrete floor, dazed.

His vision swam. His head pounded. His ears rang. He tried to get up, but a wave of dizziness kept him down. Blood trickled into his eyes. He tried to get up again, but another wave assaulted him and he fell.

Squinting up through blurred vision, he saw the vague outline of a man looming over him.

Loss. Guilt. Despair. Emotions churned.

Lethbridge-Stewart shivered and sweated as if fighting a fever. His eyes were wild and frantic, but he saw little of his surrounds. Arms wrapped around his knees, he sat in the centre of the room, rocking back and forth.

But even as all those feelings accosted him and he hit rock bottom, something else stirred.

He closed his eyes and focused on it. Memories came.

He remembered his training. He remembered all that led on from it. National Service, meeting Frank Campbell, Stan Hodgeon, his capture and escape from the Korean prison. Pemberton's patronage. Sandhurst. His graduation. His first command. The London Event. His promotion to brigadier. Everything he had worked for with the formation of the Fifth. Everything that he and his team had dealt with so far. And all the potential threats that were yet to come. Threats that needed a first line of defence. Threats that needed him and his men to stand against them.

He remembered his duty. Duty to Queen and Country.

Brigadier Lethbridge-Stewart was first and foremost a British Army Officer. It was at his core. It was what defined him. All other things, including his personal life and the emotional baggage that came with it, were secondary. He would not let his personal feelings, no matter how raw and painful they may be, stand in the way of him doing his duty.

He continued to rock back and forth, but now his eyes were alert as they scanned the room. It was a small, confined space. The walls were lined with a soundproofing material – the sort of grey foam you find on a recording studio's walls. There was a door to his left. It was also covered in the same material.

Undoubtedly locked, he thought.

He brought a hand up to his ear. The headphones were gone.

He ran through things in his mind.

He assumed Bishop had to be in a similar predicament. Since he and his men had been ambushed, chances were the same had happened to the other two teams. Younghusband and Dashner were the only other two with Erickson's headphones, so he had to assume that all the other men were more than likely incapacitated by that same dratted sound that had taken out his men when they reached the third floor. Whether or not Younghusband and Dashner were captured like him was another matter. He hoped that they had avoided his plight, but he couldn't count on it. He had to assume he was on his own, and would need to rely solely on himself to get out of this mess.

Well, if a young inexperienced Rifleman Lethbridge-Stewart could escape from that Korean prison, then seasoned officer Brigadier Lethbridge-Stewart would escape from this room.

He winced as a turmoil of emotions welled up within him again. With agonising slowness, he pushed them down. He had to concentrate. Keep his mind on the job at hand.

There were no obvious cameras in the room as far as he could see, but he found it hard to believe that he wouldn't be monitored in some way. If he, Bishop, Younghusband and Dashner were all in the same boat, there was a slim chance that attentions were divided and that he wasn't being observed every second. So, it was worth the risk of dropping the pretence and trying to break out. But he needed to do it as quickly as possible.

His eyes scanned the room one more time. There really was nothing for him to use. If the door was indeed locked, he would have to rely on brute force.

He took a couple of long, deep breaths to ready himself.

Lethbridge-Stewart sprang to his feet and rushed at the door with his shoulder. The soundproofing worked to his advantage, cushioning the impact on his bones. Although the door held, he did hear a distinct cracking sound.

Stepping back for a run up, he rushed at it again. This time he felt it give slightly. His confidence bolstered, he stepped back again, and once more put his shoulder into it.

The door burst open and he staggered out into the corridor, steadying himself on the opposite wall.

There was no hum out here. Without it, he felt his head clearing fast.

Now to find Bishop. Lord alone knows what that sound has done to him, Lethbridge-Stewart thought, thinking of how much the young lieutenant had suffered recently.

'Can I help you up, sir?' asked Langdon, reaching out a hand to Dashner.

'What? Oh! Yes. Ah, thank you.'

Langdon pulled Dashner unsteadily to his feet. He watched as his superior officer leaned against the wall for support and raised a hand to his forehead. He had a number of small cuts and scrapes on his face, and a larger gash on his temple. They needed to do something to stop the bleeding.

'Got to get him out,' mumbled Dashner, wiping blood from his eyes.

'Dermo,' called Langdon, worried that Dashner's wounds were perhaps worse than he first thought. 'Best go get the first aid kit from the vehicle.'

When Finnegan returned, Langdon left him to tend to Dashner, while he went to secure the two thugs. He dragged the unconscious body of the man who had fought with Dashner back to the truck, where the bloke he had earlier surprised was cuffed. He searched the unconscious form, retrieving another of those weird pistols that he had taken from the first, and then hoisted him up into the back, none too gently, and cuffed his hands to the bottom of the bench seat. The other bloke glared at him without saying a word. Langdon checked his cuffs just to make sure.

When he got back to Dashner, he was pleased to see that Finnegan had finished dressing the wound, but Dashner was babbling again.

'Got to help him. Save him. The captain.'

'Captain Younghusband.' Langdon realised they hadn't seen him.

'Yes,' gasped Dashner, waving at the corridor. 'He's trapped.

Langdon helped Dashner into the corridor and down to the door at the end, which was still closed.

'Damn,' grunted Dashner. 'He's still trapped in there.'

Langdon reached into his pockets and pulled out the two strange pistols he had confiscated, holding them one in each hand like a gunslinger.

'Would these help?'

'Lieutenant Bishop?'

Bishop wanted the voice to go away. He had enough to worry about. Enough filling up his mind. Enough tearing him apart emotionally. What did it matter who he was?

He felt hands grab his shoulders and shake him. 'Snap out of it, soldier,' demanded the voice. 'We've got a job to do.'

That voice. He knew that voice. It had authority.

Bishop stared up, bleary-eyed at the owner of that voice.

There was concern in those stern eyes. The moustache looked familiar. The face seemed to demand his compliance. He had a sudden urge to jump to attention, to salute, to declare 'Yes, sir!', but a wave of self-pitying indifference washed over him and pulled him back into his own private sea of despair.

He felt hands shifting, grasping him, hooking up under his armpits. He felt movement that was not caused by emotional waves.

Bishop's head lolled, his eyes lost focus and he felt a string of drool wet his chin.

Younghusband lay on the floor in a puddle of his own vomit. After the low thrumming had stopped, the experiments had continued with what the voice had described as targeted sonic bursts and wide-ranging sonic beams. Although those bursts and beams were not audible, he had certainly felt them.

Intense pain in his abdomen had made him convulse and throw up again, bringing up a thin stream of bile from an otherwise empty stomach. A sharp stab in his chest made his heart skip several beats. An overall vibration through his body had made him feel first ice-cold, and then so hot he thought his blood was literally about to boil. And, finally, there was a weird feeling in his legs and his muscles gave way.

He groaned as he braced himself for whatever was next on the agenda, his eyes gazing longingly at the door.

With an unexpected *thrum*, the door burst open.

Two soldiers came running into the room and towards him.

'No!' called Younghusband, weakly. 'The sound in here could kill you. Get out.'

As if to emphasise his point, a high-pitched whine filled the air.

But the men did not turn back. As they reached him, he

realised it was Langdon and Finnegan. They weren't wearing headphones. They would collapse at any moment. But, instead, they helped him to his feet and started to drag him to the door.

The sound screeched higher and higher. Pain stabbed at his brain.

But Langdon and Finnegan carried on. They staggered out into the corridor. Younghusband collapsed onto the floor, and Langdon slammed the door shut, blocking out the effects of the sound they couldn't hear.

Langdon and Finnegan removed plugs from their ears.

Younghusband smiled as they brandished the plugs. 'Good show,' he said weakly.

Younghusband looked around to see Dashner leaning up against the wall, a bloody bandage around his head.

'You look about as good as I feel, Lieutenant,' Younghusband gasped, holding back a hysterical giggle. Then he turned to look at his two rescuers. 'Thank you. I think you just saved my life.'

'No!' growled Delacy, slamming his fist onto the console.

The image on the screen, where he had just watched the rescue take place, jumped.

'Where are those two fools?'

He fiddled with the communications control, but neither of his thugs responded. He flicked the monitor control, deciding that, given the circumstance, it might be safer to simply kill the brigadier and his off-sider. But the screen showed an empty room with a broken door.

Delacy yelled out a particularly coarse epithet.

He flicked the switch again.

This time the screen showed Lethbridge-Stewart dragging the resisting form of his lieutenant from the sound booth.

Delacy swore again, and he slammed his fist onto the console so hard that the monitor went blank. He stabbed at a concealed button beneath his desk and the wall behind him slid away. He jumped to his feet and turned to examine the array of weaponry set out in meticulous order. His eyes gleamed.

'That's it. No more games!'

He selected a sonic rifle and thumbed off the safety.

'Hey, hey, hey!'

CHAPTER SIXTEEN
Confrontation

'LIEUTENANT?' LETHBRIDGE-STEWART propped Bishop up against the corridor wall. 'Snap out of it, man.'

Bishop looked up at him. Lethbridge-Stewart felt the pain like a punch to the gut. No man should ever feel the pain that was now clear in Bishop's eyes. Fortunately, at least, no more physical pain had been added to what the young lieutenant had already endured, but as Lethbridge-Stewart knew full well, it was the scars you couldn't see that remained with you the longest.

'Sir.' Bishop nodded weakly. 'I'm okay.'

'Good man.' Lethbridge-Stewart patted him on the shoulder. 'Rest a moment while I find us some weapons.'

He stood. They were in the corridor that led from the main area of the third floor. The device on the tripod was gone. He was certain that the door at the end would lead to Delacy. But their sidearms, not to mention their headphones, had been removed before they were placed in their cells.

Lethbridge-Stewart made his way back down the corridor. His men were still unconscious on the floor. He collected a pistol for himself and a rifle for Bishop, then hurried back to his adjutant.

Adjutant. *The man deserves a promotion after what he's been through this last year*, Lethbridge-Stewart decided. *And he's certainly earned it. I'll have to see to that soon.*

Bishop was struggling to his feet, still groggy but obviously recovering quickly. Lethbridge-Stewart handed him the weapon.

'Ready to go and find Delacy?'

'Yes, sir. I owe *him* some pain.'

Just then, the door at the end of the corridor burst apart.

Through the clearing smoke, they could see Delacy striding forward, some sort of rifle held to his shoulder.

'Seems he found us,' Bishop said.

'Sonic rifle,' shouted Delacy, and he fired the weapon again.

Lethbridge-Stewart felt the vibrations thrum down the corridor, even though the blast hit the wall ahead of them, showering them with plaster. He tried to return fire through the cloud of dust as he ordered, 'Fall back.'

He and Bishop made it to the main area of floor three just in time for another blast to take out the door frame. Taking up positions on either side of the splintered doorway, they took turns firing their weapons. Although with the clouds of plaster dust wafting through the corridor, they couldn't really see what they were aiming at.

'Are we having fun yet?' Delacy's voice echoed out through the dust.

With Dashner beside him, Younghusband rested in the driver's seat of the Bedford. He ached all over, but was willing himself to recover as he ran through the situation in his mind. He figured that if they had been ambushed, chances were, so had Lethbridge-Stewart's squad. They needed to get over to the office building to help them asap. To that end, Younghusband had the two thugs moved out of the truck and secured to the shelving units. His intent was to put his unconscious men into the vehicle and drive it back around to the front, pick up Langdon's fallen comrades, then go on to rendezvous with Lethbridge-Stewart's squad.

But as Langdon and Finnegan were about to collect the first of the unconscious soldiers, a sound came over the speakers. They all froze in anticipation. It was different to the sound that had incapacitated his team – softer, not as high-pitched.

Younghusband momentarily panicked when he realised he no longer had his Erickson-issue headphones. They must have fallen off during the rescue. He quickly put his hands to his ears. But there didn't seem to be any ill effects.

'Are you okay, sir?' asked Dashner.

Younghusband tentatively took his hands from his ears. 'It would seem so. And you?'

'All good.'

'Sir,' called Private Finnegan.

Younghusband leaned out of the truck to see that the first of the unconscious soldiers was stirring. He sent Finnegan to do a quick recce to check the others. They were all groaning and beginning to move, albeit groggily, nowhere near ready to actually get up.

Reassessing the situation, Younghusband changed plans. Leaving Finnegan to look after the recovering soldiers, he, Dashner and Langdon headed off in the Bedford.

They stopped at the gatehouse to drop Langdon off, as the soldiers there were also beginning to recover. Then Younghusband and Dashner moved on to find Lethbridge-Stewart.

'Sir!'

Lethbridge-Stewart looked at Bishop. He was pressed up against the wall on the other side of the doorway to the corridor. Bishop pointed to the soldiers on the floor. They were stirring. It was then that Lethbridge-Stewart noticed the sound. He wondered what Delacy was playing at.

Signalling to Bishop that he should go check on them, Lethbridge-Stewart peered around the splintered doorframe to see Delacy sling his sonic rifle over his shoulder. That was his chance.

Lethbridge-Stewart stepped out, aimed and fired four shots directly at Delacy. But the bullets never reached him.

'Nice try, soldier-boy,' said Delacy patting a little device attached to his belt. 'But I've got a portable sonic barrier. The only weapons that can go through it are sonic weapons. Like the sonic rifle I was just using. And...' He unholstered a pistol. 'Like this little beauty. Sonic disruptor. Doesn't do anything to inanimate objects. But it'll scramble the insides of anything that's alive. Really handy when you don't want to damage the furnishings.' He took aim and fired.

Lethbridge-Stewart ducked back out of sight, but the blast hit the recovering soldier who'd just crawled into view. The man gasped and went limp.

'What?' Delacy shouted. 'How are they recovering?' And then quieter. 'No. No, no, no.'

So, Delacy wasn't waking the soldier's up deliberately. Lethbridge-Stewart chanced another look, to see Delacy storming back to his office. Lethbridge-Stewart dashed over to check on the unfortunate private who'd chosen the wrong moment to recover. Dead. His insides oozing from his eye sockets and ears.

Lethbridge-Stewart looked up to see Bishop staring at him, and shook his head, then came over to join him.

'The others are recovering,' said Bishop, as he helped one of them into a sitting position against a wall. He had already coaxed the others up.

'Just keep them out of sight of the doorway,' said Lethbridge-Stewart. He didn't want his remaining men becoming targets in a shooting gallery for Delacy. 'I'm not sure what's happened, but it doesn't sound like Delacy was expecting the men to recover. He's returned to his office.'

'Now's our chance to get him.'

'Not unless we can find some way to get through his sound shield thing.'

The echo of stumbling footsteps made them both turn.

It was Younghusband and Dashner. The two of them looked like they'd just gone five rounds with the world heavyweight champion.

Finnegan helped the last of the recovering soldiers to their feet before addressing them.

'Right, lads, listen up.' He had to shout, as the soldiers all reported ringing ears and an inability to hear properly. He was out of his depth giving orders to soldiers that were either equal rank or above, but he was the only one unaffected by the sound weapons.

'We need to get on the move. The brigadier may need our help. Wallace. Yuen. The two of you can be responsible for our prisoners. We'll collect the security guard and his dog along the way.'

Finnegan thought of Sergeant Langdon. Of what he'd do.

'Right!' he shouted at them. 'On the double. Move out!'

'So you need a sound weapon to breach this barrier he has?' asked Younghusband.

Lethbridge-Stewart nodded. Younghusband and Dashner glanced at each other and grinned. They reached into their pockets simultaneously and produced two sonic pistols.

'Courtesy of Delacy's thugs, sir,' Younghusband explained.

'That is just what we need. Splendid work, Captain.'

Lethbridge-Stewart immediately began to formulate a plan of attack.

'Right. Delacy doesn't know we have these or that the two of you are here. Are the two of you up for action?'

'I may not look it,' said Younghusband with a grimace, 'but I'm feeling better.'

'And I'm eager for payback,' said Dashner.

'Right then. Here's what we're going to do...'

Finnegan and his little squad arrived at the gatehouse, to find Langdon and his men ready for action. They secured the two prisoners in the gatehouse, along with the security guards and the German Shepherd.

'Good job, Dermo. Now,' said Langdon, 'Time to go help the Brig.'

'What have you done to my men?' Lethbridge-Stewart demanded, as he marched into Delacy's office, Bishop at his heels.

'What do you mean?' Delacy looked up from his controls.

Lethbridge-Stewart saw the wild confusion in his eyes and thought that maybe this did have a chance of succeeding. *Start with the truth,* he thought, *then proceed to the lie in order to seed confusion and distract the opponent.*

'First you knock my men out with your sound. Then you start to bring them around. And now they're all unconscious again. Just what are you playing at?'

As he spoke, Lethbridge-Stewart and Bishop made their way to Delacy's right, keeping his attention on them.

'I don't know what's going on.' He looked down at his controls in frustration, his hands hovering over them uncertainly. 'They've all been overridden.' He looked up again and his eyes narrowed, then his hand darted out and swept up the sonic disrupter he'd left on his desk. 'But I still have control of this.' He gave it a little shake. 'And I can make sure that you die.'

Lethbridge-Stewart and Bishop both fired their weapons first. Closer this time, he was able to see exactly what his opponent's sonic barrier did. The bullets simply stopped, hovered and shivered in the air for a second, then dropped to the floor.

Delacy laughed as he slowly extended the disruptor out in front of him and took aim. He opened his mouth, for one final pithy remark, no doubt. But he didn't get to make it.

There was a staccato thrum from the doorway and the disruptor was knocked from Delacy's hand. Another thrum, and he doubled over as the sonic barrier device on his belt smashed.

'Hold it right there,' Captain Younghusband ordered, sonic pistol in hand. Dashner was right behind him, his pistol also held out in front.

Delacy fell back into is chair, still clutching his stomach.

'Right, Mr Delacy,' Lethbridge-Stewart said. 'It seems that—'

An alarm blared.

'Now what?'

'Attention! Attention please!' A voice boomed out over the speakers. 'Attention anyone who is on the Electric Soundscapes property. This is not a drill.'

'You!' spat Delacy, looking up to the speakers. 'You can't do this.'

'Who?' Lethbridge-Stewart asked.

'You have ten minutes to evacuate this property,' the voice continued. 'There are acoustic disintegrators placed in key positions throughout this property. When they are detonated, the entire area will be razed. Please leave behind all sonic weaponry, as they are also set to self-destruct.'

Lethbridge-Stewart looked at his men. This mission had not gone at all as he had anticipated, but he was completely stumped as to what to make of this latest detour.

'This is my property!' shouted Delacy, rising to his feet and looking up at the speakers. 'You can't just destroy it.'

'Your time starts... Now!'

The sound of a ticking clock echoed through the room.

'What the blazes is going on, Delacy?' Lethbridge-Stewart demanded. 'If this is some kind of trick...'

'It's not me!'

Langdon came running into the office, Finnegan and the other soldiers close behind him.

'That announcement is coming through all the outside

speakers as well,' Langdon reported, looking to Lethbridge-Stewart. 'Orders, sir?'

Lethbridge-Stewart took a moment to assess the situation. 'Well, it seems we don't have much of a choice. We need to get out of here ASAP. Delacy is coming with us. The clock is literally ticking.'

But Delacy was still staring up, looking from one speaker to the next. 'You work for me!'

'Not anymore.' The voice from the speakers finally acknowledged him.

So, it's not a recording, thought Lethbridge-Stewart. He held up his hand to stop his men rushing Delacy.

'But I'm financing your work,' insisted Delacy. 'You're nothing without me.'

'I am very pleased to say that I no longer require your financing. My final experiment today was a success, and I will soon be ready to proceed with my end goal.'

'But there's still so much to achieve,' said Delacy, his voice slipping from demanding to desperate. 'So much we can do. Together. Your scientific brilliance. My money and ambition. We could make so much more money. We could control the world!'

'I have no interest in ruling the world.' The voice was sounding tired. 'I do not share your desire for wealth. I wish merely to save one mind.'

'Well fine!' snapped Delacy. 'Go save whatever. Live in poverty. But there's no need to destroy what we've achieved so far.' He spread out his arms in a pleading gesture. 'I can continue without you.'

Lethbridge-Stewart felt like a superfluous observer in the breakdown of a relationship. He looked from Delacy to the speakers to Bishop. Bishop shrugged.

'No! Your toys of destruction were simply a means to my end. Like you and your money, they are no longer required. I cannot allow you to continue to misuse them. They will now face their own destruction.' There was a pause. 'As, I am sorry to say, will you.'

A new sound filled the room, starting low and building higher. Lethbridge-Stewart and his men all instinctively clasped hands to ears, but the sound wasn't affecting anyone except Delacy.

He shook his head, tried to run, but appeared caught by some invisible force.

'No,' he whispered.

His whole body shivered. His arms snapped back as if held from behind. As he was lifted up off the floor, his feet dangling, he screamed, 'Freiheit!'

Lethbridge-Stewart stared in astonishment as the air around Delacy shimmered and closed in on him. Then he crumpled and compressed – as if a giant pair of hands squeezed him into a football-sized mass of fleshy pulp.

What was left of Delacy fell to the floor with a wet squelch, bodily fluids splattering in all directions.

All eyes were riveted to the scene. No one moved.

'I think I'm going to be sick,' Finnegan said.

'May I remind you, gentlemen, that the destruction of this property is imminent.' The voice from the speakers was back. 'I have no wish for you to be harmed. I suggest you leave while you still can.'

'You all heard the man,' Lethbridge-Stewart snapped. He glanced at his watch. 'By my reckoning, we've got about six minutes before this place goes sky high.'

The Land Rover and Bedfords barrelled through the gates of Electric Soundscapes. They ground to a screeching halt down the road and Lethbridge-Stewart climbed out of the lead vehicle, turning to look back at where they'd come from. Soon, Bishop, Younghusband, Dashner and Langdon were with him.

'Nothing's happening,' said Langdon.

'Perhaps it was simply a ruse to get us out of there,' suggested Bishop.

As his subordinates continued to discuss the possibilities, Lethbridge-Stewart kept his eyes trained on the office building. He didn't have to wait long before he felt something. A vibration. A shiver in the air.

The perimeter floodlights flickered and died.

By the dim light of the surrounding properties, Lethbridge-Stewart and his men watched as everything within the fenced line of Electric Soundscapes shimmered, distorted and then folded in on itself. No audible sound. No explosion. It was all just gone. Disintegrated.

All that was left was a cloud of dust rising into the air.

'Good Lord!' said Lethbridge-Stewart.

The others said nothing, eyes staring in disbelief, mouths hanging open.

Lethbridge-Stewart clenched his fists. Much as he hated to admit it, there was nothing they could do right now. His men needed rest, and he needed to work out what their next course of action would be.

'Back to base,' he announced.

As the military vehicles finally moved off, a figure stepped out of the shadowed doorway of a nearby factory. The man was tall, broad and muscled. He was dressed in varying shades of grey, from steel to almost black, the collar of his overcoat pulled up high. A hand-rolled cigarette hung smouldering from his lips.

He watched the vehicles until they were completely out of sight, then turned back to look at the empty space that had been the Electric Soundscapes headquarters.

He strolled down the road as if he didn't have a care in the world, and stopped at the fence, peering through the chain link thoughtfully. He took a final drag on his cigarette, inhaling deeply, then let the remains drop to the ground.

'Now that would be a weapon worth acquiring.'

CHAPTER SEVENTEEN
Preparations

'Do you want me to come down? I can.'

Bishop smiled at Anne's concern. 'I'll be fine, I promise. And I offered to go.'

He could hear Anne's disbelief, even through the phone line.

'Of course you did. And Alistair had nothing to do with it.'

'You may be surprised to hear that he did question me first. Anne, you have to understand, I didn't join the military to take phone calls and shuffle files.'

Bishop closed his eyes. The pain was still raw. He thought he was dealing with it, but Delacy's machine had proven otherwise. What with Haltwhistle and Delacy, it seemed there was no escaping it. There probably never would be.

'I had to go,' he continued. 'For me. I can't let what happen stop me.'

'Bill, I...' Anne paused, and Bishop could hear the choking in her voice. 'I love you, and the thought of what happened to you, that you're not letting yourself heal.'

Bishop sighed. 'And I love you, but you know me, Anne. You know, just as well as I, some things don't heal by sitting around and waiting. Sitting around isn't going to help me. I need to be out there, doing something, dealing with how I feel, confront it head on.'

'You're right,' Anne said after a moment. A moment of silence sat between them. 'So, what's next?'

'I'm not sure. The Brig will decide, and I will follow. I suspect it'll be a return to the Madhouse. Either way, it's not over. Someone else is involved, pulling Delacy's strings. We need to...'

Bishop blinked. His mind drifted back to Haltwhistle, to

something he'd seen, something he'd read…

'Bill? You still there?'

'I…' Bishop shook his head. He was missing something. To do with Haltwhistle. Some connection between the old persons' home and Electric Soundscapes. Only, he couldn't quite see it. 'Just tired. It's been a draining day.'

'Then get some rest. We can talk when you return home.'

'Yes.' Bishop nodded, even though Anne couldn't see him. 'Yes, that's probably what I need. Just to see you.'

He could hear Anne's smile, and just the thought of that warmed his heart.

But even as he said goodbye and replaced the receiver on the cradle, something scratched at the back of his mind. Something to do with the voice he'd heard at Electric Soundscapes.

Lethbridge-Stewart ran a hand over his tired eyes. It had been almost twenty-four hours since he'd last slept, but he still had work to do before he could get some rest. The men had been debriefed and sent off, either to rest or be checked out by Mr Fenn, and now he needed to talk to Samson.

He had been moved from the sickbay to a private billet usually reserved for VIP visitors. There was a guard at the door.

'Any trouble, Private?'

'No, sir. As quiet as a mouse.'

'Good. Please wait here. I'll call you if I need you.'

Lethbridge-Stewart took a deep breath and walked in.

Samson was lying on the bed, a book in his good hand, his bandaged left hand by his side. He looked over the top of the book, and quickly stood when he realised who had entered. He looked tired and anxious.

'Are you okay?' he asked.

'I've felt better, to be honest with you, Samson,' Lethbridge-Stewart said, approaching his old friend. 'But more to the point, how are you? You did, after all, try to assassinate me.'

'Sorry about that, Al.' Samson looked straight into Lethbridge-Stewart's eyes. 'That wasn't me. I mean, I wasn't in control. There was this sound. And Delacy's voice and… I tried to overcome it… I…'

'Yes, I know,' said Lethbridge-Stewart, remembering his

own struggles with Delacy's mind controlling sounds. 'But how are you now?'

'I'm fine. Really, I am. When I woke up in sickbay, it was like I could see what was happening. The control. And I could fight it. And I did. And I remembered that if I had been, well, successful in doing you in…'

'Yes, I've read Corporals Fenn's and Seager's reports. It's not your fault.'

It looked to Lethbridge-Stewart like Samson wanted to deny it, to take responsibility.

Guilt, in a word.

It was a feeling Lethbridge-Stewart was all too familiar with.

'What happened with Delacy?' Samson asked instead. 'Did he ambush you? How did you get away?'

'Delacy is dead. But he wasn't working alone, and whoever he was working with decided that he'd become something of a liability. Turned Delacy's weapons on him. Then destroyed the entire Electric Soundscapes building and warehouse.'

Samson was clearly struggling to follow.

'Let's get you out of here first,' Lethbridge-Stewart said. 'Then I'll fill you in.' He indicated the door, and with a smile Samson walked with him across the room.

'Sorry about the fingers,' Lethbridge-Stewart said.

'Sorry about the assassination attempt,' Samson returned, with a brief smile. 'Shall we call it even?'

Lethbridge-Stewart smiled too. 'I think that's a good idea,' he said, and opened the door to allow Samson to walk through.

Now that they had managed to get a few hours kip, Lethbridge-Stewart, Bishop and Samson were waiting for the chopper that would take them back to Edinburgh.

Bishop was unusually quiet.

'Out with it, Lieutenant.'

'Sir?'

'There's something on your mind. What is it?'

Bishop frowned, looked down. 'I… I think we need to go to Haltwhistle ASAP.'

Lethbridge-Stewart glanced at Samson, who shrugged.

'I thought your investigations there reached a dead end.'

'Yes, sir. I thought so, too. But last night Anne and I spoke and...' Bishop shook his head. 'It's hard to explain. But it's like I've forgotten something important. And I've been wracking my brains about it. I've been going over and over it all in my mind, and I think I've finally worked it out.'

'Well, don't keep us in suspense, Mr Bishop.'

'Just before Delacy died, he called out a name. The owner of the voice we heard.'

'Yes, I remember. Fahrenheit, or something, wasn't it?'

'Sort of. Freiheit.'

'And what about...' Lethbridge-Stewart tailed off, remembering a conversation with Erickson. 'One moment, I've heard that name before. Some chap that Dr Erickson was trying to get hold of. Apparently, he was an expert in infra sound. Only he seems to have vanished.'

'Sound...? Then it can't be a coincidence.'

Lethbridge-Stewart folded his arms, and his eyebrow went up.

'At Haltwhistle,' Bishop said. 'As you know I looked through the medical records and there was a name, Greta Freiheit.'

'And you think she might be related to him?'

'It can't be a coincidence, sir. And... I'm sure the voice, Freiheit, said something about saving someone.'

'Sounds a likely lead to me,' Samson said.

'It's beginning to look like it,' Lethbridge-Stewart agreed.

'And, of course, there's the music,' Bishop said.

'What music? *Fear Frequency*'s theme?'

'No, sir. It's... It's strange. Like I had forgotten things about Haltwhistle. But it's coming back to me now. Some of the patients have been undergoing music therapy.'

'I hope they weren't strapped to a dentist's chair,' Samson said.

'I don't think...' Bishop staggered back, held a hand up. 'I'm...' He broke out in a sudden sweat, and his breathing became laboured. 'It's difficult to remember, but there was a place they go. Nearby. A music place.'

Samson gave Lethbridge-Stewart a worried look and opened his mouth to speak. Lethbridge-Stewart quickly held up a hand to stop him. He also remained silent, allowing Bishop to work through whatever was happening in his mind.

'A music... conservatorium.' His voice was strained. 'The

therapy was done there. And it was reducing the effects of Alzheimer's.' He let out a long breath and looked up.

'Sounds like someone's been tampering with your mind,' said Samson.

'There's a lot of that going around,' Lethbridge-Stewart said, and looked mock-seriously at Bishop. 'You're not planning on assassinating me, I hope.'

Erickson couldn't believe that he had missed it before.

After getting word from Lethbridge-Stewart that Freiheit was somehow involved with Delacy, and not only that but they believed that a relative of Freiheit was a resident at the Haltwhistle Aged Care Facility, he had decided to make another attempt to locate the professor.

While he awaited some returning phone calls, Erickson decided to review all the paperwork he had amassed. And now, there it was, as bright as day; a direct connection to Haltwhistle.

Future Investments, the company owned by Delacy that had funded Freiheit's research at the University of Strathclyde, owned the Haltwhistle Music Conservatorium.

'What is it the brigadier says about coincidences?' he asked himself, as he picked up the phone to be put through to the chopper bringing Lethbridge-Stewart and his men back. 'There's no such thing.'

The moment they were back at Dolerite Base, Lethbridge-Stewart sprang into action organising the new mission. Captain Miles at Stirling Castle was tasked with getting his squad briefed, while Dr Erickson was put to work creating more of the headphones.

Lethbridge-Stewart now sat in his office with Douglas, a bottle of Scotch and two glasses between them.

'So Delacy wasn't actually behind it all?' asked Douglas, taking a sip.

'Yes and no,' said Lethbridge-Stewart. 'There's no doubt in my mind that Delacy was the driving force behind creating those weapons. He was certainly providing the financing. And he was intending to profit from their sales. But it's this Professor Freiheit chap who's the creator. Erickson's research indicates he's a brilliant scientist – brilliant and quite driven. Although willing to cut corners, creating weapons seems out of character for him. It looks like it was merely a means to an end, given that he killed Delacy and destroyed all the weaponry he had at Electric Soundscapes.'

'So, not about money?'

Lethbridge-Stewart shook his head. 'Not according to what Freiheit said before he killed Delacy. He said something about saving someone.'

Douglas raised his glass and swished around the whisky. 'His mother?'

Erickson's research had revealed the filial connection between Greta Freiheit and the missing professor.

'A reasonable possibility. Although how I don't understand.'

They sat in silence for a few moments before Douglas asked, 'What about *Fear Frequency*?'

'What indeed.' Lethbridge-Stewart sipped the whisky, enjoying the warmth in the back of his throat. 'It's my understanding that Delacy was quite paranoid about the music. It was delivered to the station just prior to each broadcast on a self-erasing tape. It could only be played the once for the broadcast, with no fear of it being analysed after. Simple ego at work there, I think.'

Douglas nodded his agreement. 'Which just leaves us with Freiheit.'

'Yes. Freiheit and his connection to Haltwhistle. Bishop is slowly remembering more about his investigation, and he's convinced that the head nurse is somehow involved. So, we start there and then we continue on to this music conservatorium. Presumably, that's where we'll find Freiheit.'

'Why aren't you heading straight there, if that's where you think he is?' asked Douglas.

'I did consider it,' said Lethbridge-Stewart. 'In fact, I did initially plan on sending in two teams – one to the home and one to the conservatorium. But in the end, I thought it best to take things one step at a time. I don't want to be caught out again.' He grimaced; the events at Electric Soundscapes still gnawed at him. 'We don't really know what Freiheit is up to, but we can reasonably conclude it has something to do with his mother, and quite possibly the other patients at the old persons' home. I want to get as much information as I can before we go in to confront him.'

*

Merv Chatley arrived early for the *Fear Frequency* broadcast, the tape safely in his briefcase, where it had been since it was mysteriously delivered to him at home on Saturday night. He had spent all night wondering why Delacy had broken his own rules and delivered it early.

That morning, he had heard the shocking news that the Electric Soundscapes office and warehouse had been destroyed. The entire property flattened, according to the report on the radio. And since then nobody had heard a word from Delacy.

Merv knew this was potentially the last time he would be supplied with Delacy's music. Which left him with mixed feelings. On the one hand, he was glad he'd never have to deal with Delacy again. On the other hand, he wondered how his serial would fair without the musical controversy stirring up publicity for him. In all objectivity, the show itself was falling quite short of his expectations.

Reneging on his agreement with Delacy, he was setting up a recording to take place as tonight's episode was broadcast. If Delacy had died in the destruction, and Merv rather callously hoped that he had, then he wouldn't be around to complain. And then he, Merv Chatley, would have the latest version of the theme to continue using.

Arabella Constance cuddled up with her bottle of Beefeater Gin on the sofa in front of her television.

'God save the Queen,' she said to the cheery looking scarlet-liveried chap on the label, and took a swig. She never bothered with a glass when she was at home alone, which was when she usually drank, away from prying eyes. It helped with the loneliness.

She drew her worn dressing gown tighter about her shoulders and tucked her feet, in their pink fluffy bed socks, underneath herself. She reached out and switched on the telly.

It was a small black and white set, which she kept on a side table right next to her faded floral sofa, close enough for her to switch it on and off without having to get up. From the switch, her hand went straight to the ashtray, also sitting on the table. It was a gaudy, crown-shaped thing, which she had souvenired from a café around the corner from Buckingham Palace. A tarnished lighter and a cigarillo sat inside it. She had switched from cigarettes to cigarillos a few years back, with a brief return to the former after the last episode of *Fear Frequency*.

She lit up and settled back to watch. Taking a long drag, she justified her habit as a necessity to calm her nerves and steel herself for the televisual horrors that she was about to be assaulted with.

She was quite looking forward to tonight's episode. Beside her was a pencil and the blue-tinted, floral-emblemed notepaper that she favoured; all ready for her to take notes. She enjoyed making her notes, finding fault with the things she watched, ready to take to the public in her crusade against all that she considered unworthy.

A little thrill shivered up her spine in anticipation.

She took another swig as the theme started.

And froze.

The music grabbed her in its vice-like grip and squeezed. The fear clawed at her mind. The memories flooded through her. The gin dribbled out from the corners of her mouth.

She was five. She sat in a corner, whimpering as she clutched her grazed knee. Her parents didn't notice as they drank their cocktails and chatted with a lounge-room full of guests.

She was eleven. She sat in her room, proudly admiring the A+ in the corner of the essay she had written at school. The essay that her parents never looked at.

She was fourteen. She stood at the back of the church, alone with her tears, as someone she had never met eulogised her mother.

She was sixteen. She watched as her father wolfed down the food she had prepared, as he did every night, without so much as a thank you.

She was eighteen. Suitcase in hand, she looked back at the house she had grown up in, hoping to see her father waving to her. But the door was already shut.

She was twenty-six. Tapping away, she sat in the typing pool along with all the other girls, watching her pointless life slip away one keystroke after another.

She was twenty-nine. She sat at the bar in the local pub, sipping her G&T, watching the men buying drinks for the other, younger, prettier girls.

As the last of the gin dribbled away down her chin, the fear rose. The fear of being ignored. The fear of irrelevance. She had to do something. She had to do something right now! She had to make sure she was listened to. She had to make sure that people took notice of her. She had to make them understand.

Picking up her ashtray, Constance staggered out of the door of her tiny bedsit and out into the streets of Bexley.

Graham's eyes were closed. His hands gripped the rests on his armchair, his fingernails clawing at the fabric. His teeth clenched, and he ground them. His heart pounded in his ears. The sounds penetrated his brain.

He could hear the smash of glass as the bottle shattered on the tiles. He could smell the alcohol on his father's breath. He could see the blood trickling down the side of his mother's face as she lay crying on the kitchen floor. He could feel the sting of his father's hand on his face. He could feel the cold horror-filled anticipation of worse things to come.

The old terror surfaced from his memories like a monster ready to devour him.

He opened his eyes and screamed.

CHAPTER EIGHTEEN
Return to Haltwhistle

OH-FIVE-HUNDRED HOURS. Breath steaming in the chilly air, Douglas was again outside the New Barracks ready to see off Lethbridge-Stewart. Bishop sat behind the wheel of a Land Rover, while Samson sat in the rear. Bishop stuck his head out of the passenger window.

'All set to go, sir.'

'Very good, Lieutenant.'

'Thermos and sandwiches on the dash for you,' said Douglas.

'What would I do without you, Dougie?' said Lethbridge-Stewart, climbing into the Land Rover.

Douglas watched the vehicle head off. He always seemed to be the one left behind. He knew that was part and parcel of being the 2-in-C of the Fifth, left in charge of headquarters when the top man was off on a mission. But he did miss being out in the field. He knew that other commanders might well take a less hands-on approach, assigning him to supervise missions such as this. But really, he wouldn't have it any other way. He found it hard to imagine anyone other than Lethbridge-Stewart in charge of the Fifth Operational Corps.

He headed back inside. At least he could have a decent breakfast and a quiet cup of tea.

Davey Mills sat in his milk truck snacking on a pasty. It was just after seven-thirty in the morning and he had finished the day's milk delivery run. Looking up at the sound of approaching vehicles, he was rather surprised to see a Land Rover and a military truck come roaring down the main street of Haltwhistle.

Funny, he thought, *there are no military bases around here.* He chortled to himself. Maybe Russia was about to invade?

He returned to his pasty.

A few minutes later a black van came speeding past. The windows were tinted so he couldn't see anyone.

Maybe it really was the Russians, after all.

Bishop pulled up the Land Rover in front of the Haltwhistle Aged Care Facility, right beside a white van that was backed up to the stone step, rear doors opened. A Bedford full of troops pulled up behind them. They had met it en route, as per the plan Lethbridge-Stewart and Captain Miles had laid out. Lethbridge-Stewart climbed out. Miles was already out of the Bedford and banging on the side.

'Come on, men, look sharp!'

The troops all jumped out of the back of the Bedford and fell in, standing to attention, weapons at the ready.

'Listen up,' Lethbridge-Stewart began. 'Remember, this is an old age home, so softly does it. We do not want to unnecessarily alarm any of the residents. Having said that, I still want you all to be on alert.'

Although he was not expecting this visit to be anything like their raid on Electric Soundscapes, he was also aware that they had been taken by surprise that time. Putting two men on the front door, he sent Samson with another two around to the rear. The rest of the squad would remain at the front part of the facility, where admin and all the offices were, well away from the residential areas. He could conduct the questioning there and keep things relatively low key.

Through the glass double doors, he saw an orderly and a nurse with an old woman in a wheelchair. The nurse said something to the orderly, then headed off. The orderly, abandoning the woman in the wheelchair, charged through the door towards them.

'What the hell is going on?' he demanded, grim-faced and stalking towards Lethbridge-Stewart.

'So much for the quiet approach.'

Bishop quickly slid into place, blocking the orderly's advance. It was Miss Talley's Neanderthal.

'This facility is now under formal investigation by the Scots Guards Special Support Group,' Bishop informed him. 'You and the other staff will please ready yourself for questioning.'

'Not bloody likely,' grunted the orderly, moving to get around Bishop. 'I want to know who's in charge of this.'

Bishop stepped to block his way again. 'If you would just calm down, sir, we will explain everything to Dr Quinlan.'

But the orderly did not calm down. He seemed determined to get past him. As he put a hand on Bishop's shoulder to shove him out of the way, the lieutenant deftly grasped, stepped and twisted, bringing the larger man's arm up around and behind his back.

'If you wouldn't mind leading the way,' said Bishop, pushing the man towards the doors, wishing he'd been able to do this sooner.

'There are eleven of them,' said the man, lowering his binoculars. His voice was measured and calm, deep and melodious, filled with a natural authority. 'Three have gone around the back of the building, two have remained out the front with their vehicles, and the rest have gone inside.'

The black van was pulled over to the side of the road by the hedgerow at the intersection that led to the old persons' home. The man leaned against the door, a smouldering stub in his mouth, to address his men. He was in grey with an expensive overcoat, the collar turned up. He had the tanned complexion of a person well-travelled outside England, the lines and creases of experience and the greying buzz cut of someone who didn't care about their receding hairline. His five men wore khaki, their faces concealed behind balaclavas.

'You're going in on foot. Circle round and keep to the cover of trees as much as you can. Take out the soldiers stationed outside. Then secure the building. Try not to kill any of the officers or civilians unless you have to. I want to know what's going on in there and how it links to Delacy and the weapon used to destroy Electric Soundscapes. After we have that, then we can dispose of them.'

'Sir!' the men responded.

The man opened the door of the van and climbed in. He adjusted the radio set that was propped up on the dashboard and spoke into the microphone. 'Testing.'

'Loud and clear, sir,' responded the leader of the assault squad, holding up a hand to feel the earpiece through his balaclava.

'Report in when you have the building,' said the man. 'Move out!'

The assault squad checked their weaponry, fitted their silencers and disappeared into the trees.

The man spat out the cigarette stub, started the van and drove back along the road they had come by, to a farm driveway. He pulled the van in behind the hedgerow just inside the property. Cutting the engine, he lifted the binoculars to make sure he still had a good view of the old persons' home.

Satisfied that all was as it should be, he reached into his overcoat pocket, pulled out a pouch of tobacco and paper, and began rolling himself another cigarette.

Captain Miles approached the reception desk with two soldiers, the receptionist staring at them like a rabbit caught in the headlights of a semi-trailer. 'I assume you have a PA system for this establishment, Miss.'

She nodded, eyes still saucer-wide.

'I'll need you to make an announcement to let people know that there is an investigation under way and that there are military personnel present. Please reassure the patients that there is nothing to worry about. Ask senior staff to report to reception. Everyone else should continue with what they would normally be doing.'

Bishop remembered the old woman in the wheelchair. He had tried to talk to her before, but she hadn't been responsive. Back then he'd simply known her as Greta, but now he realised she was, in fact, Greta Freiheit.

He wheeled her through the corridors and back to her room. He parked her by the window, which looked out over the rose garden.

'Oh dear,' she said, as they entered the room. 'I thought we were going to hear music today. I've been ever so looking forward to it.'

'Have you been to the music therapy before?'

'Therapy?'

'I mean, have been to hear the music before?'

'Oh no,' Greta said, shaking her head emphatically. 'I wasn't allowed until today.'

'Weren't allowed? Why is that?'

'Well... He wasn't ready for me.'

'Who?' asked Bishop, although he was sure he knew the answer.

A big smile lit up the old lady's wrinkled features. 'My son.'

Much to Dr Quinlan's apparent consternation, Lethbridge-Stewart had commandeered his office and proceeded to question him about the goings on at the home.

'What can you tell me about Professor Waldo Freiheit?'

'Who?' Quinlan asked.

'Come now, let's not play games. His mother, Greta Freiheit, is a resident here?'

'Is she?' Quinlan stared at him defiantly.

Lethbridge-Stewart regarded the director with an inscrutable gaze. He knew his type well. Officious little empire-builders, who spent most of their lives walking all over other people in order to get to where they were. Obstinacy and intimidation were his tools of trade. Lethbridge-Stewart knew how to deal with people like that.

'Very well, Dr Quinlan, have it your way. Your files will all be confiscated, and your staff and residents will all be questioned.'

'You can't do that! This isn't a military state.'

'I think you'll find these papers give me the authority.' Lethbridge-Stewart slammed the papers in question on the desk. As Quinlan looked over them, Lethbridge-Stewart continued. 'We will be looking very closely at all your medical procedures, particularly focusing on recent deaths. We will be looking into your staff hiring practices, especially considering your hiring of a head nurse previously dismissed for stealing drugs. And, of course, your finances will be gone over with a fine-tooth comb.'

The director's eyes widened momentarily at the mention of finances, and Lethbridge-Stewart knew that he had him. The director then glared at Lethbridge-Stewart with utter loathing, before crumbling.

'Fine,' he said, looking away. 'I'll answer your questions. But as it happens, I really do have no idea about Professor Freiheit. As for his mother... She may be a patient here. I'm really not sure. I'm not in the habit of keeping track of every resident's name. Nurse Hadley is more likely to know who all our patients are.'

'Right then,' said Lethbridge-Stewart, thinking it quite likely that this man wouldn't be bothered knowing the names of people he considered beneath him. 'Tell me about this music therapy programme then.'

'I'm afraid that I don't really know anything about that either.'

Lethbridge-Stewart leaned forward across the desk, allowing his anger to show. 'Do you seriously expect me to believe that you know nothing about the medical programmes at your own facility?'

'Well…' Quinlan hesitated, looking rattled. 'It's not a real medical programme is it? From what I understand, the patients simply go to the music conservatorium and listen to music for a few hours every so often. I doubt very much that it's of any medical benefit.'

'Then why do they go for this therapy?'

'It's free.' Quinlan crossed his arms and hunched his shoulders.

Lethbridge-Stewart continued to stare at him. 'Surely there's more to it than that.'

'Oh, all right.' Quinlan unfolded his arms, looking more uncomfortable than ever. 'They pay us.'

'The conservatorium pays you to bring your patients to their music therapy sessions. Doesn't that strike you as a little odd?'

'Well, they're some sort of charity, I think. Besides… It's Nurse Hadley who organised it all. I just signed off on it.'

'Wonder what's goin' on inside?'

Private McKenzie shrugged. He really didn't care. He was quite happy standing out in front of the building and not having to deal with any of the residents. Old people made him feel funny. Their wrinkled faces and hunched shoulders and bad smells. They were a nasty reminder of what would eventually, far off in the future, happen to him. And he preferred not to think about that.

'Wish we weren't the ones stuck out here,' ventured Private Hale.

McKenzie lamented being stuck with Hale. He always yabbered on. All the time. Yak, yak, yak. He tried to ignore him.

'It's been a whole month since I got transferred, an' all I ever get to do is stand guard. I thought this was supposed to be some special corps. That's what they said anyways. But I've yet to see anythin' special.'

'Shut up!' McKenzie snapped. Hale looked mightily offended, until McKenzie pointed towards the shrubbery along the perimeter of the car park. 'I saw something move.'

'Eh?' Hale squinted in the direction McKenzie was pointing. 'Probably a squirrel or somethin'.'

'One of us should go check it out.'

'Oh, come on. There's no point.'

'Fine,' said McKenzie through gritted teeth. 'I'll go.'

He set off past the vehicles which were still bunched up in front of the building. He was halfway across the car park when he heard loud footsteps behind him and Hale's voice calling, 'Hang on. I'll come with you.'

He was about to turn and rebuke Hale for having left the door, when he heard a loud thud.

McKenzie turned to see Hale had fallen face first onto the bitumen. Another sound behind him made him spin around, just in time to catch a bullet between the eyes.

'The whole of the UK was last night plagued with odd behaviour, aggressive outbursts and a slew of arrests. Police indicate there was a rise in the reporting of domestic violence, as well as fights in the streets and damage to public property. Prominent amongst those arrested was television decency campaigner Miss Arabella Constance. She was apprehended in her dressing gown and slippers in Bexley, after having thrown a heavy crown-shaped ashtray through the window of a local electrical goods store, smashing through the screen of the latest model Philips Style70 television set. Many of Miss Constance's constant complaints have been directed at the television serial *Fear Frequency*, which was being broadcast at the time of the disturbances. As she was being taken away by local police, Miss Constance was heard railing against that very serial, claiming it as the reason for her violent behaviour.'

As soon as he heard the news report on the radio, Erickson contacted LWT and tracked down Merv Chatley.

'What can I tell you?' said Chatley, over the phone. 'The

tape with the music was delivered to me on Saturday afternoon. Yes, it was odd. We didn't usually get it until just prior to broadcast time. But frankly, this whole deal with Delacy was weird.'

'Do you still have the tape?' asked Erickson.

'Yes. Not that it'll do you any good. Like the previous tapes, it wiped itself clean as it played. I did try to record it, but no dice.'

'Yes, I discovered that too.'

'Oh.'

'Thank you for your time, Mr Chatley.'

'Hey, hang on a moment. Don't suppose you know what's happened to Delacy and Electric Soundscapes, do you? I'd like to know where things stand in terms of more music.'

'I'm afraid that information is classified,' said Erickson. 'But I wouldn't bank on any more music deliveries if I were you.'

'Yes, that's what I figured.'

'Dr Quinlan hired me because he knew that I would not question any of his decisions or look into the financial management, in exchange for him not questioning the inventory of medications.'

'I see.' Lethbridge-Stewart was a little taken aback by Nurse Hadley's forthright confession.

'I'm quite prepared to tell you everything,' said the head nurse bluntly, 'in exchange for no charges being laid against me.'

'We won't be levying any charges, Ms Hadley, that will be up to the police to do. Based on my report.'

Nurse Hadley just nodded. She was not at all what Lethbridge-Stewart had expected.

'Is that the sort of deal you made at Bainbridge Hospital?'

'I wasn't the only one there who helped themselves to the store cupboards,' Hadley said. 'No charges were laid in exchange for my silence.'

Lethbridge-Stewart noted how calmly and matter-of-factly she spoke. She had an air of confidence that indicated she expected to get off scot-free.

'Well, Nurse Hadley, as it happens, this is not the reason we are here.'

She raised an eyebrow.

'What can you tell us about Professor Waldo Freiheit?'

She looked momentarily surprised. 'He's the son of one of our patients, Mrs Greta Freiheit.'

Lethbridge-Stewart waited a couple of beats before prompting. 'And...?'

'And he runs the music conservatorium.'

'And he is behind the music therapy programme?'

'Yes.'

'What does the programme involve?'

'I don't know.' Hadley looked Lethbridge-Stewart in the eyes without wavering. 'I don't ask.'

'But you happily deliver your patients to him for this therapy without knowing what it entails?'

'He pays well.'

'Good Lord, woman, is that all that matters to you?'

'Yes.'

'But you would have noticed the effects of the therapy.' Lethbridge-Stewart pulled a file out from the stack in front of him. 'Patients going to the therapy having substantial improvements in their symptoms. Then rapid degeneration. Often followed by sudden death.'

'Old people die,' Hadley said flatly. 'It happens. And I. Don't. Ask. Questions.'

Mitch worked at the storeroom lock with a piece of wire. *Damn it*, he thought, *it always looks so easy in films.*

Mitch was not very bright. At nineteen, he was a lot younger than his large, burly form suggested to people. But even at this young age, he had managed to spend a few months in prison for a failed attempt at robbing a petrol station. After his parents had repeatedly told him that being an ex-con meant he'd never get a decent job, he surprised them by landing this current position as an orderly. They were even more astonished than him.

But Nurse Hadley didn't care about his past. All she wanted was someone strong enough to lift and/or restrain patients, do menial jobs and never ask questions – all of which he could do. He especially enjoyed restraining patients. But he did not enjoy being locked up by a bunch of Army tossers. They had no right!

Giving up on lock picking, he decided to go for a more direct approach.

He searched through the storeroom for something he could break the lock with. Finding a good, sturdy screwdriver, he smiled. That would do the trick given how cheap and nasty the locks around there were.

He wedged it into the space between the door and the frame, right where the bolt was, and heaved his weight into it. The frame splintered, releasing the bolt. Easy.

Opening the door, Mitch stepped out into the corridor and froze. Now what? He hadn't thought that far ahead. It wasn't as if he wanted to fight off the soldier blokes. He just wanted out of there. He had done nothing wrong. He'd leave and go home. That's what he'd do.

He looked up and down the short side corridor – an office and a storeroom on either side; a fire escape door at one end, and the main corridor at the other. There was no point going back into the main part of the building. That would just lead to the soldiers. His best bet would be to get outside as quickly as possible. The fire escape door led to the side of the property. From there it wasn't too far before he could jump the fence into the farm next door.

Making up his mind, he tiptoed to the door with its 'USE ONLY IN EMERGENCY' sign. Well, the place was crawling with soldiers. That was an emergency as far as he was concerned.

He opened the door.

The fire alarm started blaring.

Mitch panicked and ran blindly.

He tore along the side of the building, careening into a khaki-clad stranger.

Mitch was about to ask, 'Who are you?' when the stranger drove a knife into his stomach.

As he fell to the ground, he thought he heard gunshots.

Looking for the cause of the alarm, Samson spotted the open fire escape door down a side corridor. He raced outside just in time to see a person in khaki fatigues and a balaclava stabbing an orderly. Drawing his handgun, he fired. The assailant went down.

He ran to the fallen orderly. 'Can you stand?'

The orderly groaned in response, clutching his abdomen, blood all over his front. Samson quickly scanned the surrounds for any more intruders, then grabbed the orderly's arm, putting it around his shoulder as he lifted him. It was a little awkward given his bandaged left hand, and he winced at the discomfort. The orderly yelled with pain at being moved. With the injured man barely keeping on his feet, Samson guided him back towards the door, wondering if at any moment another assailant might appear to stab or shoot him in the back.

Private Ashe, who he'd left guarding the rear exit with Private Hollister, appeared at the end of the building just as Captain Miles, Lieutenant Hare and Private McInnie, who had come running from the foyer, exited the fire escape door.

'Unknown assailant stabbed the orderly in the stomach, sir,' reported Samson. 'I shot the man.'

Ashe reached them just as a shot rang out. He ducked as tiny stone particles showered them. The bullet had narrowly missed him, hitting the wall instead.

Miles immediately returned fire as he barked orders.

'Inside. Ashe, get that man to the hospital wing. Ware, head to the back of the building and check the rear exit. Hare, check on the building entrance.'

Hare dashed off. Samson passed the orderly over to Ashe, then headed down the corridor at a sprint. He glanced over his shoulder to see Miles and McInnie firing their weapons out into the garden.

'Offspring One to Big Daddy. Over.'

The man lowered his binoculars and reached for the radio. 'I thought I said to report in once you had secured the house. Over.'

'Ah, we've hit a snag, sir. Someone tripped a fire alarm and we've been spotted.'

'I noticed. Report back once you have secured the house. Over.' There was no response. 'Do you understand? Over.'

'Understood, sir. Out.'

Replacing the radio handset, he allowed himself a moment to be amused by his call sign. Big Daddy.

He looked out of the window to see a farmer wandering down the drive from the distant farmhouse. He'd been spotted. The man was probably on his way to check why a car was parked inside his property.

Without any great hurry, 'Big Daddy' reached behind his seat and retrieved a Colt M16 Assault Rifle. It was old – he'd had it since '64 – but it was comfortable and reliable, and when he held it to his shoulder it felt like an extension of himself.

He climbed out of the van, lined up the shot and pulled the trigger.

CHAPTER NINETEEN
Assault on Haltwhistle

'**WHAT THE** blazes is going on?' demanded Lethbridge-Stewart, almost running into Captain Miles as he burst into the office.

'We're under attack, sir. Unknown assailants, dressed in fatigues with balaclavas. Samson took down one of them, but a second one got away. And we have no idea if there are any others.'

So much for this being the easy part of the operation, thought Lethbridge-Stewart. An attack on the old age home was the last thing he expected.

'Casualties?'

'That orderly chap has been stabbed,' said Miles. 'He's been taken to the hospital wing. He was the one who set off the fire alarm. I've sent Hare to check on the men out front, and Samson to check out back.'

At that moment Hare returned. 'Hale and McKenzie are dead. I've left Atkins guarding the door.'

Lethbridge-Stewart's jaw tensed. Two men down already.

'Right. Get back to Atkins, Private.' Hare left and Lethbridge-Stewart turned back to Miles. 'We need to gather the staff and residents into a defensible position.'

'Hospital wing?'

'Yes. Then make sure all exits are covered. Get to it.'

As Miles turned to go, Lethbridge-Stewart added, 'And where the devil is Bishop?'

Bishop was crawling through the rose garden.

He had been chatting to Greta Freiheit, who had been growing vaguer by the minute, and glancing out of her window, when he noticed a figure sneaking through the undergrowth in the distance. Not something one would expect at an old age home. The moment he realised the figure was in khaki fatigues, he was through the window and crawling across the grass to the nearby rose garden.

Which was probably the most painful thing he'd done in months. Internal injuries were not quite as healed as he would have liked.

The roses occupied quite a large section of the courtyard that was bordered by the residents' wing, the administration wing and the staff car park, with trees, shrubs and assorted undergrowth in the distance beyond the lawn on the far side. Battling against the thorns, he heard the far-off sound of gunfire and quickened his pace.

He finally made it to the edge and peered out cautiously through perimeter shrubbery.

The shots had obviously riled the intruder, who was now on his feet, albeit crouching low, as he raced to the edge of the building and proceeded against the wall in Bishop's direction. The man was armed; rifle in hand and a holstered pistol.

Bishop got his own gun out. He had a pretty clear shot from his position. The further along the wall the intruder came, the closer he got. But it also meant there was a greater chance of Bishop being spotted. He carefully took aim, intending to incapacitate rather than kill. And fired!

The intruder dropped the rifle and fell to the grass, clutching his arm.

Bishop sprang to his feet and bolted.

As the khaki-clad figure scrambled for his pistol, Bishop leapt. His impact knocked the gun out of reach, but despite the wounded shoulder, the intruder fought like a madman, lashing out with his uninjured arm. Before Bishop knew what happened, the intruder had retrieved a hunting knife from his belt and stabbed it at him. Bishop managed to grasp the man's arm and force it back, then smash it into the side of the building until he released the knife.

But the man just wouldn't give up. He continued to kick and thrash.

Losing his balance, Bishop and his opponent rolled across the grass and over the discarded rifle, until he finally managed to land a punch on the man's jaw, knocking the fight out of him.

Bishop barely had time to even think about checking his own body for injuries, never mind get his breath back, before bullets ripped up the lawn next to him.

Bishop lunged for the rifle. He grasped it, rolled into a crouch and fired off two shots into the chest of the oncoming assailant. Without pausing for breath, he manhandled the first intruder into the cover of the rose bushes and ripped off his balaclava.

'You and I are going to have a little chat,' Bishop said, doing his best to ignore the pain in his abdomen.

Samson heard smashing glass and gunfire as he raced down the corridor. Bursting into the common room he found Private Hollister crouched down, firing through a broken window while a nurse cowered in the far corner with two of the residents. An elderly man crouched down behind the sofa, while on it another resident happily continued knitting a scarf while humming *The White Cliffs of Dover* out of tune, oblivious to everything going on around her.

'Someone get that woman off the sofa and under cover,' barked Samson.

As the nurse timidly crawled out to assist the old lady, Samson dropped to the floor and crawled to the rear door that stood slightly ajar.

'How many?' he called to Hollister.

'Just the one,' answered the private, ducking below the window to reload.

'Keep him busy for me.'

As Hollister popped up and shot off his entire round, Samson slowly edged the door open a little further and peered out.

And there he was, darting back behind a tree. Samson carefully took aim, cursing his injury. At this range, a steadying left hand would have made things easier. The moment the intruder revealed himself to take his next shot, Samson fired. The man was thrown back, but not before firing off his own shot.

Hollister screamed and Samson heard him thud to the floor. In a fit of anger, Samson loosed another two shots into the crumpled form of the assailant.

*

Privates McInnie and Ashe escorted three more frightened residents into the hospital wing, while Lethbridge-Stewart stood in the waiting area outside with Miles and Hare.

'Any sign of Bishop or Ware?'

'Still haven't shown up, sir,' answered Miles.

Lethbridge-Stewart swore. 'We need to regroup, then do a sweep of the building, find Bishop and Ware, pick up any staff and resident stragglers, and deal with those men outside.'

Just then Samson staggered in, supporting Private Hollister. 'Hollister's been shot,' he said.

Hare stepped forward to help Hollister into the hospital, as Samson reported.

'I got the one who shot him.'

'So, the enemy are down by two,' said Lethbridge-Stewart. 'But we still don't know how many there are.'

'There are five of them,' announced Bishop as he arrived, shoving his prisoner ahead of him. 'I've taken one down and caught this one.'

'Which leaves only one,' said Miles.

'Good to see you've been keeping busy,' Lethbridge-Stewart said, before indicating the scratches on his adjutant's face. 'Looks like he put up quite a fight.'

'Oh these.' Bishop put a hand to his face. 'I had an altercation with some rose bushes.'

Lethbridge-Stewart raised an eyebrow, before turning to the prisoner. 'And just who exactly are you people?'

The stocky, dark-haired man didn't respond. He looked down at the floor, refusing to meet Lethbridge-Stewart's eyes. He fought the urge to beat an answer out of the man. Two of his soldiers were dead and another injured. Someone was going to pay for this.

'He was a little more talkative before,' said Bishop, 'while he was still dazed. He mumbled something about arms supplies and them being after a sonic weapon, before he realised what he was saying and clammed up.'

'Delacy's legacy,' spat Lethbridge-Stewart. 'Well, we'll see if the prospect of a long prison sentence will loosen his tongue.'

Hare, accompanied by McInnie and Ashe, came out of the hospital.

'Private McInnie, secure this prisoner,' Lethbridge-Stewart ordered. 'Miles, Hare, organise the men into two groups and sweep the grounds. We need to find that last attacker before they—'

As McInnie pulled the prisoner's hands behind his back, the sound of two shots in quick succession broke into the room. McInnie and his charge fell to the floor. Everyone else ducked.

Hare scuttled across the floor to the two men. 'Prisoner's dead,' he announced. 'Private McInnie is wounded.'

'The window.' Lethbridge-Stewart pointed to the bullet holes in the glass.

Bishop was pressed up against the wall beside the window in seconds, gun in hand. Taking a deep breath, he risked a quick look. 'He's escaping.'

Lethbridge-Stewart joined him at the window. 'Where?'

'He jumped the fence,' said Bishop, 'over into the farm.'

'I can't see him.'

'Damn,' said Bishop. 'He was there a moment ago.

'Take Samson and Hare and get after him. I don't want him getting away.'

'It's a complete balls-up,' came the out-of-breath voice over the radio. 'I'm the last one left. Coming in now.' There was a pause. 'Offspring One to Big Daddy. Come in.' Another pause. 'Where the hell are you?'

Big Daddy pulled the trigger. And the last of his 'children' died. There were definite advantages to being a one-man operation; the hired help was disposable, for instance.

His Colt was certainly getting a workout today. First the curious farmer. Then his wife. And now the last of the failed assault team. In his bones, he felt that it would still have more work ahead of it before the sun set.

He tossed the rifle onto the passenger seat of the van, settled himself behind the wheel and turned over the engine. He would have to handle things himself.

Perhaps he should have done so from the start?

He pulled the vehicle out of the drive and headed off. The day was far from over.

'Over here!' called Samson.

Bishop and Hare came running. Samson pointed at the khaki-clad body, the balaclava soaked in blood.

'Dead,' said Hare. 'But who shot him.'

'There must be another one,' said Samson, looking about.

'The leader, I assume. And he obviously didn't want his men talking to us.' Bishop looked around. 'Gone now, I'd say. What do you reckon, Samson?'

Samson pointed at the farmhouse. 'We should check there, just in case.'

'Agreed.' Bishop turned to Hare. 'Take the body back. Sergeant Major Ware and I will take care of this.'

Together they set off, and Bishop smiled. It was just like old times. Finally.

CHAPTER TWENTY
Aftermath

NURSE HADLEY lurked in the foyer area. She eyed the two soldiers stationed outside the front doors. One of them held a pair of binoculars, scanning the road leading to the facility. She knew there were another two outside the back door. And the injured ones were in the hospital wing. That brigadier person was in the Director's office, with his two offsiders. Since there were no other soldiers inside the building, Hadley wandered past the reception desk and over to Dr Quinlan's door. She stopped and listened.

'So, you think there was another one?' That was the brigadier's voice. Hadley knew it well enough by now.

'Yes, sir. The final assailment was shot from a distance with a rifle.' Hadley also knew that voice. It was the nosey Lieutenant Bishop. 'I'm willing to bet that he was shot by whoever organised the assault.'

'It looks like he didn't want his men talking to us.' Although she wasn't as familiar with the third voice, Hadley knew it probably belonged to Captain Miles. 'Protecting his identity, no doubt.'

'The question is,' said Bishop, 'will he try again with more men?'

'Unlikely. With his team out of commission, he's just one man.' The brigadier paused. 'Well, assuming he is a man. I suppose it might be a woman. In any case, it's unlikely he'll be able to get another team together in the short term. Still...' Another pause. 'We had best be on our guard.'

'Do we proceed as planned to the conservatorium?' asked Miles.

'Indeed,' said the brigadier. 'The fact that we have people after the sound weapons makes it all the more imperative that we confront Freiheit ASAP. I've been in contact with Colonel Douglas, and he informs me that CID are sending in a team from London. Lieutenant, have you arranged for the local police?'

'Yes, sir. The chief inspector will be here shortly. There are also two ambulances on the way to take the injured men to the town's War Memorial Hospital. The hospital wing here is understaffed and they are busy enough with the residents. A number of them are in shock. And there have been some minor injuries, trips and falls, that sort of thing, as they were rushing about during the assault.'

Hadley heard the approaching sound of sirens.

'Sounds like the ambulances are here now,' said the brigadier. 'See to them, Bishop. Captain, get the men ready. We'll head off as soon as the chief inspector gets here.'

Hadley returned quickly to the foyer, watching everything like a hawk.

Bishop watched as the two ambulances pulled away from the old persons' home. He had supervised their collection of the wounded men, and amid all the hustle and bustle, had also managed to see Hyacinth, Jasmine and Miss Talley who, although unscathed, were being checked out in the hospital wing.

'Oh, you dear young man,' Hyacinth had gushed. 'Thank you so much for checking on us. You know, we would be delighted for you to join us any time.'

'Was it Russians?' Jasmine had asked.

'It was all rather exciting,' Miss Talley had babbled. 'Reminds me a bit of when I got mixed up with the Glasgow razor gangs. They were always trying to kill each other. Another failed suitor was responsible for that.'

Bishop had finally managed to extricate himself when the ambulances were ready to head off again.

Halfway up the road, the ambulances now had to pull off to the side so that the police car had room to come in the opposite direction. Bishop remained where he was until the car pulled up. He stepped forward to greet the local constabulary.

'Lieutenant Bishop, at your service,' he said, extending a hand to the portly older man in the rumpled uniform.

'Chief Inspector Hammond,' responded the man, taking his

hand. 'And this is Constable Barnes.'

Bishop nodded a greeting to the fresh-face redhead, who nodded back nervously.

'So, are you going to tell me what's going on,' Hammond asked, 'or do I have to wait to see someone higher up the pecking order?'

'I'll take you straight to Brigadier Lethbridge-Stewart. This way please.' Bishop led them inside to the director's office, which was again occupied by Lethbridge-Stewart.

After introductions were made, Hammond got straight down to business with a, 'So what the hell happened here?'

'Spot of bother. Probably terrorists, but we're not quite sure yet.'

Bishop noted the sceptical look on the chief inspector's face.

'I'm afraid that I can't elaborate any further,' Lethbridge-Stewart went on. 'Scotland Yard have been informed, as this is connected to a CID case in London, and they are sending a team down. No one is to leave before they get here. But it will be a while, so we need someone to keep an eye on things.'

'Do you now?' said Hammond. 'You boys not sticking around?'

'I'm afraid not. I'm down four men as it is, so I can't afford to leave anyone behind. Suffice to say that we've done our best to clean up. The wounded soldiers and the orderly have been taken to the hospital in town. The bodies of the terrorists have all been placed in one of the hospital rooms. Unfortunately, there were also two civilian deaths. A man and woman at the farm next door.'

Hammond's mouth tightened. His eyes hardened.

'Mavis and Earl!' Constable Barnes spoke up for the first time, looking to the older man, his voice squeaky, his face white.

Hammond grunted and nodded to his junior. Taking a long, audible breath, he turned to face Lethbridge-Stewart again. 'Well, how very kind of you to… clean up. And where, may I ask, are you marching off to?'

Bishop could tell by the look on the Brig's face that he did not care for the attitude of the chief inspector. But he kept his composure when he responded, undoubtedly making allowances for the fact that two people he had obviously known were dead.

'We will be moving out to the Haltwhistle Music

Conservatorium.'

'That place has been closed for years,' said Hammond. 'What could possibly be of military interest over there?'

'Not at liberty to disclose,' said Lethbridge-Stewart, his answers becoming curter.

Chief Inspector Hammond appeared to size up Lethbridge-Stewart for a few moments. 'So basically, the constable and I are here to babysit until the big boys from CID arrive.'

'That's about the size of it, yes.'

Fifteen minutes later, Dr Quinlan had reinstated himself in his office. The venetian blinds were open so he and Nurse Hadley could look out into the foyer area. They watched in silence as the last of the soldiers made their way out. The two policemen were in the foyer, also watching them leave. As the chief inspector turned to look at him, the director pulled the string to close the blinds.

His face ashen, he strode to his desk and, with shaking hands, pulled a bottle of brandy from the bottom draw. He took a swig, then noticed his head nurse watching him. He held out the bottle to her.

'A little early in the day,' ventured Nurse Hadley.

Quinlan laughed, took another swig and clutched the bottle to his chest as he sunk into his chair. 'You do realise that we're done for?'

'I realised that the moment the soldiers rolled up outside.'

'This isn't like Bainbridge Hospital,' he hissed. 'You're not getting out of it this time.'

Hadley appeared to ponder what he said, and Quinlan wondered what was going through her poisonous little mind. She had been a mistake. This was all her fault. Somehow it was all linked to the music therapy that *she* had organised. He should have said no.

He'd been making a tidy extra sum through creative financial management. And then some more on top of that through the creative management of the patients and their wills. But he had been greedy. When Hadley had suggested he could make a little more by allowing patients to go listen to music, he should have refused. It had been an odd arrangement and he should have said no. But hindsight's lessons were too late to do any good.

He scowled at the nurse. She was still looking thoughtful.

'If you will excuse me,' she said suddenly. 'I think I should make a phone call.'

As she left, the chief inspector entered. He looked disapprovingly at Quinlan's bottle of brandy before speaking.

'Just before he left, that brigadier chap suggested I should ask you about the financial records.'

'I have information that you need,' said Nurse Hadley.

'Really?' said the voice on the phone.

'Yes. It's quite urgent.'

'Well, do tell.'

'It will cost.'

There was a moment's silence. 'Very well.'

'I want five—'

'Information first,' the voice interrupted. 'Then it is I who shall decide how much it is worth.'

'Hmmm.' Nurse Hadley thought about it. But really, if she wanted to get any money out of this situation, what choice did she have. 'The Army showed up here today. Asking about you and the music therapy. Then—'

'What did you tell them?'

'I didn't tell them anything. I mean, I don't even know what your therapy is.'

'Good.'

'But there's more,' continued Hadley. 'We were attacked. I don't know by whom. They're all dead now. But I did overhear some soldiers talking about a sonic weapon.'

'Interesting.'

'And the Army is now on its way to you. The man in charge is called Brigadier Lethbridge-Stewart.'

'I need you to bring my mother here.'

'I can't,' said Hadley. 'The police are here, and no one is allowed to leave.'

'Find a way.'

'I'm not sure that—'

'If you want any sort of payment, then you will bring her.'

Hadley didn't answer as she ran the possibilities through her head. Could she get past those two policemen? Would they give chase? Sneaking Greta Freiheit out of the building was certainly possible – but there was only one highly-visible driveway off the property. Her car was bound to be seen.

'Well?' Waldo Freiheit was becoming impatient.

'Possibly,' said Hadley, finally. 'It's a matter of finding a way to—'

'Excellent! I will have a large cash settlement waiting.'

Click.

He hung up on her.

Hadley put down the receiver and plonked down into a chair. She had managed to squirrel away a reasonable amount of savings for a rainy day – and goodness knows, it was pouring now – but she was well aware that Quinlan was right. She wouldn't get away with everything this time. And even if she did manage to escape charges, she'd never work as a nurse again. Given all of this, she could certainly use a 'large cash settlement'.

She made up her mind.

The Fifth vehicles rolled through the grounds, screeching to a stop on the gravel outside the building. Bishop and Lethbridge-Stewart exited the Land Rover, to stand looking at the grand old house. They both wore a pair of Erickson's headphones.

'Remember anything?' asked Lethbridge-Stewart.

'Bits and pieces,' replied Bishop, screwing up his face in concentration. 'There was no one here when I investigated. But...'

'Yes?'

'There was something. But... I'm not sure what.' Bishop wiped a hand over his brow. He was sweating. 'And, I remember a sinking feeling.'

'Sinking?'

'Yes. I can't really explain it.'

Lethbridge-Stewart turned from Bishop and looked over his shoulder to see Captain Miles and his men disembarking from the truck. They all wore headphones. Erickson had managed to make more of them in time for this raid. And he said that he'd also manage to expand the range of sounds they could cancel out, both ultrasound and infrasound, while still allowing them to hear ordinary sounds.

'Search the building,' he said to Miles.

As Miles and his remaining men headed off, Lethbridge-

Stewart stopped Samson.

'Stay with the vehicles, Samson. And keep a sharp eye out. I don't want any more surprises.'

'I'll make sure of that.'

'Good man.'

Lethbridge-Stewart and Bishop made their way to the building.

'Music!' said Bishop as they entered the grand foyer. 'I remember hearing music. And... and other sounds.'

'In here?'

'No. Yes. Over there.' Bishop pointed to the doors under the stairs. 'The music was coming from in there.'

As the two of them approached the doors, the music began.

'Sound familiar, Lieutenant?'

Bishop's ashen face was answer enough.

'Let's proceed with extreme caution,' Lethbridge-Stewart said.

Big Daddy fitted the silencer to his Colt.

He had a clear shot, but he waited. And watched. His targets were too near the entrance. Anyone might see them go down and then the element of surprise would be lost. He didn't know if there were any other police inside, so surprise would be a good thing to keep. So, he waited. And watched.

After a few minutes, they separated. The younger policeman went back inside, the older walked out to his car. He opened the passenger side door, sat down and started going through the glove compartment. Perfect.

Big Daddy took the shot.

And the policeman slumped across the front seats. There would be one hell of a bloodstain on the driver's seat.

Big Daddy slung the rifle over his shoulder and walked across the property to the building. It didn't take him long to find and cut the phone line. Then he strolled up to the double glass doors and entered.

Time for a more direct approach.

The other policeman was standing by the front desk, chatting to the receptionist, as if he thought he was in with a chance. They both looked up. The young man's eyes locked onto the rifle. It was a pity that policemen weren't armed. Otherwise, he may have stood a chance.

Big Daddy swung the rifle off his shoulder and into his hands with an easy motion borne of much repetition, and levelled it at the man's chest. 'I wouldn't move, if I were you.'

As the policeman trembled, Big Daddy saw a patch of spreading wetness on his trousers. The young man had obviously chosen the wrong profession. He did not have the constitution for the situations police work was likely to put him in to. Big Daddy felt a moment of sympathy for him. He might be a killer, but he was not an unfeeling monster.

The receptionist went white, tears brimming in her eyes.

'How many of you are there?' asked Big Daddy.

'Huh?'

'Police? How many police are here?'

'Just... just me and the chief inspector.' The policeman raised his arms above his head.

Big Daddy looked at the receptionist. 'Get me whoever is in charge. And whoever it is that really runs things.'

The receptionist fumbled with the PA system until she finally managed to ask Dr Quinlan and Nurse Hadley to urgently come to reception.

Quinlan stumbled out of his office clutching a mostly empty brandy bottle. He took one look at the intruder with his gun, and mumbled, 'Not again.'

Hadley arrived shortly thereafter. She didn't say anything.

'Now,' said Big Daddy. 'I don't want to unnecessarily alarm any of the old people, so can we move to a more private spot? Somewhere for the five of us to have a quiet talk.'

Quinlan staggeringly led them all to his office. Once they were inside, Big Daddy closed the door and slung his rifle back over his shoulder. Everyone visibly relaxed. The policeman even released an audible sigh as he tried to position his hands to cover the patch on his trousers.

In a blur of motion, Big Daddy drew his HK P9 and promptly shot him and the receptionist. Their bodies flung backwards against the wall and slumped to the floor. He was a killer, after all.

Hadley flinched but otherwise stood stock-still. Quinlan collapsed, blubbering into his chair.

'That's just to show you how serious things really are. So please answer my questions to the best of your abilities.' Big Daddy directed his gaze and his gun at Quinlan.

He took a moment to admire the feel of the Heckler & Koch P9 semi-automatic pistol in his hand. He had acquired it in Germany a few months ago, then had a custom-made silencer fitted for occasions such as this. His silencer was smaller and less weighty than the standard sound suppressor for this model, making for better accuracy. It wasn't as comfortable and familiar as his Colt rifle – more like a trusted friend than an extension of himself. But it was more manoeuvrable in confined spaces. He shook those thoughts away to focus on the matter at hand.

'Where did the soldiers go?'

'To... to the... the... Haltwhistle Music Con... Con... Conservatorium.'

'Why?'

'Something about m... m... music therapy and a P... Professor Freiheit.'

'What is this music therapy about?'

'I... I have no idea.' Quinlan pointed to Nurse Hadley with frantic glee. '*Her!* She... she knows about it. She... she organised it. Question her! Question her!'

Big Daddy shot him and turned to Nurse Hadley. Her face remained impassive. *Tough cookie*, Big Daddy thought. But then he saw the beads of perspiration forming on her brow.

'Tell me everything you know,' he said. 'Don't leave anything out. If I get everything I need from you, then I may let you live.'

Of course, he was lying. He would kill her, as he would anyone else he encountered. He couldn't afford to leave witnesses.

CHAPTER TWENTY-ONE
Sound and Fury

LETHBRIDGE-STEWART EXPECTED the doors to be locked, but as he twisted the handles, he received no resistance. They revealed a lift shaft. Tinkling music wafted up towards them.

'Well, that's unexpected,' said Bishop. 'I was sure there would be stairs.'

Lethbridge-Stewart leaned over the shaft and looked down. 'Doesn't look far. We could climb down, I suppose. Although there would be the risk of it star—'

The cables began to move, accompanied by the grinding sound of machinery.

'Right on cue,' said Bishop. 'Do you get the feeling we might be expected?'

Miles entered from the auditorium and approached them. 'There's nothing back here, but Hare is searching the offices and the privates are…' His voice trailed away when he saw the lift car rise up out of the gloomy shaft. 'Blimey!'

'Yes,' agreed Lethbridge-Stewart, 'my thoughts exactly.'

The car came to a stop with a little *ding*.

'Well then. Shall we?'

'Do you think that's wise, sir?' Miles asked.

'Probably not. But we need to get to the bottom of things, if you'll excuse the pun. In the meantime, Captain, keep searching this place. Oh, and station one of the men up here by the lift. If we haven't reported in within half an hour, come down and fetch us.'

Lethbridge-Stewart and Bishop stepped in. Bishop pointed to the four speakers, one in each corner, through which the music was coming. Lethbridge-Stewart grimaced.

'Lift music. Just what we need.'

'Lucky we have these,' Bishop said, indicating his

headphones.

'Indeed. You know, I don't think I'll ever listen to music quite the same way ever again.'

Lethbridge-Stewart regarded the wall, and saw that there was only one unlabelled button.

'Here goes,' he said, as he stabbed it with a finger.

The lift began its descent, and the music grew more intense.

'This is the sinking feeling,' said Bishop.

Nurse Hadley's hand shook as she stabbed the needle through the membrane on the vial and drew out the liquid. She had told the man everything he wanted to know. And then she had done everything he had asked of her. She had made a lockdown announcement over the PA to ensure residents and staff were not in the corridors, and she had taken him to Greta Freiheit's room. Now she was about to give the old lady a sedative.

Hadley's usefulness was coming to an end. She felt certain that this man would kill her, shoot her, the moment she had finished. And yet, she hoped. Desperately clung to the possibility that he might show her some mercy; that he might spare her life.

'What's that for?' asked Greta.

'Just a little something to help you sleep.'

'But I'm not tired.'

Hadley patted the old lady's hand as they waited. After Greta's eyes had closed and her head lolled, Hadley straightened up and faced the man.

Head held high, shoulders squared, she looked unflinchingly into his eyes. They were surprisingly soft eyes. Gentle even. They were not at all what she would have pictured as the eyes of a killer.

But, of course, they were the eyes of a killer.

And she knew that her own eyes – cold, hard eyes though they were – were those of a victim.

The lift clunked to a stop in front of standard metal doors. Lethbridge-Stewart and Bishop held their handguns at the ready. With a *ding* the doors opened, revealing what looked like a cross between a hospital and an electronics workshop – white walls, tiled floor, lots of lights, a row of hospital beds on one side, and workbenches covered in electronics and wiring taking up the rest of the space.

'Oh dear, you're awake,' said the man in the lab coat, from the far side of the room. 'You should be asleep.'

He was a rather ordinary looking middle-aged man; pale complexion, thinning blond hair combed over a bald patch, average height. A bit of a disappointment, really. Lethbridge-Stewart had almost expected a mad scientist caricature. But there was no explosion of wiry grey hair, or thick spectacles, or even an insane glint to the eyes. Definitely ordinary.

'Ah,' Professor Freiheit said, stepping forward, peering at them intently. 'Someone's been reading my papers on using sound frequencies to cancel out other sound frequencies, haven't they?'

'They have,' Lethbridge-Stewart said. 'Fortunately for us.'

Freiheit shifted his stance, putting his hands on his hips, his face falling into a frown. 'Oh dear. You have your guns pointed at me. How disappointingly stereotypical of you. Oh well, at least you didn't shoot first, ask questions later.'

As well as ordinary looking, Lethbridge-Stewart thought he seemed pretty cheery for a mad scientist. Stepping out of the lift, Lethbridge-Stewart lowered his gun. 'So, I take it that lift music contained a frequency that would have sent us to sleep if not for our equipment.'

'Indeed!' Freiheit reached forward and flicked a switch on the dashboard of controls that rested on his bench. The lift music ceased.

Bishop lowered his gun. He gazed around the room, flinching as he looked at the hospital beds.

'Are you okay, Lieutenant?' Lethbridge-Stewart asked.

'It... looks familiar.'

'Not surprising,' said Freiheit. 'I only used a mild suggestive frequency when you were last here. Just enough to make you forget a few details. Not enough to cause any lasting problems.'

'How kind of you.'

'Sarcasm already,' said Freiheit with a smile, 'and we hardly even know each other.'

Bishop was still staring at the hospital beds. Lethbridge-Stewart followed his gaze. The beds had leather straps to hold down the patients. Overhead lamps glared down on each bed. And they were surrounded by equipment.

Of course, Lethbridge-Stewart realised. Waking up in one of those beds, strapped down, with lights and sounds disorientating you. No wonder some of the old people thought they'd been abducted by aliens. But no, it was just humans. And one particular brilliant human who had expressed his genius in the most dastardly way.

'You do realise the damaged you've done to the old people at Haltwhistle home?' Lethbridge-Stewart asked.

'It'll pass.'

'You'd be surprised the damage mental scars can have,' Bishop said with feeling. 'Whatever you did to Grantly greatly distressed him. And will probably be with him for what remains of his life.'

'Ah, yes.' Freiheit lowered his eyes and his voice. 'Regrettable. He did show improvement at first. His cognitive faculties returned. He was able to reason and remember. But it didn't last. The regression was a disappointment. Yes, quite sad really.' He looked up into Bishop's eyes. 'I am saddened.'

'But you kept on doing it, didn't you?'

'Well, of course. Every great advancement in science requires sacrifice. And Grantly's improvement was more definite and regression slower than the previous patients.'

'Those patients...' Bishop paused. 'Those patients were just lab rats to you.'

Lethbridge-Stewart thought of what Bishop had undergone at the hands of Vaar and Collins, and couldn't bring himself to be surprised at Bishop's anger. If anybody, he could relate to what the old people had gone through.

'No!' Freiheit was quite emphatic. 'No, no, no. With each one, I tried my hardest. I was trying to save them. Cure them. It was always going to be a difficult process, but with each one, the chances were improved. They were all deteriorating slowly, their minds wasting away. In the end, I may not have cured them, but... At least I gave them the chance. The hope. Never, my dear fellow, never, underestimate the power of hope. It is what keeps me going.'

Bishop turned away, but Lethbridge-Stewart noticed his finger twitching against his pistol.

Lethbridge-Stewart stepped forward. 'The power of hope,' he said. 'Like the hope of curing your mother?'

'Yes.'

'I had a little chat with your mother,' Bishop said, and turned back to Freiheit. 'Nice lady. When lucid. I notice that you didn't use her as a lab rat. With her, you waited—'

'Until I was sure!' bellowed Freiheit, suddenly losing control. 'Well, of course. She's my mother! My flesh and blood. I wasn't going to experiment on her.'

Lethbridge-Stewart tensed. Bishop looked ready to snap.

'Experiment! Suddenly it's no longer a cure, or a chance, or a hope. It's an experiment!'

'Do you think this is easy?' blasted Freiheit. 'Do you think miraculous cures just invent themselves? It's *hard!* Curing people. Repairing people. It's the most difficult thing in the world. But how could you understand? You people, with your guns and bombs and destruction. Destruction is easy! The simplest thing in the world.' He rummaged through the electronics on the bench in front of him and picked up a device that looked a bit like a gun with a speaker on the end of it. 'This!' He waved it about. 'Look at this. The sound waves from this device target living matter at a cellular level, making the cells lose their integrity.' He pointed it at Lethbridge-Stewart and Bishop. They both stepped back, raising their pistols. 'This! This is easy! But once it's done its work... Once it has destroyed something... Try putting it back together. It's almost impossible.' Freiheit threw the device back onto the bench in frustration. He looked every bit the mad scientist now, thought Lethbridge-Stewart, lowering his own weapon again. 'Repair. Cure. Creation. These things are difficult. These things take time. These things require sacrifices.'

'Yes, that's all very well and good,' Lethbridge-Stewart said. 'But what about the weapons you created? You rant and rail about destruction, and yet you supplied Delacy with all sorts of destructive equipment.'

'A necessary evil.' Freiheit's voice lowered and he looked almost ashamed. 'He had financed my work. But in exchange, I had to provide him with what he wanted. The scientific community often moralises about the ends and the means and the justification and the whatnot. It's not a luxury I had if I wanted to save my mother. The longer I took, the more she deteriorated...' He took a long deep breath. 'It's a moot point now, anyway. The moment I achieved my goal, the moment I no longer needed his filthy money, I ended our arrangement.

And I destroyed all the weapons I made for him.'

'And you murdered him,' pointed out Bishop.

'He deserved to die,' said Freiheit, in such a matter-of-fact way as to suggest the discussion was closed. He was back in control. 'Now, gentlemen. I need your help for a moment.' He reached out to his controls and music filled the air.

'What are you doing?'

'Relax,' said Freiheit, his hands still moving across the switches and dials.

Bishop yawned.

Lethbridge-Stewart began to feel fuzzy and heavy.

'Tell me when you start to feel sleepy,' continued Freiheit.

'What are you doing?' Lethbridge-Stewart demanded, stumbling around the equipment towards the scientist.

'Good,' said Freiheit. 'Found the correct frequency.'

Lethbridge-Stewart heard Bishop groan and fall behind him. He tried to aim his pistol at Freiheit, but couldn't focus properly. He tried to pull the trigger, but couldn't find the strength. All he wanted to do was sleep.

He closed his eyes.

Was that dust? Samson lowered the binoculars and rubbed at his eyes, then raised them again. Yes. Way off in the distance, a trail of dust was rising up off the road. There was a vehicle travelling in their direction.

'Mayhem four to Mayhem two,' he said into his walkie-talkie.

No response. Just static.

'Dammit!'

Music suddenly came out of nowhere. Only, he couldn't hear it. But he could *feel* it.

He tried to stifle a yawn. His eyes felt heavy. His mind fuzzy. This wasn't right.

'Dammit, Erickson,' he hissed. The headphones were supposed to protect him.

'Bloody hell!'

The headphones! The music was coming through the headphones.

Samson tried to take them off, but he barely got a chance as consciousness slipped away.

*

Private Ashe stepped back from the lift shaft. Looking down made him feel woozy. Still feeling unstable, he leaned back against the wall under the grand staircase. He yawned and stretched out his tired arm muscles. The early morning was finally catching up to him. He closed his eyes for a moment and relaxed as he listened to the music. Music?

A thudding sound made him struggle to open his eyes again. He staggered out from under the staircase to find Hare unconscious on the bottom step. He got down on his knees to check on the lieutenant, only to find himself going all the way down to the floor.

Everything went dark.

Lethbridge-Stewart couldn't move.

He opened his eyes. He was lying in a bed. Strapped down. The headphones no longer on his ears. Blast! He'd fallen asleep. So much for Erickson's headphones. Twice they'd failed him now.

Anne wouldn't have failed me, Lethbridge-Stewart thought unkindly.

A groan made him turn his head to see Bishop waking up in the next bed.

'Wakey-wakey,' said Professor Freiheit, coming to join them. 'Have a nice nap?'

'But how did you...?' Bishop's voice trailed away.

'How did I put you to sleep? Simple, really. Your headphones are based on my research. It was easy to modify the frequencies they were emitting. So, it was the headphones that put you to sleep.' Freiheit came to stand between their two beds. 'And I am sorry about the restraints. But I couldn't allow you to keep waving your guns around. Nurse Hadley should be here soon with my mother. After I have administered the sonic treatment that will cure her of Alzheimer's, I'll play you some nice music to help you forget all of this. Then you can go back to marching and saluting and whatever else it is you do when you're playing soldiers.'

Lethbridge-Stewart struggled against his restraints. 'You won't get away with this.'

'Get away with what? Finding a cure to a disease which affects so much of our aging population? Oh, Alzheimer's may not be popularly known, but it's there. Always there.'

Freiheit moved over to the end bed and started to fuss over the equipment that surrounded it.

Lethbridge-Stewart looked over at Bishop, who was trying to work his hand out of the restraints. Lethbridge-Stewart angled his head down to look at his own straps. He swivelled his hand around to see how far he could reach. It was hopeless.

Big Daddy jabbed the end of his beloved Colt into the coloured soldier's stomach, hard. The man didn't move. He crouched down beside the Land Rover to examine the man more closely. A warrant officer. Was he snoring? Big Daddy slapped the man across the face, knocking the strange headphones off his ears. No reaction. Very odd indeed.

He straightened up and considered shooting the soldier just to be sure.

No. No point. It would be a wasted bullet. Just as he didn't see the need to kill unnecessarily, he also didn't see the need to waste ammunition.

With a final look down at the man, he headed off to unpack his van.

Still adjusting the equipment around the hospital bed, Freiheit's attention was grabbed by the *ding* of the lift. He let go of the wiring and rushed over in anticipation.

The doors slid open to reveal Greta Freiheit, seated in her wheelchair, head lolling, fast asleep. But, instead of Nurse Hadley, standing behind her was a tall man in a grey overcoat, wielding a rifle.

Panicked, the professor stumbled backwards, turned and made for the workbench with his controls. Gunfire made him stop and crouch to the floor. Amid the descending plaster dust, he turned and looked up to see the man pointing his rifle to the ceiling. Slowly the rifle moved down until the barrel was pointing at him.

'Next bullet will be for you,' said the man, his voice calm, measured and deep. 'So, don't give me a reason to pull the trigger.'

Professor Freiheit nodded, wondering who this man was, why Nurse Hadley wasn't here, but most of all, how he was going to get out of this.

The man stepped out from behind the wheelchair and into the room, leaving Freiheit's mother where she was in the lift car. The man gazed around, his eyes resting on the two soldiers strapped to the hospital beds. He smirked.

'You seem to have done a fine job incapacitating the military.'

'Who the blazes are you?' Lethbridge-Stewart demanded, his struggles renewed with vigour.

'You can call me Big Daddy.'

'You can't be serious.'

'Don't provoke him,' begged Freiheit. The situation was bad enough without stupid soldiers making it worse with their bravado.

But Big Daddy smiled. 'My line of work doesn't provide much in the way of amusement. I take what I can get.' The smile faded. 'You were at the old persons' home when my assault team struck. And you were at Electric Soundscapes when it was destroyed. I'll need to ask you some questions before I kill you.'

Big Daddy turned his attention to Freiheit. 'But first, you and me need to have a little chat.'

Freiheit slowly rose to a standing position from where he had been cowering on the floor. 'What do you want?'

'For starters, whatever weapon you used to destroy Electric Soundscapes.'

'The acoustic disintegrators?'

'I really don't care what they're called. But I want them. And whatever it is you used to influence people's minds. I don't care about selling cigarettes, but there are a lot of other things I could get people to do. And whatever it was you used to send those soldiers to sleep. Can you imagine how useful that would be? And any and every other weapon you may have developed.'

'Weapons!' spat Freiheit. 'Destruction! Is that what this is all about?'

'Well,' said Big Daddy. 'Death and destruction is my line of work. So, I am always on the lookout for equipment that could improve business.'

'No,' said Freiheit. 'No. Delacy was one thing. I knew I could stop him before he actually did any widespread harm. But I will not be responsible for releasing wholesale destruction upon this world.'

'You don't have a choice,' said the man.

'I would rather die,' said Freiheit, defiantly.

'Waldo?' The voice came from the lift. His mother had woken up. 'What's going on?'

The man slowly turned to point his rifle at the woman in the wheelchair.

Professor Freiheit's face fell.

He was defeated, and he knew it.

CHAPTER TWENTY-TWO
The Cavalry

SAMSON GROANED as he woke. His head pounded, his cheek stung, and his gut ached. How many times had he been put to sleep now? He'd be having strong words with Erickson when he returned to the Madhouse – the headphones were supposed to protect him, not put him to sleep.

The headphones. He wasn't even wearing them anymore. He didn't remember taking them off. He stumbled to his feet and immediately saw the black van parked beside the truck.

Damn! Someone was there. Someone had got past him.

Drawing his weapon, he raced for the building, stopping dead as he entered. Hare and Ashe lay in a crumpled heap at the foot of the staircase. He could see Miles through the open door on the right. They were all still wearing the headphones.

He approached Hare and Ashe and crouched down beside them. He could hear music coming from their headphones. He yanked the headphones off them, then moved on to Miles.

As soon as his mother's life had been threatened, Freiheit had caved in to the demands. Not only that, within minutes he had eagerly suggested an ongoing alliance, offering to not only hand over all the weapons he had, but also to continue developing new ones, if, and only if, he was allowed to cure his mother – right here, right now.

Big Daddy agreed.

Freiheit was now kneeing down beside his mother's wheelchair, her hands clasped in his. 'Don't worry,' he reassured her. 'Everything will be all right. I will take care of you.'

'But Waldo…' She looked from him to her surroundings in confusion, her eyes coming to rest on Big Daddy and his rifle, which was still pointed at her. 'Why has that man got a gun?'

'It doesn't matter, Mother.'

'I don't like guns, Waldo.' Her voice was quavering as her eyes returned to her son. 'They frighten me.'

'I know, Mother.' He gave her hands a squeeze, and looked into her eyes.

Eyes that recognised his, for the moment. Eyes that too often didn't know their own son. Eyes that glazed over as each little part of her life crumbled from her memory. Of course he was doing the right thing, he told himself. His mother was more important than anything else in the world. And as for that criminal... Well, he would work it out later. Deal with him as he had dealt with Delacy.

Big Daddy was, after all, just another means to his end. What was one more justification in his pursuit of the ultimate good.

'There's no need to be frightened. I'm here with you. The treatment is finally ready. I'm going to cure you.'

'Cure? Treatment?' His mother's face crinkled in confusion.

'The music, Mother,' he reminded her gently. 'We talked about it, remember? I'm going to play you some special music.'

'Oh... I do so like music.' Her face lit up. 'I remember dancing with your father to...' Her brow creased, and her eyes lost their sparkle. 'It was a waltz... I think.'

Freiheit's eyes brimmed with tears as he got to his feet. 'Let's get you over to the bed.' He turned the wheelchair around.

'Waldo!' His mother's voice was cracked and frightened. 'That man over there. That man has a gun, Waldo!'

'I know, Mother,' he said patiently, as he wheeled her towards the bed.

'I'm frightened, Waldo. I don't like guns.'

'It's okay, Mother. I won't let him hurt you.' Stopping beside a bed, he turned to Big Daddy. 'Can you help me get her up onto the bed?'

'No.'

Freiheit opened his mouth to protest, but Big Daddy cut him off.

'Do what you need to do. But don't expect my help. I'm here for one reason and one reason only. To that end, this rifle stays in my hands and remains trained on my insurance policy.'

'Waldo? Why is that man holding a gun?'

Freiheit scowled at the criminal. Maybe he was making a mistake. He shot a glance at the two officers strapped down into their beds. But it was too late to turn back now. Not when he was so close.

He bent down awkwardly, lifted his mother from the chair, one arm under her knees the other around her shoulders. He stumbled as he moved her to the bed, almost letting her slip.

Big Daddy made no move to help.

Finally getting her into the bed, Freiheit positioned the equipment around her, adjusting the settings.

'What's going on?' she asked, her voice frail and shaky. 'Where am I?'

'Shhhh,' hushed Freiheit, as he pressed speakers to her ears and temples. 'Relax and listen to the music.'

You'll be back to your old self soon, he thought.

'I like music,' she whispered, closing her eyes and drifting off to sleep.

'Right,' said Big Daddy. 'Now that's done, let's talk business.'

'What?' Freiheit looked up from the equipment. 'Done? It's not done. I need to monitor the treatment carefully.'

Big Daddy paused, then nodded. 'Just remember there's a limit to my patience.'

Freiheit returned his attention to the instruments.

'One other thing,' said Big Daddy. 'The soldiers upstairs.'

'Oh, don't worry about them,' said Freiheit absently. 'They'll stay unconscious until I'm ready to wake them.'

'Good. I'd hate to have to kill them as well.'

'As well?' Freiheit looked up, alarmed.

'Don't worry, Professor. Not you or your mother. Just those two you so helpfully incapacitated.' He indicated Lethbridge-Stewart and Bishop.

'Why do you want to kill them?'

'They've seen me, haven't they? If someone sees me… they die. That, or they come work for me. And I don't think there's much chance of these two changing sides quite so readily as you.'

'He's not wrong, Waldo,' Lethbridge-Stewart said. 'And if you think he'll let you go, think again. He killed two of my men.'

'Not me. That was the hired help,' Big Daddy said.

'Ah yes. The last of whom you killed.'

Freiheit glanced at Lethbridge-Stewart.

Big Daddy smiled. 'I'm a killer. Everybody has their uses, and when they don't...'

Freiheit knew Lethbridge-Stewart was right. Even if he were wrong, what would happen to his mother? There was no way she would join that man. She would be appalled by him and his deeds. So, either Big Daddy would kill her, or she would need to remain his captive. An insurance policy, guaranteeing Freiheit's continued cooperation. Cooperation in creating more instruments of death and destruction.

The blood drained from Freiheit's face as the truth finally hit him.

What had he got himself into?

Samson came down the stairs, arm supporting the private who had been searching upstairs when the music in his headphones had knocked him out.

'What happened?' asked Hare, looking up from where he was seated on the bottom step.

'Yes,' said Miles, now standing in the doorway to the auditorium. 'Where are the headphones? I thought they were supposed to protect us.'

'I think they were hijacked,' said Samson. 'You all woke up after I took them off you.'

'But how?' asked Hare.

'I don't know. But we've got more trouble.'

'More?' Miles looked far from pleased. 'What now?'

'We had a visitor while we were unconscious. There's a van parked outside. Probably the last guy from the assault on the old folks' home.'

'No prizes for guessing where he's gone,' Hare said.

'No,' Miles agreed. He looked down the lift shaft and checked his watch. 'Well, it *has* been well over an hour.'

'Then we need to get down there.'

'Agreed.' Miles turned to Hare and his men. 'Search this place, just in case our visitor is elsewhere. Be careful. He took out one of his own men, he won't have any qualms about shooting first.'

Hare put together a quick search pattern, and the three men set off in different directions.

'Right,' said Miles. 'We need to get down there.'

'There's no button,' Samson said.

'What?'

'To call up the lift.'

'Then we'll climb down, Sergeant Major.' Miles looked over the edge again, shining a torch. 'There's a hatch in the top of the car.'

'Okay then.' Samson glanced down at his bandaged hand. 'What we need is rope.'

'Let's see what we can find.'

And with that, the two men set off to find something – anything – that might act as abseiling gear.

Keeping an eye on where Big Daddy was at all times, Lethbridge-Stewart worked at the leather restraints. Things had progressed since Mrs Freiheit's treatment had begun. Professor Freiheit continued to fiddle with controls, rush about anxiously and fuss over her. Big Daddy had pulled up the discarded wheelchair and sat himself down, resting his rifle over his crossed legs, the barrel unwaveringly pointed at the old woman. 'Just in case,' he had explained.

As Freiheit continued to run back and forth, Lethbridge-Stewart saw him surreptitiously nudge the device he had earlier shown them to the edge of the bench. What did it do? Target peoples' cells? He wasn't even sure what that meant.

Their eyes met briefly and Freiheit looked down at the device pointedly. Then, when he passed by the bed to which Lethbridge-Stewart was secured, he tripped. As he steadied himself against the bed, he pressed a penknife into Lethbridge-Stewart's hand.

He'd been working on his bonds ever since. The one securing his left wrist was now cut through and he was working on the strap that held down his torso. As he finished, he tried to catch Freiheit's eye. Eventually he did, giving the scientist a little nod.

Freiheit scurried to the opposite end of the room and retrieved a screen, which he wheeled over to his mother's bed. It was made of foil-like sheeting, stretched over three metal frames secured with hinges.

'What's that?' asked Big Daddy, sitting up straighter and lifting his rifle.

'This is to contain the next bombardment of sonic waves,' said Freiheit with confidence. 'It intensifies them for the patient. And stops stray waves hitting the rest of us.' He positioned the screen at the top end of the bed, with the hinged flaps coming down either side.

Lethbridge-Stewart saw that it mostly blocked his view of Big Daddy. Freiheit stood himself at the edge of the screen, obscuring the man completely.

Clever.

Lethbridge-Stewart reached over his body and unbuckled the strap on his other wrist. He then carefully stretched across to Bishop in the next bed and undid the restraint on his closest wrist. As Bishop set to undoing the rest of his straps, Lethbridge-Stewart sat up so he could reach the straps on his legs. But leaning forward would most likely put him into view of Big Daddy. He held off, and waited until Bishop had reached the same point of unrestraint as himself.

He and Bishop looked at each other. This last part would be a risk. There was a high probability of them being spotted. But he would be damned if he let that man and his ridiculous name get the better of him without a fight.

Lethbridge-Stewart held a hand up, and counted down.

Three, two, one.

They both leaned forward and got to work on the final restraints.

Lethbridge-Stewart managed to get one leg free before Big Daddy was on his feet pointing his rifle.

'Stop right there!' he bellowed.

Freiheit knocked the screen out of the way as he groped for the equipment around his mother's head. Pulling the speakers away from her, he angled them at Big Daddy and hit a switch. There was a loud *thrum*, and the man was knocked off his feet, his rifle thrown across the room out of reach.

Lethbridge-Stewart and Bishop took the opportunity to finish freeing themselves. Not knowing what Freiheit had done with their handguns, Lethbridge-Stewart dashed for the workbench and the device Freiheit had indicated to him. He had no idea how it worked or what it did, but it was a weapon he could use against Big Daddy.

Bishop, meanwhile, rushed the man and threw himself at Big Daddy as he tried to right himself. The two of them went crashing to the floor.

As all this commotion was happening, Freiheit repositioned the equipment around his mother and adjusted the controls, obviously determined to finish the treatment.

Lethbridge-Stewart aimed the weapon, but didn't dare fire it. Bishop was struggling with Big Daddy, rolling across the floor and knocking into equipment. Freiheit shrieked as they knocked into his mother's bed. He struggled to right the speakers and keep the treatment on track.

As Bishop and the man continued to struggle, Lethbridge-Stewart tracked the progress with the weapon, pointing it out in front, finger on the trigger. He watched as Bishop smashed his fist into Big Daddy's face. Blood sprayed from his nose, but he kept fighting, oblivious to any damage Bishop was inflicting. Pulling his feet up, he kicked out at Bishop, catching him in the stomach. Bishop was flung backwards, smashing into a bench and falling to the floor. He tried to get back up, but collapsed, clutching his abdomen and vomiting.

Big Daddy couldn't have known it, but there couldn't have been a better place to strike to take Bishop down. Anger bubbled up inside Lethbridge-Stewart. Rage at what his man had been through, but before he could do anything, Bishop passed out.

Big Daddy jumped to his feet and drew his pistol.

Finally having a clear shot, Lethbridge-Stewart pulled the trigger.

Nothing happened.

'You have to switch it on first,' yelled Freiheit.

Big Daddy began shooting.

'Blasted thing!' Lethbridge-Stewart hissed, and ducked behind the bench. He looked down at the device in his hand, completely baffled by the controls. There were no labels on anything.

Looking up he saw Freiheit, down on all fours, crawling across the floor, under benches and around equipment, towards him.

Placing the device on the floor, Lethbridge-Stewart slid it across the tiles towards Freiheit. The scientist scooped it up and adjusted the settings.

'The box under the desk,' he said, and slowly rose to his feet, the device raised and pointed at Big Daddy.

'Big Daddy,' he said. 'What a stupid name!'

The two men eyed each other.

'I appear to have underestimated you,' said Big Daddy, pointing his pistol, not at Freiheit, but at his mother. 'But I still have the upper hand. I've killed a lot of people, young and old. One more here or there means nothing to me. She means nothing to me. But she obviously does to you.'

Freiheit remained where he was, although his hands were shaking uncontrollably.

Lethbridge-Stewart spilled out the contents of the box, which included his and Bishop's handguns. He grabbed both and stood, pointing them at the criminal.

'I think this has gone on long enough.'

Crash!

The top of the lift fell into the car, followed by Samson.

And the room exploded into chaos.

Big Daddy whirled around, firing as he went.

Freiheit screamed and fell, clutching his right thigh, his device skittering across the floor.

Lethbridge-Stewart managed to get off two shots, one from each pistol, before he had to duck as bullets went whizzing over his head. Neither hit their mark.

Samson remained in the lift, pressing himself against the wall to avoid the shots that came his way as Big Daddy finished his arc.

His nine shots spent, Big Daddy smoothly lowered himself into a crouch and snapped another cartridge in place, before leaping up and over to the hospital bed. The muzzle of his gun pressed against Mrs Freiheit's nose.

'All right,' he called. 'I've had enough of this. Everyone up and out where I can see you, weapons on the floor, or Mummy Dearest will need a new face.'

Lethbridge-Stewart saw Freiheit trailing blood as he inched his way across the tiles to his device. Dropping the guns, Lethbridge-Stewart raised his hands above his head and stood. Seeing Samson giving him an enquiring look from the lift, he nodded. Samson also put down his weapon, raised his hands and stepped out from cover.

'You too, Professor,' Big Daddy said.

Freiheit remained out of view.

'Do you need some incentive?' Big Daddy drew his hand

back and brought the butt of his pistol down heavily on the equipment surrounding Mrs Freiheit.

Sparks erupted with a flash as a piercing screech filled the air. The old woman, eyes still closed, began a mournful wailing.

Everyone instinctively brought their hands up to their ears as the sound drilled into their brains. The screeching died down as the equipment sparked again, then sizzled and popped.

'What have you done?' screamed Freiheit, staggering to his feet, stumbling forward, blood soaking his clothes, device outstretched before him.

Big Daddy still had his pistol trained on Mrs Freiheit. 'Demonstrated just how serious this—'

Freiheit pulled the trigger.

There was no sound. No flash of light. No apparent indication that the weapon had been used. Except...

Lethbridge-Stewart watched in horrid fascination as Big Daddy's cells literally fell apart. In a matter of seconds, his skin sagged, as if everything inside of him had dissolved, and as he slumped, even his skin liquefied, pouring out of his clothes onto the floor. It was, without a doubt, the most ghastly sight Lethbridge-Stewart had ever witnessed.

Freiheit dropped the device and lurched across the room towards his mother, trailing blood. Ripping aside the damaged equipment he threw himself at her and cradled her wailing form.

Bishop groaned as he started to regain consciousness. Lethbridge-Stewart indicated to Samson that he should go and help him. Then he crossed the room to Freiheit.

The scientist was leaning awkwardly across the bed, holding his mother by her shoulders and rocking back and forth. Her eyes were glazed, vacant and staring wide. Her lips were parted as she continued her anguished sound.

'No, no, no, no, no, no, no,' Freiheit murmured, patting at her face helplessly. 'We were so close. I almost had you back.'

'I'm sorry, Professor,' said Lethbridge-Stewart coming up behind him. Even though everything that had happened had been caused by this man and his inventions, Lethbridge-Stewart couldn't help but feel pity for him at this moment. Freiheit's feelings for his mother were undeniable.

'Sorry?' whispered Freiheit. 'The procedure was almost done. She was minutes away from having her mind back. Not just cured, but better. And instead... the overload has wiped everything. She's just a shell.'

Lethbridge-Stewart placed a hand on the man's shoulder. An inadequate gesture, he knew, but it was all he could offer.

With a sudden shout Freiheit smacked his hand away. Dropping his mother, he lunged at Lethbridge-Stewart, knocking him off his feet. He fell back onto the wheelchair and skidded into the wall, while Freiheit, clutching his injured leg, tore across the room, knocking over equipment as he went, until he reached his workbench. His hands flew across the controls.

'Out!' he shrieked. 'Get out!'

Samson approached cautiously from one side, hands held with palms up, and Lethbridge-Stewart from the other with a similar stance.

'I'm a dead man standing,' announced Freiheit. 'Do you really want to join me?'

Lethbridge-Stewart and Samson both stopped.

'My hand is on a dead man's switch,' Freiheit explained, his face haggard. 'I'm losing blood fast and I don't know how long I'll be able to hold out. This entire property is wired just like Electric Soundscapes.'

Lethbridge-Stewart weighed up the possibility of rushing Freiheit and keeping his hand on the switch. Perhaps replacing his hand with something heavy. Perhaps he could...

He stopped himself. You can't always win, he told himself. And it was not worth risking more men to save Freiheit and his research.

He looked over at the barely conscious Bishop. Anne would never forgive him, Lethbridge-Stewart knew, if he didn't return her fiancé home to her.

He wouldn't forgive himself.

'Professor?' he asked, one last time.

'Just leave!' Freiheit's face was devoid of all hope.

'Samson,' Lethbridge-Stewart said, 'help me with Bishop.'

It was like a repeat of their raid on Electric Soundscapes. Their quarry had been stopped, but was not in custody to face justice. Given all that had happened as a result of Freiheit's quest to cure his mother – the men the Fifth had lost, the old people at the home who had been experimented upon – his quick death seemed somehow inadequate. But then again, thought Lethbridge-Stewart, was it really his place to judge? After all, he was just a soldier. And the threat had been neutralised.

Lethbridge-Stewart and his men watched from the road as the conservatorium and everything within the grounds, without sight or sound, disintegrated. It was no less terrifying than the last time they had seen the devastating force unleashed. Although there was some comfort in knowing it was the last time.

It was some moments before Lethbridge-Stewart gave the order to move out.

'I'm scared,' said Tommy.

Graham saw the fear in his son's eyes and was ashamed that it was not merely fear of the upcoming television serial, but fear of his father's behaviour.

'Here. Come sit by me.'

He awkwardly put his arm around his son as *Fear Frequency* began. He was unused to displays of affection. They had always made him uncomfortable. He would have to work on overcoming that.

He turned his attention to the screen. It was interesting – the visuals, although identical to the previous time, didn't have the same impact with the new music. Although discordant and sinister, the orchestral piece was just a piece of music. There was no underlying fear or desire.

'It's not as scary,' said Tommy, leaning into his father.

Graham's heart swelled as he made himself a new vow. A promise to be a better and more understanding parent. A determination to not be like his own father.

If there was anything good to have come out of this strange experience with a theme from a cheap television serial, it was this.

EPILOGUE

'Turns out CID has been after that Big Daddy chap for a while,' said Douglas. 'He had links with a number of terrorist-for-hire organisations overseas. Reggie says they are quite pleased to have him out of the picture.'

'So, they owe us one,' said Lethbridge-Stewart with a smile.

'Well, I'm not sure Reggie would see it that way.' Douglas laughed and took a swig of his ale.

Lethbridge-Stewart mentally filed away the connection anyway. CID's help might come in handy in the future. And being able to remind them of the part played by the Fifth in bringing down Big Daddy could be to their advantage.

It had been a week since Freiheit had destroyed his work and himself, and loose ends were still being tidied up. For now, though, Lethbridge-Stewart and Douglas were enjoying a quiet drink in *The Auld Hundred*.

'What about the sonic weapons? Any luck with tracing them?' Lethbridge-Stewart asked, after taking a long draught of his own ale.

'Afraid not. Erickson and his team have literally sifted through the dust at both the Electric Soundscapes property and the conservatorium. They found nothing. Whatever devices were used to clear those areas, destroyed themselves in the process.'

'And Freiheit left nothing anywhere else?'

Douglas shook his head. 'Erickson has checked with the University of Strathclyde where the professor used to work. He took all his notes with him when he left. And the other researchers there had all been working on their own discrete projects, or providing support to Freiheit without actually knowing what the end result was. It seems that he was quite good at keeping his research to himself.'

'Perhaps it's better that way.'

They both proceeded to sip their drinks in silence for a while. *Let it Be* began playing on the radio in the distance.

'So, I hear there was a distinct lack of alien involvement,' said Anne, as she and Bishop joined them, drinks in hand.

Lethbridge-Stewart noted the tenderness to Bishop's walk, but didn't draw attention to it. Anne was already paying him close attention. As was her right.

Funny, Lethbridge-Stewart thought, *how I never saw their connection in the first place. Am I really so blind as all that?* Their bond had always been there, ever since the first day they met. Lethbridge-Stewart smiled to himself; if only he was to be that lucky in love.

'I thought you'd be at home watching *Fear Frequency*,' he said.

Anne laughed. 'No, I think we've all had enough of science fiction programmes.'

'Congratulations on your promotion, Captain,' Douglas said, and stood, offering Bishop his hand.

'Thank you, sir. More responsibilities.'

'And no more chasing phone calls, or worrying about filing,' Anne added with a grin.

'Indeed,' said Lethbridge-Stewart. 'Well, for a change,' he added, returning the subject back to the previous one, 'the threat was entirely human.'

'Old Colonel Grantly's imagination was getting away from him,' said Captain Bishop, gingerly taking a seat next to Anne. She placed a gentle hand on his.

'I am sorry I didn't get to see any of the sonic technology Freiheit had developed,' said Anne. She took a cursory taste of her shandy, a wistfulness in her expression. 'Not so much the weapons, of course, but the medical equipment.'

'Yes,' Lethbridge-Stewart said, 'you were missed.'

Anne raised her eyebrows, and Lethbridge-Stewart almost blushed. He hadn't meant to say that out loud.

'So, I take it Jeff isn't working out so well?' she asked.

'Quite well,' said Lethbridge-Stewart. 'He's not you, of course, but… he did well.'

A look passed between Anne and Bishop.

'I know it's not my place to say, sir,' Bishop began, and held up his hand to shush Anne before she could interrupt. 'But Anne and I have been talking. She's none too happy about you putting me in the line of fire. Her words not mine.'

'Well, it can't be helped, and now you're a captain it's only going to get worse,' Lethbridge-Stewart said. 'Life at the Fifth is no picnic.'

'No, sir. And—'

'What Bill is trying to say,' Anne said, interrupting this time. 'Is that I can't just sit on the side-lines. I thought I could, but Bill is never going to leave the Fifth, and... Well. I'm not sure I should have either.'

Lethbridge-Stewart nodded. In truth he wasn't surprised. As dangerous as their work was, the things they saw, the incredible sights they witnessed... Nobody could walk away from that. Sometimes, even the highest cost was worth the wonder.

'Okay, Anne. I have a proposal. How would you feel about unlimited access to the Warehouse and its facilities?'

Anne looked at Bishop, then eyed Lethbridge-Stewart suspiciously.

'In exchange for?'

'In exchange for some occasional assistance. I mean, it wouldn't do to just dump Dr Erickson. He has much to learn, but he did his best, and I've no doubt he'll do better.'

'Oh, he will.' Anne nodded, her eyes now alight. 'So, this proposition. You want me to be a consultant? I would need more than just access, though.'

'Really?'

'Space of course,' she said. 'A permanent lab.'

'Very well,' Lethbridge-Stewart said, sounding as if she had just convinced him.

Anne nodded and smiled. 'I think that would work very well.'

'Excellent. Then it's all settled.'

Douglas and Bishop were both smiling broadly.

'It'll be good to have you back,' said Bishop.

Douglas raised his glass. 'To Anne's return to the fold.'

They all clinked glasses.

'Celebrating without me,' said Samson, finally arriving. 'Sorry I'm late.' He seated himself next to Lethbridge-Stewart and placed his drink down on the table. 'Good evening,

Captain,' he said, smiling at Bishop.

'As you were, Sergeant Major,' Bishop returned with mock-severity.

Everybody laughed and Lethbridge-Stewart regarded them.

'Well, now that we're all here,' he said, reaching for his glass. His face sobered as he paused for a moment. 'To our fallen comrades. Let us never forget the cost of protecting this world.' He raised his glass and drank.

His companions followed suit.

After a moment's silence, conversations resumed. Anne and Bishop excitedly talked about her return to the Fifth. Samson held out his bandaged hand and told Douglas about expected recovery time given that he had managed to re-break it while abseiling down the lift shaft.

Lethbridge-Stewart sat back and watched. They were a good team.

Actually, no.

Somewhere along the line Anne and Bishop – not Bishop, *Bill* – had graduated beyond that. They were all more than just his team, Lethbridge-Stewart realised with a deeply satisfied smile, they were his friends.

'What you thinking, Al?' Samson asked.

'What? Oh. Just wondering what our next problem will be.'

Whatever it did turn out to be, he knew that Samson and Dougie, and now Anne and Bill as well, would be there to face it with him. And that was a good position to be in.

Available from Candy Jar Books

KKLAK! THE DOCTOR WHO ART OF CHRIS ACHILLÉOS

Kklak!: The Doctor Who Art of Chris Achilléos covers for the official Target novelisations, which began in the early '70s, defined a generation's image of the Doctor and his adventures – particularly after the show disappeared from British screens in the late '80s.

Lavishly detailed, with psychedelic overtones and an unapologetically pulpy sensibility, these covers perfectly captured the eccentric appeal of the classic series.

Kklak!: The Doctor Who Art of Chris Achilléos collects the entirety of Achilléos' *Doctor Who* artwork in chronological order, along with commentary from Achilléos himself (as well as some fans) – presenting the definitive guide to his seminal work. The book also includes a small contribution from twelfth Doctor Peter Capaldi and a foreword from Achilléos' long-time friend and collaborator, the late Terrance Dicks.

Available from www.candyjarbooks.co.uk

Coming soon from Candy Jar Books

100 OBJECTS OF DR WHO BY PHILIP BATES

"So, all of time and space, everything that ever happened or ever will: where do you want to start…?"

100 Objects of Dr Who is a celebration of everyone's favourite sci-fi show. Perfect for fans, no matter your mileage – whether you've just started your journey through all of time and space, or have lived through the highs, the lows, the Wildernesses, the Androzanis, and the Twin Dilemmas.

Inside, you'll find: A terrifying army of three Daleks! Death's Head's head! A really quite astonishingly heavy door! Dinosaur fossils! A framed piece of wall!

And much, much more!

This is a book about *Doctor Who*. But probably not the one you're expecting..

Available from www.candyjarbooks.co.uk

Also available soon from Candy Jar Books

LETHBRIDGE-STEWART COLOURING BOOK

Art by Martin Baines

This fantastic collection of artwork is a must for all *Doctor Who* fans, as well as collectors of adult colouring books. It features twenty brand new pieces of art by *Thunderbirds*, *Danger Mouse* and *Doctor Who* artist Martin Baines.

The artwork concentrates on the Lethbridge-Stewart series of novels and features the Dominators, Quarks, Yeti, Anne Travers, Bandrils and much more. Added to this, the book also explores the UNIT era of *Doctor Who*.

Available from www.candyjarbooks.co.uk

Also available from Candy Jar Books

LETHBRIDGE-STEWART: DOMINATION GAME
By Aly Leeds & Megan Fizell

It's time to move on.

Sally Wright has had enough of the Fifth Operational Corps to last a lifetime. She has been chased, kidnapped, and dogged by unknown horrors – and to top it all, the end of her engagement to Brigadier Alistair Lethbridge-Stewart has cast a shadow over her career. In an effort to leave it all behind, she requests a transfer back to the Regular Army... But, after everything she's seen, is it possible to return to normal life? And will the Brigadier let her go?

Harold Chorley cannot move on. While searching for answers to the missing gaps in his memory, he makes an alarming discovery; the Dominator war lord, Dominic Vaar, is no longer in prison. Hot on Vaar's trail, Chorley discovers an experimental military project that seems sinister in its appetite for volunteers. Volunteers who are never heard from again.

William Bishop is not looking forward to life at the Madhouse without Anne Travers, but in heading up a mission to Gloucestershire with Sally and Chorley, he soon finds other things to worry about.

One thing is for sure, not everybody will survive this encounter with the Dominators!

Available from www.candyjarbooks.co.uk